Table of Contents

Part 2

Robin Renounced and Reformed

PREFACE

Flamborough Village and Headland, where the story of Robin Lyth takes place, is a real place located on the east coast of Yorkshire in Great Britain. R.D. Blackmore who wrote the original story of Robin Lyth under the title "Mary Anerley", must have stayed there for some considerable time in order to describe the place so accurately.

North Landing can still be seen just as Blackmore described it, although little or no fishing is done there any more. Nevertheless, setting up crab and lobster pots is still undertaken by the local fishermen and their catch is a distinct delicacy which I have enjoyed many times.

The old tower, located near the new lighthouse has recently been renovated and is a magnificent sight, with its white limestone bricks which match the high, white chalk cliffs a short way off. It is generally recognized to have been built in the 17th century and was used as a warning of the dangerous rocks off the headland by burning a bonfire on the top. It was also one of a series of beacons placed along the east coast of Britain which were to be lit to spread word in case of a Spanish or French invasion.

For many years it was supposed that Danes Dyke had been been dug by the Danes who settled on Flamborough Head in the 800's A.D. It was said that their intention was to cut off the headland entirely from the mainland and make it an island, and therefore easier to defend. Certainly the Danes settled on

Flamborough Head, for some of the villagers' dialect and customs which survive to this day, derive from those days. In addition, Flamborough was often referred to as Little Denmark. However archeologists tell us that the dyke dates much further back than the Danes. Whomever we have to thank for it, it is today, a beautiful place for a shady, woodland walk, from one side of the headland to the other, on a warm summer's day

Perhaps the most awe inspiring place mentioned in the book is Robin Lyth's Cave or 'Hole' as it is locally called. This cave can only be entered at low tide from the North landing. Its entrance is not unlike many other caves on Flamborough Head, but once inside, it opens up into a large cavern of glistening rock, wet from the retreating sea. At the far end, the roar of the waves can be heard and a very small shingly beach opens up towards the open sea.

Whether or not Robin Lyth was a real person, a legendary person or simply Blackmore's imaginary hero in "Mary Anerley", I have been unable to determine. I don't know if the fishermen named the cave after Blackmore's hero or if the cave was known as Robin Lyth's Hole before Blackmore wrote his book. This may never be known. It doesn't really matter for "Mary Anerley" is a wonderful book full of delightful descriptions of Flamborough and its tight knit dwellers. It is salted with wry humor and held together by a romantic, adventurous plot.

Nevertheless, for today's readers it is slow-paced and bogged down by a plethora of characters, with enough material to make two books. Because of my love for Flamborough, (I lived there during my growing up years), I have tried to edit and revise the book, keeping only to the theme of Robin Lyth. Believing as I do that the book has merit as literature, I have tried to leave much of Blackmore's vocabulary, style of writing and his humor, undisturbed.

The reader should note that being literature, this book cannot be enjoyed and consumed as a meal at a fast food store, but should be approached slowly and carefully, savoring the flavor as one who dines at a gourmet meal.

Christine A. Jones
2005

Chapter One

A DANE IN THE DYKE

1798

Bridlington Bay is one vast expansive curve that stretches from the north, where the high, white chalk cliffs of Flamborough Head thrust six miles out into the cold North Sea, to the south, where lies the sand spit known as Spurn Point. The bay is only thirty miles across as the crow flies, from point to point. But when a strong north-easter blows, there's many a sailor who is thankful to find shelter behind the Smethwick sand bar that shields the bay from the frightful pounding of the breakers. Those who know the Yorkshire coast, know better than to venture northwards around the headland at such a time. Beyond the point, the winds have a keen knife-edge to them and the waves turn savage, like a wild animal. If that were not enough, the treacherous rocky coastline combines with the winds and the waves to wreck the unwary ship that dares to venture forth, and sends him to join the scores of others which litter the infamous sea bed.

In contrast to everything that Flamborough Head is, a narrow wooded valley separates the village of Flamborough from the rest of the world. Known as Danes Dyke, it cuts the headland into a triangle. Here, the land is lushly green, and filled with ferns, mosses and young trees. Here, the winds are tamed and the sun shines with a warmth unknown on the headland.

One day in August, a pretty country maid guided her pony gently through the glen of Danes Dyke on her way down to the white pebbled beach that looked out over the bay. Though it was still very early morning, the air was warm and heavy with the fragrance of damp earth, grasses and ferns. It was Mary's favorite time of day and her favorite place to explore. The stern words from her mother a few days ago, that one day she might meet a free-trader or other such villain in these woods Mary had thrown to the winds. She should be behaving more like a lady, said her mother. Her father, Stephen Anerley of Anerley Farm, a loyal, stout, thorough going farmer of thriving Yorkshire stock, shushed his wife and bade young Mary enjoy the Dyke while she was young. There were not many summer days at the threshold of bold Flamborough Head and it was his desire that Mary should enjoy them to the full before settling down to become a farmer's wife as her kinfolk had done generations before her.

Since this was not the time for spring flowers, Mary went on her way to find another kind of nature's bounty – the intricate seashells, urchins and starfish that the white pebbled beach might yield. She let her pony, Lord Kepple as she had named him, choose his pace, which he did from long years of experience and knowing the gentle hand that guided him. Although she was wearing a pretty pink, checked dress, she had taken the precaution of covering it with a russet brown riding skirt that matched the bonnet covering the clusters of her soft sun-colored curls.

Suddenly the beauty of the time and place was broken by the sharp, angry sound of muskets fired from the mouth of the Dyke and echoing up the winding glen. She was startled but not frightened, for the sound was common enough when the "Yorkshire Invincibles", that gallant, volunteer regiment of soldiers, would come down to the Dyke to practice their shooting skills in readiness against the invasion of the French or "Frogs" as they were commonly called.

Before the girl had time to wonder at the noise, another volley broke forth and around a bend in the trail someone came running very swiftly towards her. Mary jerked her pony aside to give the man space to run for his life. Then without a second thought she beckoned him to her and he came running, so out of breath that he was unable to talk.

"Poor man!" cried Mary Anerley, "Are they shooting at you?"

The run-away nodded and doffed his hat. Though he was heaving in great gulps of air, that action showed that he had been raised well. But he clapped it swiftly back on his head again and set off at a run.

"Not that way!" cried Mary, "Over here! I can show you a place where they will never find you." The young man stopped and turned to her. Though he was thoroughly out of breath there was no sign of fear in the handsome, dark eyes that met hers.

"Look ! That little hole -- up there -- by that clump of ferns. Up, at once, and take this to put over you!" She had untied her riding skirt in an instant.

He snatched it, and was gone up the side of the Dyke, like a darting, brown salamander disappearing into the shrubs. At the same instant, Mary quickly rode forward to meet the men who were now appearing around the bend.

A thousand years ago, Dane's Dyke must have been a very grand entrenchment. In spite of its name, there were many learned men who were sure that it never was the work of any Dane. But there was no arguing that the folk who peopled the headland beyond the trench were the descendants of a colony of Danes who had settled there centuries ago. They had left the distinct imprint of their speech and manners upon the tight knit band of villagers. It was said by them that the Danes, when they settled the village of

Flamborough, had tried to sever the headland from the mainland and make it an island, being so much the easier to defend. The closest they had come to success was at this access to the sea on the south side, where Mary and her pony were heading.

There were four men. Three broad and sturdy, running at a good pace, their muskets at the ready, and a fourth, a tall, bony man with a cutlass, that he was swinging in the air, while swearing loudly.

"Coast-riders," thought Mary, "and he is a free-trader, I'm sure! But four against one is unfair." If the dark brown eyes of the young man had not made their mark, the stamp of a free-trader would have done it instead. For although, as all England knew, especially all who dwelt in Flamborough or any other fishing village on the east coast of Yorkshire, free-trading was illegal, yet there were many who winked at their misdeeds and enjoyed their booty for keeping quiet. Indeed, some said that entire villages were in league with the smugglers. But it was impossible to get at the truth of that from these closed-mouthed northerners.

"Halt!" cried the tall man as his small company of men were about to run past her. "Put down your arms. It would not do to be scaring young lasses." Then he took off his hat with a flourish. "Young Mistress Anerley, I'm afraid we are spoiling your ride. But his Majesty's duty must be done. Hats off, fellows, at the name of your king!" and he waved his own in the direction of the men who were breathing heavily from their exertions. "Mary, my dear, the most daring villain, the devil's own son, has just run up here. You must have seen him. Tell us the truth now. Your father will be proud of you, for I know he is a most loyal subject of the king. Did you see the man? Which way did he go?"

"Was it a man you say?" said Mary, her blue eyes opened wide. "Oh, surely not a man, Captain Carroway. Never say so!"

"A man? Is it likely that we were shooting at a woman? But you are trifling with me. You saw him I've no doubt. Forgive my bluntness, but we are on the king's business. Which way did he go?"

"Was he a Flamborough man?" asked Mary, in all innocence. Not that it mattered, for she herself was not considered a Flamborian. The triangular headland was known for years as Little Denmark and its people seemed to feel somewhat of a contempt for those on the outside, designating them as "furriners". Although Anerley Farm lay altogether on the outside of Danes Dyke, it did not bother Mary to be considered a "furriner" for she rarely left the scope of her father's farm land.

"Flamborough! Filey! Whitby! What's the difference?" cried the Captain. "They're all hand in glove with the smugglers."

"Why, you always used to be so polite, sir. I can hardly believe that this is the same Captain Carroway that loves to smoke a pipe with my father. And those guns look so dreadful! Surely my father would be shocked to see me so escorted home as if the French had just landed!"

All this time Mary had been cleverly contriving to exaggerate her pony's fear and trotted him further up into the Dyke away from the young man's hiding place. Her attempts to mishandle him puzzled the pony so that she became entangled in the harness and reins. "Oh, what a troublesome little horse he is," she cried when they were far enough away. She jumped down and handing the reins to Captain Carroway, she appealed to him with all the innocence of the sweet, young maid that she was, "Oh, Captain Carroway, would you hold him for just a moment, so I can calm him and untangle these reins?" She glanced up at him from under her pretty brown bonnet.

"No, no my dear," he blustered, "How can I hold him when I cannot get out of his way. No, my dear, brace him up sharp and stand him clear of me."

"But you wanted to know about some enemy, Captain. Was it an enemy as bad as my poor Lord Kepple here?"

"Mary my dear, the very biggest villain. He has a hundred golden guineas on his head and there's half for you if you can direct us to him. Think now, think of the beautiful Sunday gowns you will be able to buy and how well they will look on you, such a beautiful lass as you are. Your father would be proud to have you on his arm at Sunday church. Now tell us the truth, my dear. Which way did he go?"

"Captain, you are pressing me so hard for an answer and I'm sure I don't like the thought of betraying anybody. I think that will not please my father either."

"Of course not, Mary, my dear," said the captain, seeing her logic. "No-one asks you to betray someone. But you cannot hurt him now, for he must be a half mile from here by now."

"Oh I'm sure you're right, captain, because he was running so speedily. Well, I will tell you if you are sure it is too late to catch him... for I do not like to think that I was the cause of someone's imprisonment. Poor man, he looked so tired out."

"Yes, to be sure! A worn out fox! We have been chasing him for two hours. Now which way did he go?"

"I will not say for certain, but I did see a man. He was running slowly -- so slowly, because he was tired. I think he might have set off again towards Sewerby. But perhaps he was not the man you are seeking,"

"To be sure he was," stated the Captain doggedly. "Forward men, on the double!. We have him now. There's five guineas in it for each of you -- dead or alive! Thank you young mistress, thank you most heartily."

The small company of men rushed off with gun and sword in readiness. But one of the men, John Cadman by name, looked back at Mary suspiciously. He had very little trust of women in general, even his own wife. He knew that it was often thanks to the women of a village that the men could carry out their contraband trade.

Mary had the grace to blush at her deceit, but her bonnet's shade hid her rosy cheeks. She disguised her discomfort by giving Lord Kepple a light whack with a fern and followed the men slowly, until they were well out of sight on their way to Sewerby.

She paused a moment or two longer, and then turned her pony's head back toward the sea again. Truth to tell, she was more concerned about her riding skirt, (for which her mother had paid six shillings at Bridlington fair), than she was for the hidden young man. More than that, it would be worse than losing ten times that amount of money if her father were to discover how she lost it. Mr. Stephen Anerley was a straight-backed man with a mild interest in politics as well as farming. He was especially hot against free traders, even if it meant his wife had to make a bad bargain on occasion, rather than patronize contraband.

Not that Mary could believe that such a brave young man would likely steal her skirt. In fact, as she thought more about it, there was something down right honest and almost noble in the face of that poor persecuted man. How brave he was! What a runner too! How clever to escape those cowardly coast runners as they shot to the left and right of him! As she stood and surveyed the side of the glen, she wondered if perhaps he had made good his escape, and with her skirt at that. Perhaps he had taken off toward Flamborough or the Bempton Cliffs.

Before she could be certain that the fugitive had indeed made good his escape, a quick shadow glanced across the middle of the path and the young man leaped from his hiding place. To look at him, no-one could have guessed how close he had been to losing his life, nor how deep into the hole he had hidden. For he stood there as clean and spruce, as any sailor home from the sea might have been, with a careless smile lighting his face. He was tall and agile, but sturdy too. His black hair fell in a wave across his brow and above the keen brown eyes that now studied Mary. With his sun-browned face, he looked the perfect sailor; but circumstances had made him a smuggler, or to put it more kindly, a free trader.

Indeed, he looked so clean and handsome standing in the pathway, that Mary at first doubted it was the man she had seen. But then she saw her skirt folded neatly in his hand.

"How do you do, sir?" she asked hesitantly, a little shy at being confronted so unexpectedly by such a handsome young man.

The free trader looked at her with equal surprise. He had been in such a hurry that he had scarce the time to take in what a pretty picture young Mary made. Her golden curls tumbled from under her brown sun hat, and her slim figure, so gently rounded in the right places, yet she had an air of unmistakable girlish innocence. His breath taken from him yet again, but this time it was not from running.

"I think you should run again now," said Mary "and do please hurry."

"What have I to run away from now?" he answered in a deep, kind voice. "I run from enemies, but not from friends."

"That is wise," answered Mary with a self -conscious blush. "But your enemies are not so very far away. They will come back with great anger when they don't find you."

"I'm not afraid, fair lady, for I know them only too well. I have led them on many a dance such as this, before. Though this may well have been my last, were it not for your help. They will look all morning before Captain Carroway will return here. He is the most stubborn of men to admit to a mistake. They will hunt through the fields and the hedges until they cannot take another step, and then they will return to Anerley for breakfast."

"I dare say you are right, and we will be glad to see them. My father is a part time soldier and it is his duty to aid the king's men."

"Then you are young Mistress Anerley? I thought you were, for there cannot be two such fair ladies as I have heard you described. And you saved my life! It is truly something to be saved by one so fair."

The young man wanted to kiss Mary's hand, but she, not being used to such gallantry, held out her hand to take back her skirt. He parted with it reluctantly for he looked for an excuse to meet her again. But he was not entirely without ideas.

Mary gave him a farewell smile, took up her pony's bridle and with the good sense of a properly brought up young woman, realized plainly that she must leave.

"Fair lady," he began, sensing that she enjoyed being called a lady, "though I owe you more than I could ever repay, may I ask a little more?" His quick wits served him well. "Since you are on your way down to the sea, if you should chance to see the other earring to match this," he showed her the one he had taken from his ear, (for it was quite customary in those days that a sailor should wear them), " I would be most grateful if you would pick it up for me. Look at this one so as to recognize the other. It was shot away and flew against the large stone at the left of the mouth of the Dyke. I dare not stop to look for it or go back that way just now. It is worth more than a hat-full of gold to me, though it is worth little to anyone else."

He had unerringly caught Mary's attention once again. "You mean they really shot away your earring!" she gasped. "Cruel, careless men! What could they be thinking of?"

"They were thinking of getting what is called 'blood money'. One hundred pounds for Robin Lyth. Dead or alive--one hundred pounds."

Mary shivered, though the sun was warm upon her. "Of course they must offer money for people -- *bad* people-- but to offer a hundred pounds for a free trader, and to try to shoot him dead, why that is to make themselves criminals!. I should not have thought it of Captain Carroway."

Robin smiled grimly. "Captain Carroway only does his duty. I like him none the worse for it. He is a fool of course. I could have had his life fifty times before now, but I will never take it. He will be killed sooner or later I'm sure, for he rushes ahead without thinking. But it will never be my doing."

Mary looked admiringly at Robin. She liked his noble words and indeed his noble figure. "Then you are the famous Robin Lyth—the new Robin Hood as he is called. They say you are a man who can do anything."

"Mistress Anerley, I am Robin Lyth, but I can do very little. I cannot even search for my own earring."

"Then I will search for it until I find it. Cowardly, cowardly men! How could they shoot at you in such a way!" Her sense of injustice was intensified by his gentleness and fine manner. "You are well known for your honor, sir. I am sure I will find it, but how shall I get it back to you when I do?" she asked, her heart racing as she realized that she might see this fine young man again.

Robin's mind raced as he too thought how to devise a second meeting. "Perhaps you could keep it for me until one week from today. Then along about four o'clock in the afternoon, in the lane that leads towards Bempton Cliffs, you can return it to me there. Tonight we are going away on some important business for a few days, but I will return and you can give it to me then."

"Yes, yes, but you must hurry now." His winning manner had made her all but forget Captain Carroway's return. Her fear for him returned afresh. "What will you do if they come back?"

"I will run away as gallantly as I did before, but this time there will be a difference. My thanks to you, I will be fresh for the chase, but they will be stiff and tired. They will be angry at having missed the best chance they ever had at me. If they shot at me again, they would do little harm. Crooked mood makes crooked mode." And he laughed at his joke.

To Mary it sounded the best and bravest laugh that ever she had heard. "Do not think of such a thing!" she cried.

"I shall think only of you," he said, serious once more. "... that is, I shall think only of your kindness in keeping my earring for me. Please say nothing of this to anyone, or Carroway will be upon me like a tiger. Farewell, young Mistress Anerley, farewell until one week from today."

With a wave and a smile he was gone, up into the Dyke, dodging lightly between the shrubs and the ferns, disappearing into the undergrowth.

Mary waved, a little uncertain that this was what a lady should do, since her mother had told her to wait until she had been introduced before behaving so forwardly. Yet it was a little late for that, she thought ruefully. Not only had they not been introduced but they were to meet again—secretly. But the brightness of his smile, the kindness of his face and the nobility of his reputation conspired to make her think that this assignation was not so very shocking.

She turned towards the sea, pulling gently at Lord Kepple and wandered on slowly, to look for the smuggler's trinket.

Chapter Two

VISITORS AT ANERLEY FARM

Anerley Farm boasted an old porch of stone, with a bench of stone on either side, and pointed windows trying to look out under brows of ivy. The porch opened into a long low hall where breakfast was about to begin. The table was laden with hearty country fare and Farmer Stephen Anerley readied himself to fortify the inner man. But the farmer was vexed because there were no shrimps on the table. Not that he especially delighted in shrimp, but he appeared to like them, because Mary, the delight of his life and the flower of his flock, made it a point to see that her father was supplied with them. She hunted for them when they were in season, down at the mouth of the Dyke. She would bring them back to be cooked in butter, as her special treat for him. Farmer Anerley was not only a little vexed, but also somewhat discomforted because it seemed that his darling Mary was keeping something from him. She led a good clean life, but to be a farmer's wife, as he knew she would be, would demand from her the strength and stamina of a cart horse. Though Mary was strong and healthy, she was no cart horse. Stephen had watched her go across the field in the early morning and through the gate where the pathway led into the Dyke. She was a beauty, and no mistake, even more beautiful than her mother had been at the same age. He knew he spoiled her, but he knew too, the long hard years he and his wife had labored to make a prosperous living from his own farmland. That time would come soon enough for Mary. She had so much grace and charm. Perhaps she was a little too strong willed and independent but she was an obedient lass for all that. At least until now.

Mary, who could read him like a sailor reads a compass, darted back and forth into the kitchen to help her mother lay the table, hoping to avoid her father's questioning eye.

Just as she was sure she had avoided his looks for as long as she could hope to, there came the noise of the dogs barking and men's boots stomping into the porch. Then a tall man, with a body full of corners, and a face of grim temper, stood in the doorway.

"Well, well now, Captain!" cried Stephen Anerley, getting up to greet the visitors. "Come ye in and sit doon to the table, and your men along o' ye. Ye've been hard at work doing the king's business, I'm sure. The breath of us all is hard to get when we're doing our duty"

"Aye, but the men be damned! They shall have all the victuals they want in good time." Captain Carroway barked. He was starving, and the sight of the heavily loaded table and the farmer's half-full mouth, made his own emptiness the more bitter. So he was resolved to adhere to strict discipline. He would feed himself first and then his men, in proper order.

"Coom in, coom in, gentlemen all," said Master Anerley, side-stepping the captain's intentions. Though he believed in discipline, his big heart would not suffer men in the king's service to wait upon their hunger. "Glad to see all of ye, that I am. You've hit upon the right time for coming too. Mary, there's a dear, run and fetch some more plates and we'll fill them up for all the gentlemen, Sophie lass, call our Willie down and have him get that black pitcher full of our best malt brew."

The farmer knew well enough that young Willie, though a year or two older than Mary, was still a-bed and it grieved him to admit that his wife favored young Willie's laggardly ways just as much as he favored his beautiful Mary.

"Ah, poor lad, our Willie has a bad chest this morning," said the mistress of the house. "I fear he overheated himself in the barley harvest yesterday."

"Aye, aye, I forgot. And he has to heat himself in bed again this morning! Mary, lof, how many hours was ye up already, lass?"

"Your daughter, sir," answered the captain, with a glance at the maiden from over the top of the gleaming froth of his ale, "your daughter has been down the Dyke before the sun rose high enough to cast a shade and was doing of her duty by the king and his revenue men. Mistress Anerley, your good health! Master Anerley the like to you and your daughter and to all of your good household." He drank deep and set down the tankard. "A very pretty brew, sir, very pretty indeed." He heaved a contented sigh and then bellowed at his men, "Fall back, men! Fall back I say! Have a heed to discipline. Mistress Anerley, if you'd just give them a bench back against the wall, they'll wait their turn. And if you have any beer brewed for the workmen, that'll do the right thing for their bellies, when the time comes. They've not the refined taste of such as me and you, Mr. Anerley."

"But surely, Captain Carroway, you wouldn't sit down to eat without them. Look at the dust and the dirt on them. Poor creatures, they've done a day's work already," said Mistress Carroway.

"Yes, Madam, that they have. But they're always looking for a free bit of victuals whatever their state. They can wait their proper time."

"Their proper time is now, sir," thrust in Farmer Anerley. "I'll not see men starve in me own house. That I won't. Sophie,

Mary, fill up their tankards and plates." The captain scowled but his men set themselves down to eat swiftly and heartily.

The farmer, pleased with his hospitality, then sat himself down to enjoy the pertinent conversation as to how the war with 'Boney' was going. "His majesty has made an officer of me," he boomed. "Put me in charge of the Filey Briggers, he has, in fear of the invasion. 'Brigadiers' he calls them. Not that I stand on ceremony o'er the name o' them.... Mary, lof, the captain's plate is empty. Whatever will he think of us?"

Mary stood up with a bright blush to make her way to the kitchen.

"But hold up your head, lass. 'Tis nothing to be ashamed of," her father said with a tiny smile of pride, and a pat on her shoulder. "To my mind, captain, and I may be wrong, but to my mind, that little lass could stand upright with the best of them." Mary ran off to do her father's bidding, glad to be out of the sight of so many men. "Ye never heard me say that she were any booty'" the farmer continued, "but God has made her as she is, with straight legs and eyes. Howsomever, there may be many a lass worse favored than she in the East Riding."

"You may ride all the way to London and not find a maid fit to hold a candle to your Mary!" exclaimed the captain. The farmer hurrumphed in agreement, happy to have his daughter so appreciated.

"Come, Captain Carroway," he said, pushing away from the table at last. "How goes the fighting with the froggies, now. Put up your legs, and light your pipe and tell us all the news."

"Men! Be off with you," the captain shouted. "Ye've fed well. No more neglect of duty! Place an outpost at the fork of

Sewerby road and watch out for the enemy while I hold a council of war, with my brother officer here."

The men made themselves scarce.

"Well, now the rogues are gone let us make ourselves at home. Ay, but this is uncommonly fine stuff," said he, wiping his mouth on his sleeve. He took another swig of the new jug Anerley had brought out. "How the devil has this slipped through our fingers?.....Well, well, never mind that.... between friends," he added, as Anerley began to flush. "But as to the war, sir," he hurried on, "the soldiers is going to the devil, for the want of simple discipline and principle."

The farmer nodded, "Tell us more, sir,"

"Well now, you see this little slash across my eye, sir? Got that when I was in the navy with Lord Nelson. Been in the navy and in the army I have and now I'm in the Revenue. It's a nasty business compared to the navy, but I owe my duty to my family first, now."

"Do take care, sir," broke in Mistress Anerley, "Those free-traders now have come to such a place that they might shoot you, any day or night."

"Not they, Madam. They are not murderers. In a hand to hand conflict they might do it, as I might do the same to them. Why, this very morning my men shot at the captain of all smugglers, Robin Lyth of Flamborough, with a hundred guineas on his head. I don't wish to see him dead, but a man with a family like mine can never despise a hundred guineas."

"Why, Sophie," said the farmer, thinking slowly with a frown, "that must have been the noise I heard through the window when I was getting up this morning. Three gunshots, or might a' been four.

Thought it was one of them there poachers. How many men was you shooting at?" He wrinkled his brow a bit.

"The force under my command was in pursuit of one notorious criminal; that well known villain, Robin Lyth."

"Captain," exclaimed Farmer Anerley. "You have to do your duty but I'm amazed to hear that you would have brought down four gun muzzles on only one man." His brow wrinkled some more. Then his face reddened at criticizing a guest in his own home. But Farmer Anerley's sense of fairness, rightfully inherited by his daughter, didn't sit well with four against one.

"The force under my command carried only three guns, sir" replied the captain pompously, drawing himself up straight in the old chair and glowering at him.

"Captain, I would never have done the same if I'd been in your place. I call it ungentlemanly, that I do!" He paused, and added in a kinder tone, "But then…. many things are done in haste. I take it that this was one of them."

"It was not, indeed. All was done correctly. We was never so much as a cable's length behind him, --as close as I've ever been in all my years."

"Ah," heaved Farmer Anerley, "I ask your pardon. You and your men must have been too far back to holler then. " He nodded, thoughtfully. "At our age, the breath in us dies a bit quicker than we'd like. So you used your guns instead of your breath, hey?"

"Stuff and nonsense!" cried the captain. "Who was as fresh as a new caught herring when he came to your door this very morning? Nay, but I tell the truth. I said 'Fire!' and fire they did. Hurrrumph! What do you volunteers know of the revenoo'er's. duty?" He sucked hard on his pipe.

"Stephen, you shall not say another word," Mistress Anerley stopped her husband.

"These matters are quite out of your line altogether. You've never taken anybody's blood. The captain here is used to it. He was a soldier. It's part of his job."

Captain Carroway bowed to his hostess, while his gaunt and bristly countenance gave way to a pleasant smile. At the same time Master Anerley was thinking he had spoken a might too frankly to one who was a guest in his home. All this considered, he stretched forth his right hand to the officer and the two strengthened their mutual esteem once again. Then the farmer lifted his sturdy frame from the bench and explained that he had to see a man who had come about some hay ricks. But he urged his comrade to sit a while longer and take his ease after such a hard morning's work and left.

Carroway denied that he had need of rest, but when the farmer's good wife urged him to stay, since she had something in particular to tell him, he was persuaded to smoke another pipe. She left him at ease in the warmth of the hall for a few moments, while she took care of some house-wifely matters, and explained she would be back directly to tell him what was on her mind.

Carroway settled into the chair, but Mistress Anerley's work took longer than she had anticipated. Before long, he was in a vapory dream of ease. His breathing deepened and there might have been the faint beginnings of a snore, though the man would have denied it.

Then somewhere in the midst of his hazy dreams, he heard a sweet, soft voice. Mary had crept back silently to the breakfast scene. "It was me who helped him. Will you forgive me? But I couldn't help it. You would have been so sorry if you'd shot him."

The captain gave a little snort and grunt.

"I could not be happy without telling you the truth," the soft voice continued, "because I told you such a dreadful untruth. And now—oh! Here comes mother!" The Captain continued to drift in a cloud of comfort and warmth. The whispered words dissipated in his dreams.

Mary ran swiftly to the table and began to rattle dishes as she collected them for the kitchen. She looked all innocence as her mother appeared in the doorway.

"Whatever has come over you this morning, Mary. You cannot let the captain rest. Go now and look for the hens' eggs, this very moment."

Mary left the dishes and ran with relief into the sunshine and far from her guilt at deceiving the captain.

Chapter Three

MRS. ANERLEY ENLIGHTENS CAPTAIN CARROWAY

Captain Carroway stirred drowsily as he heard Mrs. Anerley's sharp words to Mary. He forced himself to alertness.

"Rest, madam? She's never disturbing my rest. Rest is for those who have finished their day's duty and mine's not done yet," he blustered. "I never felt more wide awake in my life. We of the King's men must snatch a wink whenever we can, but with one eye open, and it's not often we see such a delightful sight as you and your daughter."

The farmer's wife blushed a little at the compliment, since after she'd finished her tasks she had put on her second best Sunday cap in honor of the officer. Even so, the compliment did little to disturb her. She had seen too much of life to be as flattered as a young country miss might have been.

"Ah, Captain Carroway, you know how to get along with us farming folk. I expect it comes of all your experience with foreign wars. You are never at a loss to find favor with any company you're in." Then remembering her self-appointed task, she added, "except one place. There's one place you can never curry favor with, it's my belief. Anyone but those born among them is a foreigner. Not even Boneypart himself could conquer that place, I'll be bound."

"Ah, you mean Flamborough—Flamborough. Yes! It is a nest of cockatrices," muttered the captain.

"Captain, it is nothing of the sort!" cried Mrs. Anerley with indignation. It is the most honest place in all the world. A man may lose a golden guinea at the crossroads one night and the good Reverend Doctor Upandown of the Flamborough parish would have it and return it any time within seven years. But you ought to know by this time, who they and what they are. Hard as it is to be accepted by them."

"I only know that they're a closed mouthed lot, and the devil himself never could get them to speak if they hadn't a mind to it."

"You are right, sir. I know their manner well. Although they are open as the sky with one another, but close as the grave to all the world outside, and close most of all to people in authority like you."

"Mistress Anerley, you're absolutely right. Not a word can I get out of any of them about the scurrilous doings of such as Robin Lyth. Not even the king's name carries any weight with them."

"And you won't get anything out of them, sir, not by money or even living among them. The only way to do it is by kinship or marriage. That is how I come to know more about them than almost anybody else this side of Dane's Dyke. My husband, as kind and as well spoken as he is, can't get near them; and neither might I if it weren't for Joan Cockscroft. Being Joan's cousin, I am like one of themselves."

"Cockscroft! Cockscroft? I know that name. Do they keep the public house there?"

"The Cockscrofts keep no public house," Mrs. Anerley answered with a flush of pride. "Why, she was half-niece to my grandmother and never was beer in the family! No, you are thinking of Widow Precious, licensed to the Cod and Hook." She sat down cozily in the chair at the other side of the fireplace. "Now I have something to tell you. Something as I hope you will hear clearly and note what I say." She smoothed out her apron and turned her attention to the captain. "I have to tell you of a time a'fore you came to this coast, sir. It was about the time when everybody in these parts thought to make a fortune in banking rather than fishing. Poor Cousin Joan was robbed of her money through the fault of her own trustees. And Robin, her husband was driven to fishing for a living again."

"I've heard that kind of story often," said Captain Carroway puffing on his pipe, "and it served them right. Others knew how to keep their money safe, ma'am."

"Neither Captain Robin Cockscroft nor his wife was in any way to blame," answered Mrs. Anerley firmly. "Now I've set my mind to tell you something and I will do it truly, if I am not interrupted."

The captain settled lower in his chair, saying with a shadow of chagrin, "Madam, you remind me of my own wife."

"Aye, Mistress Carroway must understand you well, Captain." She took a deep breath and continued, "I was on the point of telling you about my cousin Joan and how she was married when she was young and good looking and long before her money gave out. I was just a child at the time. I remember running along the shore to see the wedding feast. It must have been midsummer when the weather was fit for bathing and the sea was as smooth as a duck pond. Captain Robin, being well-to-do, and well established with everything but a wife, was known to be pleased with the pretty smile and the quiet ways of Joan -- for he had never heard of her money, mind. It wouldn't have mattered if he had. Robin was known as the handsomest man and the best fisher of the Landing, with three boats of his own, and good birth along sea-lines. Well, that day, he set in his oar and rowed from Flamborough all the way to Filey Brigg, and thirty-five fisherman rowed after him, for the Flamborough people make a point of seeing one another through, in good times or in bad. When they arrived there they met my cousin Joan, with her trustees, having come overland in four wagons. There, they were married. They had a great feast there and burned seaweed on the shore, for there was no fear of invasion from Old Boney in those days. Then after the merry day they'd had, they rowed back to Flamborough in the moonshine. Everyone liked and respected Captain Cockscroft on account of his skill with the deep-sea fishing lines and the openness of his hands when they were full—a wonderful quiet and harmless man, as the manner is of all great fishermen. They had bacon for breakfast whenever they liked and a guinea to lend to anyone in distress." She leaned forward towards the Captain, so that he might not miss anything she was about to tell him.

"Then suddenly one morning when his hair was growing grey, there came to them a shocking piece of news. All his wife's bit o' money and his own as well which he had been putting by from year to year, was lost in a new-fangled bank that was supposed to be as secure as the Bible. Joan was very near crazed about it, but Captain Cockscroft never heaved a sigh, though they say it was nearly seven hundred guineas. 'There are still enough fish in the sea,' he said, 'and God has spared our children. I will build a new boat and not think of feather beds.'

"Captain Carroway, that's just what he did. Everybody knows the story. The new boat built with his own hands was called the Mercy Robin after his only son and daughter little Mercy and poor Robin. You can still see the boat there as bright as ever, scarlet outside and white within; but the name is painted off now, because the little dears are in their graves. The nicer little children you never saw, -- clever and sprightly and quick to learn. They loved all the little things the Lord made as if with foreknowledge they knew of their early going home to Him."

Mrs. Anerley sniffed a little and wiped a tear from her eye with the corner of her apron. Then seeing Captain Carroway was about to interrupt, she hurried on. "Their father came back tired very early one morning, after a long night of fishing and went up the hill to his breakfast. The children, as children will, got into the boat and pushed off in imitation of their daddy. It came on to blow all of a sudden, as it sometimes does off Flamborough Head, without a whiff of warning. When Robin awoke for his mid-day meal, there on the table lay the bodies of his two little ones washed up on the shore by the cold North Sea. From that very day Captain Cockscroft and his wife began to grow old very quickly. The boat was recovered without much damage and there he sits in it, on dry land, whenever there is no one on the cliffs to see him, with hands in his lap and his eyes upon the place where his dear little children used to sit."

"Madam," the lieutenant exclaimed. "It is a long time since I heard so sad a tale. If one of my own little ones was drowned like that I cannot tell what I should be like. To lose them both at once, and perhaps only because he was thinking of his breakfast! And at such a time when he had lost all his wealth in addition!"

"Captain, I'm sure you have not heard the like of it," said Mistress Anerley wiping away yet another tear. She drew herself up, and with a firm gleam in her eye, she added, "And I'm sure you would never have the heart to destroy that poor old couple by striking the last prop out from under them. They are broken down enough and are hobbling towards their graves. Surely you would not be the man to come and strike them down again after all their troubles."

Captain Carroway sat up straight, took the pipe from his mouth and looked at her in amazement. "Have you ever heard that I am such a brute, that I would be so inhuman as to do such a thing? Madam, I have no less than seven children of my own and would love to have more."

Mistress Anerley straightened her cap, smoothed her apron and then looked Captain Carroway in the eye. "I would hope with all my heart you may. You would deserve them all," and she paused briefly before continuing very quietly, but very clearly, "for promising not to shoot poor Robin Lyth."

"Robin Lyth!" exclaimed the Captain. "We have not been speaking about him, Madam. He is an outlaw, condemned, with a price upon his head"

"Blood money," said Mrs. Anerley, "and for it, you will have taken three lives. Robin's, Captain Cockcroft's and my dear cousin Joan's. "

The Captain stood up flustered, "My dear Mistress Anerley, I cannot but do my duty and my duty is to catch Robin Lyth. My duty is also to my dear wife and our children for whom the capture of Robin Lyth would bring much bounty. We would be without want for many a year if I were to capture this rascal. Indeed, perhaps you shouldn't tell me anymore, since it might interfere with me doing my duty."

Mrs. Anerley stood up in an agitated fashion. "I can see that my story has not swayed you from your duty, Captain, but I am not finished."

"No indeed it has not, Ma'm. In fact, it has reminded me that I must be on my way to carry out those orders which have been entrusted to me." He hesitated momentarily, "But what is it about him that makes you think that the lives of such an excellent couple as the Cockscrofts depend upon Robin Lyth?" He was already buttoning his coat and fastening on his sword.

Mrs. Anerley knew that her moment was lost and besides the story would take too long in the telling. "If you would but come and dine with us next Sunday, Captain Carroway, I will finish my story. Perhaps when you have heard all of it you may reconsider. For then I will tell you how Robin Lyth came from the sea, sent by God to fill the empty hearts of my cousins, the Cockscrofts."

"Ah, Mrs. Anerley, a man may only do what is his duty and he should know well what is his duty if he has been serving our king as long and as faithfully as I. I will gladly dine with you Sunday next, at one o'clock, if the parson lets us out in time, but I cannot but say that I will do nothing for Robin Lyth but what is my duty" With that, he marched out, leaving Mrs. Anerley quite certain that the rest of her story would be unlikely to move this man. There was no doubt he had well earned and much enjoyed the power his position gave him.

So it was, that Captain Carroway left Anerley Farm the next Sunday afternoon with not a sliver of a change in his attitude. His stomach was once again filled with fine fare, which might change his waistline, but the tale told by Mistress Carroway of how Robin Lyth came to Flamborough did nothing to change his intentions towards that free-trader.

Chapter Four

HOW ROBIN LYTH CAME TO FLAMBOROUGH

Half a league on the north side of bold Flamborough Head, the intrepid North Sea has carved out from the white, chalk cliffs, a little cove. It is more like a grain-shoot than a bay, for the cliffs angle a steep causeway down to a narrow strip of shingly sand at the edge of the water. Truly, in bad weather and at high tide there is no shingle at all, for the waves crest and surf up the steep incline itself. The cove, although sheltered from some quarters, receives the full brunt of north easterly gales, which means there is no safe anchorage there. But the hardy Flamborough fishermen make the most of its quiet times and gratefully call it, "North Landing", even though the wind and the tide must be in the right mood for anything to land there except rough, breaking waves.

Here, the long, desolate sea rolls in with a sound of melancholy, and the grey fog drizzles over the cliffs which provide the scant shelter for a fishing boat. Yet here too, upon this narrow ledge of sand and seaweed, it is said, the rugged men who peopled Flamborough in the time of the Danes, first landed.

And it is here, it must be remembered, that even today, uncommonly fine cod are landed.

Landed, that is, if that word can truly describe the arduous task the fishermen undertake, to bring ashore, not only their catch, but their boats, from the reach of the ugly waves that would threaten to dash them all.   Here, the heavy boats beach themselves and wallow and yaw in the shingly roar. With the gunwales of the boats swinging and rolling from side to side, and the hull and stern going up and down like a pair of lads on a see-saw, the crew unload their catch into baskets heaved over the backs of forlorn but intrepid donkeys. These, laden with three hundred-weight of fish apiece, with a flick of their tails and harsh braying, mount the steep slide at the urging of the fishermen.

No sooner are the fish disposed of at the top of the cliff, than the toughest work begins. For after all that these heavy boats have endured at sea, they must now be hauled far up the slide out of the reach of the powerful waves. A big rope from the capstan at the summit is made fast and each boat is tugged, with a groaning and a grinding, to her berth of safety. Each boat has her own special place on the steep bluff and reaches it by dint of the men's sheer effort of arm, legs and lungs. With a pant and a shout in steady time together, the fishermen hoist and haul the boats, (which have a keel especially designed for this endeavor), until all are displayed in a long row, gallantly balanced on the steep incline. Once there, they make a bright show upon the dreariness of the cove. Painted on the outside with the brightest of scarlet, and the inside with purest white, from a distance they resemble butterflies, poised and preening their wings in readiness for taking flight into the seething depths below them.

Little could be seen of that bright array of fishing boats in the dark of the early morning on St. Swithin's Day, 1782. The summer weather on Flamborough Head had been worse than usual and the fishing no better. But word had swept over the village that the long looked for fish had at last arrived. All Flamborough gathered together at North Landing long before daylight, along with as much paraphernalia as could be rounded up for the urgent task that lay ahead. Rollers, buoys, nets, kegs, swabs, tenders, blocks, buckets, kedges, corks, oars, gaffs and every kind of fishing gear imaginable, was collected at the top of the slip and dispersed among the lined up boats. Several ancient tin lanterns gave feeble light as bodies and gear jumbled about in the dark. The moon was just setting over the western highland, while away in the northeast, over the sea, a slender wisp of grey began to materialize, betokening the rise of a fine sunny day.

With haste and bustle the rugged boats were launched down the slipway one by one. The timber shores were jerked out from under them. Then, guided by the rope from the capstan and their strong-armed crew, each boat slipped away down to the shingly shoreline and splashed into the water.

Just as they got to boat number seven, which used to be the Mercy Robin, came the urgent cry, "Hold hard!" The closest fisherman lunged against the boat with his sturdy shoulders stopping it in its flight. The men at the top pulled hard on the rope to delay the descent.

Captain Robin Cockscroft, had spotted something white under the stern. He put out a hand to touch it and felt the warmth of a bundled baby. It was in imminent peril of being crushed to death. He stooped underneath the boat as the men held it steady and pulled out a small child, sound asleep. It was still too dark for the men to see what Robin had discovered and the urgency of the launch could not be held back. Quickly Robin looked around for his wife, but she had fallen back into the dark shadows to cry a little, remembering the days when her small children had been with her enjoying the excitement of the launch. The nearest woman Robin could spy, who was not running around in the midst of the action giving help and last minute advice to their husbands, was an old lady sitting on a tuft of stubbly grass on the side of the cliff nearest the slope. Swiftly, Robin laid the child next to her with swift and terse instructions to make sure the babe was given to his wife. Then he covered the sleeping child with an old sail and rushed back to join his ship-mates.

Throughout the tramping of feet, shouts of command, creaking of capstans, the grating roar of the boats across the shingle and the plunging into the waves, the babe slept on peacefully near the old lady and under the sail cloth.

Gradually the noise and turmoil subsided and the dark night lightened to morning. The village folk left behind, mostly fisher-wives, gathered up their bits and pieces and climbed the steep slope to the top of the cliff to watch the progress of the boats. When the sun was really up and every chalk cliff face had a color of its own, the remaining few women and children came up from the water's edge. It was then that they discovered the poor old woman fallen asleep with the babe at her side.

"Nanny Pegler, get oop wi ye!" cried an older lady. "Shame on ye to lie aboot so." Then spotting the child, she laughed coarsely, "Have ye been brought to bed at this toime o' life? That's a wonderful foine baby for sich an owd moother!" More women gathered around. "Some foine swaddles too, wi' solid gowd on them," she continued.

Nanny, struggling to her feet and shielding the babe with her arms outstretched cried, "Stand every one of you away. Master Robin Cockscroft gie me the bairn, an' nawbody shall have him but Joan Cockscroft, which is just as he told me."

Joan Cockscroft had been lingering with the other wives on the cliffs, watching their men-folk leave for the wiles of the cold North Sea. Her heart was heavy as she watched until the last boat was a speck on the waves. She knew she had to return to her own empty cottage and remembered the days when the joys of caring for her children would distract her from her husband's departures.

The cackling of the women drew her attention. Then hearing her name mentioned, Joan moved towards the circle of women.

"Tell ye what, but that yon bairn's a frogman," pronounced the eldest old woman. This caused some stir among the women, and they retreated a little, for the threat of Napoleon still created an uneasiness among the people of that coast.

"Frogman!" cried another old woman. "Naw, there's no sign of the frogs about him. He's as fair and as clean as a tyke. A' might almost a' been born in Flamborough."

At that moment Mrs. Cockscroft approached. The women stood aside for her, for she had been kind to everyone, and all knew how she had taken to heart the loss of her children. At first glance, Joan's face was hard. What was this child compared to her own two lost children?

But suddenly the child opened its eyes and his clear gaze cut to Joan's heart. With an outburst of tears, she flew straight to the little one, snatched him up into her arms and tried to cover him with kisses. But the child was of the age when he wanted no-one but his mother. His little face screwed up and a burst of tears came from him. He tried to say some words which no-one could make out. But Joan knew children, and soothed him down with delicate hands and a gentle look. She cuddled him to her, warming up his little hands and cheeks, so that before long he smiled and snuggled into her. In another moment, she turned to pass the women, with the child, his arms flung round her neck and his cheek laid on her shoulder. She said as she passed, "The Lord hath sent him."

Chapter Five

HOW ROBIN LYTH CAME TO FLAMBOROUGH (continued)

Now the people of Flamborough would listen fairly to anything that might be said by one of their own, but from experience, they feared two great powers -- the law and the Lord. Living in such a stormy place, their experience of the Lord was frequent, whereas they knew much less of the law. Even so, their fear of the law was greater than their fear of the Lord, for they never knew what the law might cost them. With this in mind, the ladies of the village took it upon themselves to persuade Joan that she would be more secure in the raising of the child if they could discover the law's opinion of her plan.

For the Flamborians, there was one great advantage when they needed advice from either the law or the Lord. It happened that in the parish of Flamborough, both of these powers were centered on one man, known familiarly as "Parson Upandown". His name in truth was the Reverend Turner Upround. The villagers' name for him derived from an incident early in his years of ministry at Flamborough, when it seemed that the good Doctor Upround could never feel comfortable with himself when preaching condemnation of sin, without softening the sinner's judgment by recanting all the perils he had threatened previously. As a consequence, the rector became known far and wide as 'Dr. Upandown,' even among those who loved him the best.

It is a fact that Dr. Upround was both a Doctor of Divinity and a Justice of the Peace. In either capacity he was loved by all that knew him. Indeed they loved him the more for just what his nickname implied. He was a kind and tender man who thought twice about it before he said anything to rub sore consciences, even when he had them at his mercy. Happy in his calling, this pleasant, inoffensive man was blessed with a good wife, who blessed him with two fine young boys and a younger daughter. Happier still, he had a solid income of his own and so his wife and parishioners were proud to have the doctor in his pulpit every Sunday. His wife took care that his rich, red hood, kerseymere small-clothes and his black silk stockings, set upon calves of such dignity, were the envy of other congregations all the way to Beverley.

It was to this man, on that St. Swithin's morning, that the grannies and wives of the village brought good Joan Cockscroft and the young child – but not before ten o'clock of that morning.

Dr. Upround had long ago decided that the fishers of fish had to comply with the habits of the fish, but the fishers of *men* need not be up at the small hours of the morning as were his congregation. The Flamborians were happy with that custom, since they certainly did not want him among their boats, where the sight of a parson before going to sea was said to be the worst of bad luck and would set the burliest of fishers shaking in his boots. Joan had had time then to feed and wash the little toddler and wrap him up in her own woolen shawl. All this time the child stared about him with wondering eyes. He spoke out at great length, but Mrs. Cockscroft could not make out the gibberish, except once or twice when he flew into a tantrum at not being understood. Then she fancied he pronounced a word or two, which made Mrs. Cockscroft hope that her ears were wrong --or else they were foreign words and meant no harm. When she asked him his name, he answered over and over again—"Izunsabe, Izunsabe!"

By the time she brought him before Dr. Upround, with the other women surrounding her, the boy looked so calm and peaceful that none could think that he was other than of pure English stock.

"Set him down, ma'am," the doctor said, after hearing the story from the half a dozen women. "Mistress Cockscroft, put him on his feet and let me question him." As she set him down, the child resisted. He dug in his heels, spun around and swore with all his might. Then he threw himself into a tantrum, waving his little hands and legs and twirling his thumbs in a very odd and foreign way.

"What a shocking child!" exclaimed Mrs. Upround, who had joined the gathering in the doctor's library, with her daughter close behind. "Jane!" she cried to the parlor maid, "Take our Janetta away upstairs. I'll not have her hear such language."

"The child is not to blame," said the rector kindly, "but only the people that have brought him up. I never saw a handsomer child in all my life." He held out his hands to the child. "Come, my little fellow, shake hands with me."

The boy broke off his tantrum, and looked up at this tall gentleman with great surprise. His dark eyes dwelt upon the parson's kindly face with a questioning look. Then he put his hands into the gentleman's and burst into a torrent of tears.

"Poor little man!" said the rector very gently, taking him up in his arms and patting the silky black curls, while great tears dropped on his robe and a nose was rubbed on his shoulder." But the good doctor cared not a whit, for he had only put on his daily robe and not his best one. "You are very young to be having such bad times. Why, how old are you, if you please?"

The little boy sat upon the kind man's arm and poked a small investigating finger in the man's ear, and then he said proudly, with a toss of his chin, "Sore." The women drew a long breath and nudged one another.

"Well done! Four years old, my dear. You see that he understands English well enough," said the parson to his parishioners. "He will tell us all about himself by-and-by, if we do not hurry him. You think him a French child. I do not. Though the name you say he calls himself, 'Izansabe' has a French sound to it. Let me think. I will try him again with a French question, *Parley-vous Francais, mon enfant?*"

Dr. Upround watched the effect of these words upon him a little anxiously, in case the child replied in French. For the good doctor knew no more of that language than the words he had spoken and wondered how he should look before his congregation if he were unable to translate any reply. Luckily, the child looked none the wiser and the doctor's reputation was saved.

"Aha!" the parson said. "I was sure he was no Frenchman. But tell me, if he were found from the sea, how is it that his clothes are dry and even quite lately ironed, from their look?"

"Please your worship," cried Mrs. Cockscroft, who had watched the proceeding with more anxiety than all. "I did up all his little thing hours 'ere you and your hoose was up."

"Ah, you had night work! To be sure." returned the parson quite unruffled by the allusion to his working hours. "Were his clothes dry or wet, when you took them off?"

"Not to say dry, your worship; and not to say very wet. Betwixt and between, like my good man's when he comes out of a pouring rain, or a heavy spray from the waves. And there was some ground dirt on them here and there. And the gold tags on his outer coat were sewn with something wonderful. My best pair of scissors could not remove them. I was frightened to put them in the wash tub, your worship; but they come up and shone lovely, like a tailor's buttons."

Then she grasped his arm, "'Twas my man as found him, sir, and it was him as says we must keep him." Her lip trembled and a look of pain crossed her face. "The Lord took away our own," she whispered.

"It is true," said Doctor Upround gently placing the child in her arms again. "But this child is not mine to dispose of, -- nor yours. But if he is a comfort to you, keep him till we hear anything of him. I will take down the particulars in writing, then you or Captain Robin can sign them, and they shall be published. For you know, Mrs. Cockscroft," he said softly, "however much you are taken with the child, you must not turn kidnapper. It may be that there has been some shipwreck we have not heard of, though I think it unlikely. So then if nothing is heard about him, you can keep him, and may the Lord bless him to you."

Without any more ado, Joan kissed the child and after curtseying to his worship, carried him straight away to her cottage.

Thus was the future of the toddler settled, for nothing came of the doctor's published report. The boy grew up tall, brave and comely and as full of the spirit of adventure as might be expected from any boy cast on the winds of Flamborough Head.

He took upon him the name of his foster father, Robin, though not his craft. No matter how hard he tried, it was in vain that the older Robin strove to cast his mantle of fishing over the boy. The boy's love of excitement, versatility and daring demanded a livelier outlet than the slow toil of deep-sea fishing.

The boy was much brighter than most, and thrived when the parson took his schooling under his wing. Yet for all that he could run, jump, throw a stone or climb a rock with the best of them. His playmates shunned him; first because he was not truly of the village, and then because his learning far surpassed theirs. Far from letting this unnerve him, Robin became more resolute. No crag was too steep for him, no cave too dangerous and wave-beaten, no race of the tide so strong and swirling as to scare him of his wits. Indoor life never suited him at all. He seemed to rejoice in danger. His nimble ways, on land and sea, (for he was handy with a boat, if not interested in fishing), won for himself the name of 'Lithe,' or 'Lyth.'

So he took his name, Robin Lyth and made it famous even far inland. The gifts of this youth were brighter and higher than all other callings, for he showed an inborn fitness for the lofty vocation of a free-trader.

Chapter Six

IN A LANE BUT NOT ALONE

Mary Anerley was not by nature deceitful, but she did resist when her mother plied her with questions with a suspicious curiosity. After hearing from Captain Carroway about her daughter's encounter with Robin Lyth, Mistress Anerley pressed Mary for information. Being truthful at heart, Mary told her mother no lies about it; but on the other hand she did not tell *all* about the encounter. She said nothing about the earring, or the smuggling run that was to take place that week. Nor did she mention the riding skirt with which she had hidden Robin Lyth. She especially forbore to mention her promise to visit Bempton Lane in a week's time.

She did consider telling her father however, to ask his opinion about her plan. Unfortunately, her father was a little out of sorts with the world that evening. Remembering that her father's duties as 'an officer of the king' sometimes made him preoccupied, Mary also realized that her father might feel bound to report her information about Robin's impending smuggler's run. To Mary, that would be a breach of honor, since she was quite sure Robin Lyth had told her in confidence.

All in all, not liking to deceive her parents, and yet uncomfortable about her promise, the more Mary thought about it, the more she began to wish she had never met Robin Lyth. But then, she reasoned, this would mean he might now be lying dead in the Dyke. What good would it do to have Robin Lyth dead? Free trade was bound to continue, she decided. Indeed it *needed* to continue, for the sake of everybody, including Captain Carroway himself, who without it, would find himself without the most important part of his duties. Then again, she reasoned, what if Robin, who was young and generous, was replaced by a smuggler who was old, ugly and greedy? Why, all the women of the county who admired Robin would blame her for that misfortune.

Clearly, Mary decided, after looking at the matter loftily, it did not matter what anyone else thought, for they could not judge the situation as well as she. Thus she was forced to reach the strong conclusion that she must keep her promise. Not only had she made a promise, but she was now in possession of the small valuable which, in all honesty, needed to be returned to its owner. She had spent two hours looking for it and after all that trouble, she was reluctant to perhaps be accused of theft just because her mother wanted to know everything and her father was a little out of sorts with the world.

The trinket, which she had found after much searching that morning, seemed to be a very unusual and possibly precious piece of jewelry. It was made of pure gold, and was minutely chased and threaded with a curious workmanship, rather like the skin of a melon. It also seemed to bear some letters on it, in what might have been some foreign language. Looking at it in its hiding place, where she had wrapped it in lamb's wool, Mary even convinced herself it would certainly be better to return it to its owner, since there might be a spell or even witchcraft in it. Nevertheless, she peeked at it many times a day and doing so made her think of its owner just as often. It also brought to her mind all the stories and wonders she had heard of him.

As luck would have it, on the very day that Mary was to take her innocent stroll down Bempton Lane, her father had business at Driffield corn market, which would keep him from home nearly all day. Mary was at first worried, since she had hoped that her father would have been working on the northern edge of the farm, which was not too far away from Bempton Lane. Knowing the impropriety of her intentions, it had comforted her conscience to think that he would not be so very far away, when she met with Robin Lyth again.

Since her oldest brother Jack had run away to the war, Mary had to enlist her other brother Willie, who, though five years older than Mary, was not nearly so sensible. As part of his education, Willie had spent a month at Glasgow and another month in Edinburgh, where he had become vastly popular for his superior mind and many exceptional ideas and inventions. There the ladies of his acquaintance, both doted on him and spoiled him, so that when he returned home, he felt himself vastly superior to the demands of the farm. As a result he spent much of his time lying around, idly imagining newfangled inventions that were more new-fangled than they were inventions of worth.

"Willie, dear, will you come with me?" Mary said to him that day, just as he came running down the stairs to try out some great new inspiration. "Will you come with me for just one hour? I wish you would and I would be so thankful."

"Child, it is quite impossible," he answered with a frown, which set off his delicate features. "You have caught me just as I have the most important work to do."

"Oh but Willie," Mary begged, "remember how many times I have helped you. Do come with me for once, Willie. If you refuse you will be so sorry."

Willie Ancrley was as good-natured as any such self-indulgent youth could be. He loved his sister in his way. He was indebted to her for getting him out of a great many little scrapes.

Besides, he saw that she was in earnest and was curious to know what she wanted.

"Well, you can have me for a while. My good-nature is my downfall," he bemoaned. Mary gave him a kiss, which anyone else might have sought after, but Willie just wiped his face. Presently the two of them set off upon the path towards Bempton.

Robin Lyth had carefully chosen his place for meeting Mary. The lane, of which he knew every inch as well as he knew the rocks and ferns, was deep and winding, and fringed with bushes. An active, keen-eyed man such as Robin himself, might easily leap into a thicket, before any coast rider or king's man could shoot at him. He knew well enough that he could trust Mary, but he could never be sure that some bold person anxious for the weight of gold in his pocket would not set up a snare for him. Such a consideration made him careful.

The brother and sister went on their way by the footpath, northwards across the uplands of the farm towards the other side of the headland. The wheat on her father's farm looked healthy and the barley too. Even the four-acre patch of potatoes smelled sweetly in the breeze. Willie strode along loftily in front of his sister, casting over his shoulder a stream of words as he went. He could talk of nothing else but his latest brilliant invention, through which he was sure he would become famous over all the world. Mary barely interrupted him, for she knew only too well that more than likely nothing would come of his bright ideas. Instead she indulged him his lengthy speech because she wanted his company. As they stepped comfortably northward, they left the pleasant warmth and bounty of their farmland. Here toward the north of the headland, jutting out into the cold North Sea, the land was damp and cold. The chalk cliffs looked slimy and greenish instead of creamy white. The fields were littered with white limestone rocks and the now sparse trees were bent like old men heading into the cold east wind, their craggy branches and sparse leaves looking like wrinkled faces and wiry beards.

This change in climate caused a new spate of ideas to issue forth from Willie. He began to elaborate on an idea which to him seemed so simple, yet cleverly contrived that he was sure it could possibly make his fortune. He decided that the change in climate in the place where they were now walking, was the result of the warm air to the south of the headland, not moving far enough to the north. He explained his theory to Mary.

"Why the air is always blowing up here," interrupted Mary, "It almost blows away my bonnet."

"You don't understand," replied Willie irritably, "You never do, Mary. My plan is to invent a simple machine that will move the stagnant air from the south to the north and thereby produce a uniformity of climate from which all Flamborians could benefit."

"How clever you are, Willie!" said Mary. She assured him that he must surely make his fortune from just such a plan. Willie lengthily continued his dissertation, expanding and elaborating upon the need for some type of a fan which, when rotated, would turn the air for miles around, thereby preventing the growth of the moss and green scum of the northerly reaches of the headland.

Just as he finished this discourse they turned a bend in the lane and came upon a large windmill, with arms revolving merrily.

"Why, Willie dear, here is Farmer Topping's mill doing just as you have described," broke in Mary. Then looking about her added, " but I do not see a decrease in the moss and scum, and the land is as bleak and bare as ever."

"Stuff and nonsense!" cried Willie. "You just don't understand. I'm not wasting any more of my precious time on you," he announced peevishly. He turned around and strode off back the way they had come, muttering something about girls and having no brains.

Mary had not the least intention of offending him, but offend him she did. She hadn't yet had the chance to explain to him the purpose of her walk. In fact·she had resolved not to tell him anything until the last minute, in case he would be overcome with the desire to put the Revenue-men onto the smuggler. So now she had to go on alone or else break her promise. She was a little anxious but she was certain that Captain Robin Lyth, whose fame for chivalry was recognized everywhere, and who was loved by the ladies for his silks and laces, must surely be all that was proper. With those thoughts she quieted her misgivings.

The lane that descended down towards the beach from here, was as bare and wild as the first part of it had been green and luxurious in growth.. It could not be compared to the pretty lanes in Devonshire where the fern, crystal brooks, and dog roses and honeysuckle entwined among the hedges. Yet the lane was a very fine one for Yorkshire. On the other hand, Mary had a prettier pair of ankles, and a more graceful and lighter step than any Devonshire lane might be accustomed to. Mary had put on her best hat, a pretty thing made of peach-colored silk with ribbons that were tied in the neatest of knots at her bosom. She had assured herself that to dress in her finery was in acknowledgment of walking with her handsome and tall brother, Willie. She was sure it had nothing in the least to do with the smuggler fellow she expected to meet.

She was deep in thought now that she was alone, as to how she would convince her father the next day that she had merely done her duty by returning the trinket. At that moment, a figure came into sight at a bend in the lane and with quick steps advanced towards Mary. He wore a broad hat, looped to the side, with a pointed black crown, and a scarlet feather perched on the dove-colored brim. It sat well upon a mass of crisp, black curls. A short blue jacket of the finest Flemish cloth bore silver buttons and was left properly open at the strong brown neck. Under this was a shirt of pale blue silk, with a turned down collar of fine needlework, which fitted the broad chest without a wrinkle. His brown leather belt with an anchor-shaped clasp supported true sailor's trousers of the purest white. At their broad bottoms, appeared a pair of shoes with glistening buckles. Mary was so amazed at the splendor of this person's apparel that she barely recognized Robin Lyth. The young gentleman moved towards her and smiled warmly at Mary.

"Young lady…" he began. Mary warmed to him immediately for his politeness.

"Young lady, I was quite sure you would keep your word."

Casting her eyes downward modestly, she replied, "I wouldn't dream of doing anything else," and stretched out her hand, scarcely looking at him, for now she felt keenly the impropriety of her being there. "I have found your earring for you." Her heart pounded as she dared to look up at the tall, fashionable young man before her. "Now I must be going," she added hastily. "So goodbye."

"Surely you will wait to hear my thanks. Perhaps you should know what made me ask you to do such a thing. After all, you had already saved me from the revenue men. I have such a reputation as an outcast. I should never have asked you."

"I never saw anyone look less like an outcast," Mary said, gazing at the saucy red feather and smiling a little at her boldness.

"Ladies who live on the land can never understand what we free-traders go through," Robin replied, his voice soft and rich as the murmur of the summer sea. "We try to look our best, especially when we expect such a great honor as meeting with you.

Unhappily, free-traders' days are short if the coast guarders have their way. So we must make the most of it."

"Oh please do not speak of such dreadful things," said Mary.

"You remind me of my dear friend, Dr. Upround, the very best man in the whole world, I believe. He will never let me dwell on such a fate."

Mary looked up at him in amazement, "Is Dr. Upandown a friend of yours?" she exclaimed.

"Dr. Upandown, as some people call him," said the smuggler with slightest note of reproof, "is the best and dearest friend I have, next to Captain and Mistress Cockscroft, whom I think you all know at Anerley Manor. Dr. Upround is our magistrate and clergyman. He doesn't mind what people say about me, and honors me with his friendship. In fact I am to be at the good doctor's at seven this evening, for supper and a game of chess."

"Oh my! Oh my!" exclaimed Mary in puzzlement. "He is a Justice and you were being chased by the soldiers of the king just last week. How can you be the Justice's dear friend?"

"Young lady, it is truly to be wondered at. What a shameful murder it would have been to shoot me. Yet, but for you I surely would have been shot."

"You mustn't think of such a thing!" exclaimed Mary, her cheeks pink, as she remembered her kind deed. Then, remembering that she should not be lingering here in the lane, she added, "but I shall not keep you from the good Doctor's company. I must go."

"Ah yes, of course, but I would be most ungrateful if I did not see you safely on your way. You have already been put to so much trouble for me. I'm on my way to Flamborough so we are going in the same direction. Come, I shall tell you what made me so anxious about this mere trinket, as we walk along. It is now worth ten times as much to me as before, because of the one who found it for me."

"I should like to hear about it, sir, if I had the time," said Mary with a fine blush. "But my brother, who came with me, may perhaps be waiting for me." Mary knew that this was not very likely, but she wanted to let the smuggler know that she had not come alone to meet him.

"It will not take but two minutes, I assure you," Robin replied. "I have learned to talk quickly in my trade." He grinned mischievously at her. "May I tell you then, about this earring?"

"If you begin at once and finish before we reach that corner in the path," said Mary primly.

"I'll admit that does not give me much time," said Robin. But he liked her all the more for showing her sense of what is proper. "However, I will try. Only we must walk a little more slowly."

"Nobody knows, where I was born," he began. "They only know that I was found upon this coast as a very little boy, lying among the fishing boats of North Landing. Of course I was too young to remember anything but they say I was wearing a linen tunic when I was found, which was adorned with gold buttons and gold lace. Dr. Upround gave me to my new parents, as I now call them, (for they have been as good and as kind to me as if I were truly their own son,) and instructed them to keep these buttons and eventually give them to me. Sadly, all of them were lost as I grew up except for two of them. When I determined to take to the sea in night trading, I had them turned into earrings." He paused and looked at her earnestly. "There now, Mistress Anerley, I have not taken long in telling you, as I promised."

Mary peeked up at him from under the brim of her bonnet looking very concerned. "How very lonesome it must be for you, without your real parents," she said, her gentle gaze thrusting into his heart. "I am sure I cannot tell you whatever I would do if I did not know my father, or mother or even a cousin."

"All the ladies seem to think it is very hard on me," Robin answered with a fair attempt at a deep sigh. "But I do my best to get along without benefit of true relatives." Then he added, giving a sidelong glance at her, "What helps the most is when kind ladies who have good hearts, allow me to talk to them as if they were my sister. This helps me to forget my unfortunate past."

"But you should never forget who you are!" exclaimed Mary, "For everyone speaks so highly of you. Even that cruel Lieutenant Carroway cannot help admiring you. And though you have taken to free trading, who could blame you when you had no friends or family?"

"Perhaps," said Robin, "but I took to free trading for the sake of my friends, not because I had none. That is, I did it in order to support the kind old couple who have raised me as their son and who have been so good to me."

"That is even a better reason. It shows gratitude and good scruples." said Mary warmly. Then as they approached the corner she added, "but I must not stop any longer. I really should say good bye."

"Miss Anerley, I will not take further advantage of your kindness. You must know that I will never forget what you have said. I have met many ladies who have been kind to me, and many on the Continent at that. But none have been so kind as you. A minute of talk with you is worth an hour with anyone else. But perhaps you are laughing at me and will be glad to see me gone. Goodbye. May I kiss your hand? God bless you."

Mary had no time to reply, for as swift as a bird, the great free-trader vanished into the bushes. She had decided as they had talked, to let him walk with her a few more yards, but he was gone in a moment. For Mary, he had left an emptiness behind him. She was left breathless. She was sure that she had never met such a wonderful man. So active, strong and astonishingly brave. He was so sweet in his manner and voice and looks, and so unconscious of his fame. Indeed, he was so polite and unassuming, that he really seemed almost afraid of her. It frightened her a little also to think of that, but she didn't know why.

Chapter Seven

SERIOUS TALKS AT ANERLEY FARM

A few days after that momentous meeting in Bempton Lane, Mrs. Anerley had a serious talk with her husband. The farmer was anxious to be off to the fields to cut the clover, but his wife was determined that he would hear her out first.

"Stephen, if I were to tell you this about anyone else, you would listen to me in a minute. But because it is our Mary, you don't want to hear it. I tell you Mary has mischief on her mind. You've always told me I had good common sense. Well now, Captain Anerley, I'm using it."

The farmer loved to hear her call him 'Captain Anerley'. It reminded him of his dignified position. So he stopped on his way out of the door. "My dear," he said in a kindly tone. "You may be right, but who am I to understand what goes on in a young girl's mind?"

"You used to once upon a time, Stephen, when we were young. You knew then, when I would say sweet things about your hair and your smile. You knew what was betwixt you and me, my dear."

"Aye, that I did, Sophy," said Stephen remembering, "and I have the Lord to thank for it. I'm glad that we two stuck firm." he added tenderly.

"And so am I, Stephen. But now it's the turn of our young 'uns. With Willie and our Jack, now there's not much chance for either of them at the moment, but Mary, your darling of the lot, our Mary – her mind is unsettled and there's a worry coming over her, the same as was with me when first I saw you."

"It's the Lord that directs those things, " protested the farmer, "and our Mary has your good common sense. If the lass has taken a fancy to someone, it will pass, as long as we don't make too much of it. Why, how many fancies had you, Sophy, before you settled on me."

"That is neither here nor there," his wife replied. "Young girls are not a bit like they used to be in my time--no steadiness, no diligence, no duty to their parents. Gadding about is all they think of, light-headed chatter and saucy ribbons."

"That may be so with some of them, but I never see none of that in our Mary," protested Stephen.

"Mary is a good girl, and well brought up," her mother could not help admitting. "She's fond of her home, and industrious. But for all that, she must be looked after sharply. I'll tell you one thing, Master Stephen, your daughter Mary has more strong will of her own than the rest of the family all put together, including me."

"Amazing!" cried the farmer rubbing his hands together and laughing. "Amazing! A man might almost say impossible! A young lass like Mary? Such a coaxing little poppet, and as tender as a lambkin -- more strong will than her mother!"

"There's two sides to every coin. So there is to Mary," said her mother, ignoring his comments. "I know her better a long sight than you do, and I say that if ever our Mary sets her heart on any one, have him she will – be he cow-boy, thief or chimney sweep. So now you know what to expect, Mister Anerley." His wife folded her arms and nodded at him, her jaw set in a firm line.

He wasn't one to make light of his wife's opinions, mainly because they so seldom differed from his own. He knew she deserved to be heard. "All right Sophy, " he said, as he buttoned up his coat, "I'll remember what you've said. But you be the one a-watching of the little wench. Harry Tanfield is the man I would choose for her, though never would I force a husband on the lass."

"Very well, then. I'll not say more. But I've an inkling that there is more to her ways than either of us knows as yet. I might be doing the lass a great wrong, but she's keeping something from us and I might just make a guess as to what – or whom. I will not say another word until I know for sure. But if I'm right – which the Lord forbid—if I'm right, we shall both be ashamed of her Stephen."

"The Lord forbid! The Lord forbid! I don't want to hear another word. She's a good lass." He paused, then he added triumphantly, "—why I know what the trouble is. Mary has not had even a new frock for going on a year and a half. Now you get those couple of bright new guineas I was keeping in the biscuit barrel for her birthday. You take them and don't worry. We'll turn up the lass sweet with a new frock. You see if we don't."

His wife didn't move, not even to unfold her arms. "She shall not have sixpence, unless it is deserved." she stated.

The farmer snatched up his hat. "Of course, of course, my dear. I'll leave it all in your hands." He hastened off without hearing more. He knew that some long hours of labor lay before him. To face the day with a heavy heart was not a new thing for him. He had ploughed through the unstable years of Willie's fits and starts, and the sudden run Jack made for the life of the navy. If

Mary, the pride of his heart, were also to plough a crooked furrow, that would be a sad day indeed.

Mary was in the garden, innocently working on her flowers, when her mother called her. "Mary, can you spare a little time to talk with me? You seem wonderfully busy, as usual."

"Mother, my flowers depend upon the weather, so I must help water them once in a while."

"That's true, but let them stay awhile and sit down and talk with me."

Mary was a little irritated, because she could see from her mother's eyes that a lecture was coming. However, she took off her hat, and sat down without the least sign of impatience, -- or guilt.

"Mary," her mother began sternly, "you know that I am your mother and bound to look after you while you are so young. For though you are sensible in some ways, Mary, you are but a child in experience of the world. You always think the best of everybody and don't understand the traps and the wickedness of people. Still it is my duty to warn you, that the world is not made up of people such as your father and mother and brothers are. There are always bad folk who go prowling about like wolves in – wolves in...."

"In sheep's clothing," the maiden suggested, a little mischievous smile lurking at the corner of her lips at being able to finish the verse of Scripture for her mother.

"Don't be pert, miss! When do you ever read your Bible? What do you know about wolves in sheep's clothing. Perhaps you've met some of them."

"How would I know, Mother? You haven't told me what they are like."

Her mother ignored this comment and warmed to her task. "It is your place to tell me, my lady. What is more, I insist upon it. What is going on with you, that is making you behave so foolishly? Why, on Tuesday I saw you sewing with a double thread. Your father had eyes in his potatoes that you prepared for him, on his dinner plate last Sunday. You tried to hang up the dish cover the wrong way this morning. You've been wandering in and out of the house like a lost sheep, and them -- the bosom of your Sunday frock was undone by two buttons in church and it was not at all hot. In fact there was even a wasp in the next pew! All these things make me unhappy Mary. Now my dear, please tell me what it is."

Mary listened in amazement to this list of her crimes for she had never given a thought to any of the -- except for the potato on her father's plate. She blushed when she thought of the buttons of her frock -- which she had only undone because of tightness, for she had been wearing it for more than a year."

"Mother dear," she said softly, "you know so much better than I do. I don't remember the mistakes you speak of. There's nothing the matter with me. Tell me what you mean about the wolves."

"My child," said her mother, trying another tack and putting her arms around her daughter, "Don't hide anything from me. Either you have something on your mind, or you have not -- which is it?"

"Mother, what can I have on my mind? I have never hurt anyone and everyone is kind to me. I always have plenty to do. My father loves me and so do you. What more can I want? I have only one problem in all the world…"

"And what is that?" broke in her mother.

"Surely you must know! It is my brother Jack, of course. He was so wonderfully good to me. I miss him so much."

"Such nonsense, child. Jack ran away of his own free will. He has repented it more than once I dare say. I wish he was home again, too, with all my heart. Mary, is that your only trouble? Stand up where I can see your face plainly. Put your hair back from your eyes now and tell me the very words of truth".

"Mother, I am telling the truth. What more can I say?" asked Mary, a little vexed with her mother, as she stood proudly before her, her hands clasped behind her back. I have told you everything I know -- except, -- except one little thing which I am not sure about."

"What little thing, if you please?" her mother cried, her eyes flashing. "How can you not be sure about it since you always seem to be so positive about everything else, madam."

"I mean that I was not sure that I ought to tell you. I meant to tell father first and see if he thought you needed to know."

"Mary, I can scarce believe my ears. To tell your father before your mother! I insist on knowing what it is at once. I knew you were hiding something. It is very unlike you."

"It's nothing to be disturbed about, Mother dear. It's nothing of importance to me -- though it may be considered important to other people. That's why I kept it to myself."

"Ah, now we've come to it. You think you know better than your mother. Now, miss, if you please I'll be the judge of what's important. Tell me. What is it that you have been hiding so long?"

Mary's face grew red, but more with anger than with shame. She was sure she'd never thought twice about Robin Lyth -- except with nothing warmer than pity. Her mother's attitude was more likely to push her into dwelling more upon him than she should.

She drew herself up to her full height and speaking a little primly, looking steadfastly at her mother, she said clearly, "What I have been hiding, is only that I have had two talks with that great free-trader, Robin Lyth."

"What?' cried her mother, "That arrogant smuggler! That leader of all outlaws! You have been meeting him on the sly?"

"Certainly not!" declared Mary. I met him once by chance and the second time I had to see him again on a matter of business."

"This is too much for me," said Mrs. Anerley throwing her hands up in the air. You'll have to answer to your father for this."

"Very well, Mother. I'd rather do that anyway. May I go now and finish my gardening?"

"Certainly you may. You are making the death of me! To think that a child of mine, my one and only daughter, who looks as if butter wouldn't melt in her mouth, should be hand-in -glove with the wickedest smuggler of the age! The rogue everybody shoots at but cannot hit him, -- because -- because he was born to be hanged. The by-name, the by-word, the by-blow, Robin Lyth! Oh, it is too much!" Mrs. Anerley threw up her pinafore over her face, and buried her head in her hands.

"How would you like your own second cousin, Mistress Cockscroft to hear you speak of their Robin in such away?" said Mary, spiritedly. "He supports them at the risk of his own life every day. He may do wrong, that is not for me to say, but he does it very well, and he does it nobly."

"You wicked, undutiful child!" moaned Mrs. Anerley. "Go away. I have nothing more to say to you."

"No, I will not go away," cried Mary, her eyes sparking, "when false and cruel charges are brought against me. I have a right to speak. I am not hand-in-glove with Robin Lyth, or any other Robin! If I have done wrong, I will take my punishment. I ought to have told you before this, perhaps, but that is the worst that I have done. I never attached much importance to it. When a man is being hunted so unequally, four against one, as he was, should I have joined with his enemies? I have seen him only twice. The second time was only to give him back a piece of his own property which he had lost. And then I took my brother, Willie with me -- only he ran off as usual. He should have stayed with me."

"Oh yes! Blame everyone but yourself. I cannot believe what I am hearing. The whole sky will fall on us if Captain Anerley, your father, approves of Robin Lyth as a sweetheart for his daughter."

"Mother!" exclaimed Mary, "I never thought of Captain Lyth in that way, nor he of me. You accuse me very unjustly."

"Go back to your flowers," said her mother haughtily. "I've heard they grow very fine ones in Holland. Perhaps you are growing some smuggled tulips."

Mary did not condescend to answer this last thrust by her mother. She returned to her flower-beds. "Tulips in August!" she thought disgustedly. "But I am not going to let her upset me when I have done nothing wrong."

Late that afternoon, Mr. Anerley returned from the clover fields, hungry and tired, as well as put out because one of his workers had drunk a little too much ale. And Willie, whose help he could have used, was nowhere to be found. But he said nothing of it when he saw the look on his wife's face. She, for her part said nothing to him just yet, for she saw his mind was on other things. So after supper and before going to sleep that night the farmer heard it all.

At first, because he had enjoyed a full supper, a mug of ale and smoked a pipe or two, he was inclined to think very little of Mary's escapade. He was too comfortable now to have his day upset at the very end. But in the morning, in the clear light of day, he took a stronger view. He pronounced that Mary was only a young lass yet, and one could never tell with young lasses. At last he agreed with his wife, that Mary should go on an extended visit to her Uncle Popplewell, some miles the other side of Filey. He declared they could spare Mary from the farm for a few weeks and Mr. and Mrs. Popplewell, a snug and comfortable pair, would be only too glad to have their niece stay, for she was like a daughter to them.

Chapter Eight

CAUGHT AT LAST!

Meanwhile, successful smugglers' runs continued off Flamborough Head and that man whose responsibility it was to put an end to them, became increasingly disgruntled.

"Why was I born?" cried Captain Carroway. "I was thoroughly trained and educated in the services of the king. I was expected to be a top star of the king's brigade and now here am I sent down to this hole of a place, so cold and windy, among such closed-mouthed people, to be starved and laughed at; to be bamboozled by a mere boy. Another lucky run he had again last night and the whole revenue was sent upon a wild goose chase. Now every gapped-toothed, zany Flamborian is grinning at me knowing full well that Robin Lyth has made a fool of me yet again. Me-- a man who has battled for his country…"

"Charles, are you coming in for dinner?" his wife called to him from their cottage on Bridlington Bay.

"No I am not! There's no dinner worth coming to. You and the children are likely to be eating rat pie, if this state of affairs continues," grumbled the Captain.

"Come in, Charles," his wife begged. "There is very little left already. The children are eating as if their lives depended on it."

"And so they may," the Captain complained bitterly. "I just want to think a little."

"You may think by and by," replied his wife, Matilda, "but if you want to eat you must do it now or never."

The commander of the coast-guard turned abruptly, and entered his cottage.

Small as it was, it was beautifully clean and neat. Everyone wondered how Mrs. Carroway kept it so. In spite of all her troubles and many children, she was very proud of this little house, with its healthful position and beautiful view over the bay of Bridlington. It stood in a niche of the low, soft cliff, where now the sea-promenade extends from the northern pier of Bridlington Quay. Often the bay was filled with a fleet of craft of every kind, especially if the winds off Flamborough Head were treacherous, as they frequently were. Here in the bay, one of his Majesty's cutters would often shelter and the skipper would come ashore to visit her vigilant officer husband.

Yes, if the truth were known, the gallant officer of the King's guard had only two main troubles in his life. The first being the growth of the number of mouths to feed in his family and second, the growth of rampant smuggling, led by that upstart Robin Lyth.

Now when the Captain had exhausted his unusually intense grumble, and just as he sat down to eat the dinner provided by his wife, there came a loud knock at his cottage door. The sharp, gruff voice of Robert Cadman, the one of his men whom Carroway distrusted the most and whom he suspected made a mock of his authority behind his back, called out, "Can I see his Honor immediately?"

"No you cannot," replied Mrs. Carroway, "No sooner does he sit down than…"

"Ah Matilda, my love," broke in the Captain, "you know my rule, 'Duty first, dinner afterwards.' Now put my dinner on the hob and cover it with a basin. Cadman, I will come with you."

The revenue officer took up his hat and followed Cadman to their usual place for holding privy councils. This was under the heel of the pier at a spot where the outer wall broke the crest of the surges that came in the height of a heavy easterly gale. In moderate weather, this place was dry, with a fine salt smell with nothing in front of it but the sea, and behind it only the solid stone wall. Here, Captain Carroway believed that all conversation was sacred, secret and secluded from eaves droppers.

Yet that was not true, as Robert Cadman well knew. Over against the parapet under the pier there was a small gully-hole with an iron grid, which had been made to carry off the rain or the spray that broke over the walkway above. Captain Carroway never dreamed that the outlet of this little gully at the other end was the reason for so many of his frustrated efforts to ensnare the smugglers. For it was possible, by gently lifting the iron grid above, that a person might hear every word that was spoken in the recess below. If Cadman was aware of this fact, he was not disposed to reveal it to his commander. He too often felt himself unfairly ill-used by the Captain and was too often blamed for the failure of their plans to capture Robin Lyth.

The Captain settled himself against the rough stone work and nodded at Cadman, "Well out with it. What's so important as to take me from my dinner yet again."

Cadman, short and stocky with crafty eyes quickly set about delivering his news. "Captain, I've got it at last. I was set wrong the last time I brought you news, but this time I've no doubt about it. Old Hackerby sent me word last time through a wench who couldn't be trusted. But this time I heard it from his own lips. There's no woman go- between involved now.   At the new moon, Tuesday, is the next run. If we slips first into that cave we know, on Monday night, we've got 'im. E'll have 'ad 'is last good run."

"I'm sick of all the talk about those three caves. It's all old woman's talk. We've never had any luck there. How much is supposed to be coming in his time?" said the Captain skeptically."

"Captain, it's the biggest run of the summer. Near two thousand pounds in it. There's no woman involved in it this time. We'll have the right pig by the ear this time, you see if we don't," finished Cadman with some indignation at the reference to old woman's talk.

"Now don't look like that at me Cadman. If you had not been in such a flurry and haste with this news, just like a woman carrying gossip, you would not have spoiled my dinner. There'd better be something worthwhile in it this time."

With these words Carroway hastened home leaving Cadman growling to himself.

"Never a day or an hour goes by without which he insults me. A woman indeed! We'll see about that. He'll be sorry to speak of me in such a way -- that he'll be."

So it was, that the day after the new moon, there was a great flurry at the good Doctor Upround's house. Dr. Upround himself was taking a break from his reading and notes for Sunday's sermon and chanced to look through his spyglass that was mounted on a stand in his study. It was placed carefully, to look through the window and out over the south shore of Flamborough Head, with a grand sweep of Bridlington Bay. He turned his eye to the tranquil anchorage that lay to the south of Flamborough Head. There he saw a vessel and people all about her and at the landing too. There was a great to-do going on. In the midst of all this flurry was a tall man flourishing his sword about excitedly.

"Why, it's Captain Carroway," said Dr. Upround to himself. "Whatever is making him so excited. There's been rumors of some contraband proceeding on the Yorkshire coast this week, but surely not in Flamborough." The doctor liked to think that his parishioners were taking better heed of his sermons. Though in clearer moments, it occurred to him that they were probably no better than the other inhabitants of the coast.

He focused the spy-glass more clearly. "Well, bless my soul! Captain Carroway has found somebody of importance. He has got a man by the collar and he is dancing with delight. Ah, there he goes dragging him along the deck like a codfish. I declare, now he is lashing his arms and legs with a thick rope." He watched the proceedings keenly. Then he straightened up quickly. "My goodness me. They're all coming here!"

He swiftly put away his notes and rummaged in the cupboard for his justice robe. He barely had time to express the thought that he hoped it was not his favorite chess adversary, Robin Lyth who was being brought before him, to be sent to jail. More than once he had striven hard to lead that youth into some better path than free-trading, but Robin, from force of nature and circumstances, he knew, continued to follow his old pursuits. So the doctor, continued to make believe that Robin was leading an exemplary life.

There was a violent ringing of the gate bell, followed swiftly by a thumping of equal urgency upon the front door. "The poor boy," he said to himself. "Poor boy! From Carroway's excitement I greatly fear that it is indeed poor Robin. How many a grand game of chess we have had. If I have to commit him, when shall we ever meet again? However, I must be stern and not partial." He drew his robe around him with a heavy heart and bid the maid bring in the visitors.

There was a noise of strong language in the hall and something was dragged across the floor and then about a dozen rough looking men entered the room.

"You will have the manners to take off your caps," said the magistrate, with all his dignity, "not from deference to me, but to his Majesty, whom I represent."

"Off with your covers, you sons of _____" shouted Captain Carroway with his sword still drawn.

"Sheathe your sword, sir," said Dr. Upround in an awful voice.

"I beg your Worship's pardon," began Captain Carroway, his grim face flushing purple. He laid his sword to rest. "If you knew but half of the worry I have had over this miscreant, you would not rebuke me. Cadman, have you got him by the neck? Keep your knuckles into him while I make my deposition to his Worship, here."

"Cast that man free!" Dr Upround commanded sternly. "I receive no depositions with a man half strangled before me."

The men of the coast guard glanced at their commander. Receiving a surly nod from him, they obeyed. The prisoner could hardly stand as yet. He gasped for breath and someone set him on a chair.

"Your worship, this is a mere routine matter. If it were up to me, I would not trouble you at all, for the man is without doubt, an outlaw and not entitled to any grace of law. But I must follow my orders, which is to bring him to the nearest Justice of the Peace."

"And so you should, Lieutenant Carroway. Come give me your sworn statement." The worthy magistrate began to write down the captain's tale.

In brief, the tale was this: being under orders to seize Robin Lyth, wherever he might find him, and being certain that this same Robin was aboard the vessel, *Elizabeth of Goole,* which was laden with contraband goods, he, Charles Carroway, had gently laid hands on him and brought him here to Dr. Upround to obtain an order of commitment to jail.

All of this took near to half an hour for the magistrate to set down in his own neat hand writing, during which time several men black with coal dust, could scarce be kept from interrupting. But upon noticing the magistrate smile slightly once or twice to himself, they quieted down sensing something unexpected about to happen.

"Very good, Captain Carroway," said Dr. Upround, at last. "Be so kind as to sign your deposition and I will commit the prisoner upon his clear identification. That I must have first, so let us hear what he has to say. Robin Lyth, stand forward."

"Me no Robin Lyth , sar. No Robin anyone, man or woman. Me, only a poor Frenchie, make liberty to what you call—row row, sweem, sweem, sail, sail, from la belle France. For why? Zat is of no import to nobody,"

"Your worship, he keeps going on about imports," Cadman said respectfully, "that is surely enough to know who he is." He had a satisfied smile on his face.

"Enough Cadman! You may trust me to know him," cried Lieutenant Carroway. Then, turning to the prisoner, he said, "No more of that stuff! Robin Lyth can pass himself off as any countryman whatever. Put a cork between his teeth, Cadman. I never did see such a noisy rogue. He is Robin Lyth all over!"

"I'll be blest if he is!" cried the biggest of the men of coal. That there froggy come out of a Chaise and Mary as had run up from Dunkirk. I know Robin Lyth as well as my own face and that there froggy isn't him."

At this all his friends set up a good laugh, cheering their man for giving such a good speech.

"Lieutenant Carroway," his Worship said after an impressive silence, and fixing him with a steely gaze, "I greatly fear that you have let your zeal outrun your discretion. Robin Lyth is a young, and in many ways, highly respected parishioner of mine. He may have been guilty of occasional breaches of law concerning importation. We all know how frequently these laws fluctuate from year to year at the whim of the authorities. It requires a keen knowledge of legislation to keep up with them all. Sir, you would have discharged your duty in a truly exemplary manner, if only the example had been the right man. This gentleman is no more Robin Lyth than I am."

Chapter Nine

TROUBLE IN GOYLE BAY

Mary's banishment to her Uncle Popplewell's home was no hardship for anyone but Master Anerley, who keenly missed his gentle daughter. His wife, however, frequently assured him it was for the best. Old John Popplewell, as people called Mr. Anerley's brother, had made a good living as a tanner, and having no children, he sold his business as soon as he turned his sixtieth year. "I have worked hard all of my life," he said, "and I mean to rest, for the rest of it." Consequently, the tanner bought a snug little place which he called "Byrsa Cottage." It was situated about ten miles the other side of Filey.

Here at her Uncle's cottage, Mary was as blithe as a lark – or perhaps as petted as a robin redbreast. By no means was she pining or languishing for any other robin. For truthfully, until now, she regarded the smuggler more with pity than admiration; first because of his constant running from the coast guard and then because her gentle heart was touched by his story of having no real family. In some ways she was like her father, whom she dearly loved, and was as law-abiding as was he. She could not wholly approve of Robin's occupation as a free-trader.

Her Uncle Popplewell was a law abiding man too, yet he was less strict and much under the influence of his wife, as so often happens to a man without children. As for Mistress Popplewell, she was both thorough and conscientious in her chosen occupation -- that of the free-trader's friend.

Far to the right of Byrsa cottage, looking away down towards the sea, there is a high ridge of scrubby grass that runs up to a bold cliff. Below this ridge a dark and narrow bay can be seen. It is a lonely and rugged place and even dangerous for unwary visitors. Mary's aunt and uncle, having retired to the area, spent no time exploring the local inlets and bays. They were content to enjoy the fresh sea air and hard work necessary to keep their garden in order. For them to understand the sea, it was too late in life. They knew too, that Mary was well accustomed to the fits and starts of the sea, since she had been playing there since a small child. So when there came a day that Mary, having explored all the new places on the sands near her uncle's cottage, decided to explore Goyle Bay, her plan went forward without any word of caution from her aunt or uncle.

Taking her faithful pony, Lord Kepple, she led him down to their usual haunts along the strands. The weather had been very fine and gentle for some time, and the idea of storms seemed remote after such calm seas. Mary had heard there were many pretty things to be found in Golyle Bay at the time of the spring tides. The bay itself was less than a mile wide, but at certain times of the year when the tides fell back much further than usual, a deep hollow basin in the bay was left empty. In this hollow, which was barely a quarter of a mile across, Mary had heard that there were many pretty shells, richly tinted stones, unusual seaweeds and even crystals to be found. The bay was accessible only by rounding the headland beyond her familiar terrritory from the beach and then only when these exceptional tides were ebbing. The cliffs down into the bay were much too steep and treacherous to climb down easily.

So taking advantage of the tide, Mary and Lord Kepple turned the headland and ventured into the Goyle Bay. The tide was far out and ebbing still, but the wind had shifted to the east rather stiffly and with increasing force.   Beguiled by the long spell of good weather, Mary felt she had timed her visit carefully.   She thought she had about an hour and a half to spare. In fact her uncle had bade her return by one o'clock for dinner and she had every intention of obeying him.   Without any misgivings, Mary led Lord Kepple to the slippery basin.   At the mouth of the bay, a barrier of black rocks formed a crescent.   On their seaward side the sand sloped smoothly up to their edge.   But the inside, where Mary now picked her way, was the renowned bowl of slippery, smooth rock that lay below the normal level of the sea. Here lay the enticing tide pools and unusual seaweeds.   What Mary didn't know was that by some quirk of nature, there were hollow tubes running through these rocks, through which the sea easily drained at the tide's ebbing, yet at the tide's returning, the sea would build up behind the barrier of black rocks without refilling the basin.   At these times, the volume of water held back would become so deep, that with the tide and wind behind, it would suddenly spill over the brim into the bowl with a great roar, swift and powerful, and with the speed of a lion.

Mary was entranced by what she saw in the bowl. It was a lovely place, so deep and full of bright wet colors. She hooked the pony's bridle over a convenient boulder and set off to explore. She was delighted beyond description. She had never before come upon such treasures of the sea. There were so many of them she hardly knew which to take first. The sea-weeds had such intricate shapes and colors, the shells were so delicate and of so many different kinds. Then she noticed the pebbles. Some, when she held them up to the light, shone with stripes and patterns so that they looked like jewels. Fortunately she had brought a strong canvas bag with her and quickly set to work to fill it.

At every step she spied something to take home, --for her mother—for her father and, -- oh! What would Willie think of this one?

So engrossed was Mary with her task that the time flew by. The mutter of the sea became a roar, and the breeze stiffened into a heavy gale. Even when foamy spray, like suds, wafted past her, Mary barely noticed it. She could still see that the waves had not yet covered the rampart of black rocks and she believed she could easily get back around the point into her own bay.

As time went by, Mary became more discriminating about her finds. She began to hunt for the more rare treasures and cast away those she had at first picked up in her enthusiasm. More and more she became engrossed with her collection. Her bag was nearly full, and just as she stooped with a long stretch, to reach for an almost hidden jewel, she was suddenly doused with a wave like a heavy bucketful of water thrown across her back. She looked up, but even then was not fully aware of her danger.

She began to shake the water from her dress and then coming back to reality, she looked around in earnest. She swept back her salty hair from her face and suddenly realized her peril. She was standing several yards below the level of the sea and great surges were heaving towards her. The first billow of waves thumped into the basin and rushed swiftly around her ankles.

"Don't think you frighten me," said Mary boldly, yet at the same time moving towards safety. "I know your ways, and I mean to take my time." But even as she spoke, a great, black wall with a fringe of creamy foam curled on top, hung for a second above the rampart and then lashed down upon Mary with such force that it knocked her backwards. She sprung nimbly to her feet again and hastily made her way through the swiftly rising water towards her pony. But her weighty bag of sea treasures hindered her. Higher and higher the surges crashed over the rampart. Over the swirling waters, great bursts of foam and spray blew around her. She could swim pretty well, but in these turbulent waters, swimming would be of little use.

She finally fought her way to her poor old pony and here her distress was multiplied. For Lord Kepple looked anything but lordly. He was up to his knees in the rushing waters, prancing and twisting, his eyes rolling in fear. Mary flung her arms around his neck.

"I know, I know", she cried, "I'm so sorry, but I will not leave you to drown." But the pony could not be moved. His tether had become entangled under the boulder as he pranced in fear and Mary's hands were too cramped from the cold water to undo his bridle. "Oh if only I had a knife!" she cried as the waters rushed around her. She pushed at the horse and jerked at the reins, but they would not come loose. She tried to unbuckle his reins with her stiff and numbed fingers, but all to no avail. The horse in his fear was pulling with all his might to get away from the angry waves so that his headgear was tightly strained against him and nothing could snap it.

"Oh how could I ever be so stupid!" she cried as the water was now up to her waist. She burst into tears and clutched desperately at Lord Kepple as yet another surge threatened to sweep her off her feet. Suddenly she heard a loud shout and a splash and felt herself caught up and carried away like a child in someone's arms.

"Stay still. Never mind your pony. I'll come back for him afterwards. You first-- you first of all, in the world, my Mary".

She tried to speak but words would not come. She was carried quickly through the whirl of tossing waters, out of the basin and gently laid upon a pile of kelp.

Then Robin Lyth said, "You are quite safe here for at least another hour. Stay still and I will go and get your pony."

"No, no, it's too dangerous! The waves will knock you down!" She could scarcely see the pony in all the scud and froth.

But the young man was already halfway towards the struggling pony.

Now Robin was quite at home in seas such as this. He had landed many kegs in seas as strong or stronger. He also knew how to deal with horses in the surf. "Don't worry," he called back to Mary, "We've at least five minutes to spare before the basin fills entirely. There's no danger." Mary could hardly believe him. She fell to her knees with arms outstretched, crying for him to come back.

Rapidly and skillfully he made his way, meeting the larger waves sideways and rising with them. At last he had to swim the final stretch to where the little horse was also swimming desperately to keep afloat. The tether, still jammed in some crevice at the bottom, was jerking his chin downwards. His eyes were screwed up like a new-born kitten's and his dainty nose looked like a jelly-fish. Suddenly, with a stroke of Robin's knife he was free. He tossed up his nose and blew out the salt water with a sputter. Then turning swiftly against the rollers towards the dry land, he kicked out his hind feet, catching Robin on the elbow. "Such is gratitude!" muttered the smuggler. Bearing up against the waves, Robin stowed his long knife away, and struck off for the shore after him.

Mary waded into the water to meet him, shivering with fright and cold. As they met, he clasped her hands to him while Lord Kepple snorted and panted a little way off.

"How cold you are!" Robin exclaimed. "You must not stay here another moment. Please don't talk, though I love to hear your voice. You are not quite safe yet. We cannot get back around the point. See, the waves are dashing up against it already. `We must climb the cliff and that is no easy task for a lady, even in the best of weather. In a couple of hours the tide, a fathom deep, will cover this whole beach. We must climb the cliff, and at once, before you get any colder."

"Then will my poor pony be drowned after all?"

The smuggler looked at her with a crooked smile, thinking her gratitude was about the same magnitude as that of her pony. "There is time enough for him. I will not let him drown," he assured her—though he was by no means as sure as he sounded. "We must get you out of danger first. When you are safe, I will fetch up the pony. Now you must follow me step by step, carefully and steadily. I would carry you up if I could but even a giant could scarcely do that, in this gale and with the crags so wet and slippery."

Mary looked up with a shiver of dismay. She was brave and nimble usually, but now she was so wet and cold and the cliff looked so steep and slippery, she cried, "It is useless. I can never get up there. Captain Lyth, save yourself and leave me!"

"That would be a pretty thing to do!" he responded, "And where would that leave me? No, I am not at my wit's end yet." Then with a gleam in his eye he added, "I have a neat little hoisting crane up there. We brought it here for when we ran our last goods into land. None of my lads are about now to help me, but I could hoist you very well if you would let me."

Mary straightened herself indignantly. "I would never think of such a thing! To come up like a keg! Captain Lyth I would never be so disgraced."

"I was afraid you might think that." He grinned at her spirited reply. "Though I cannot see why. We often hoist up our last man that way."

"That may be so," said Mary, "but you will not do that with me. I will not have it!"

The free-trader looked at her bright eyes and the colour returning to her face. His words had aroused her spirits as he'd hoped. "Forgive me, Miss Anerley," he said. "I meant no harm. It is your life I was thinking about." He gazed at her with undisguised admiration. "But right now, you look as if you could do almost anything."

"Yes, I am warm again. I'm not afraid. I will certainly not go up like a keg. I will go on my own two feet and I can do it without help from anybody!"

"Do please take care not to cut your hands on the rocks," said Robin as he began to climb ahead of her. "Follow me."

"My hands are my own and I will cut them if I choose," said Mary thoroughly riled. "Please, do not look back at me. I am not in the least afraid of anything."

The cliff was not of the soft, easily crumbled stuff to be found at Bridlington, but was hard and slippery sandstone, with bulky ribs, bulging out here and there, which threatened to send any climbers back down again. But at the worst spots, niches for the feet had been cut out, or broken with a hammer, though they were scarcely more than a foothold. To surmount these bulges, Mary had to resort almost to crawling at times. With her heart in her mouth, she began to wish she had taken the hoisting crane. Luckily the cliffs were not very high, only difficult. Almost to the top, her courage failed at last and she cried out for help. A short lanyard was thrown to her immediately and Robin Lyth pulled her up on to the top of the bluff, where she lay for a moment, panting and breathless.

"Well done!" he cried, when she sat up again. He gazed at her with such admiration that she had to turn her face away. "Why, you could almost teach my sailors to climb. Not all of them can get up this cliff, you know." Mary blushed furiously at his praise. "Now, run back to Master Popplewell's as fast as you can, and your aunt will take care of you."

"You seem well acquainted with my affairs," said Mary half-smiling now that she was finally safe. "Pray, how do you even know where I am staying."

"Little birds tell me everything—especially about the best, most gentle and most beautiful of all birds."

At first, Mary felt a little cross to think how much he knew of her habits. Then looking back out over the bay at the steely grey breakers, pounding the point, and remembering how much he had done and how little gratitude she had shown, she forgave him the impertinence and asked him to come back to the cottage with her.

"I will bring up the little horse first," he said. "Have no fear, I will not come at all unless I bring him. But it may take two or three hours."

With a wave of his hand he set off along the cliffs as if the Coast riders were after him. He knew that Lord Kepple would have to be hoisted by the crane and he could not manage that alone. And the tide would wait for none of them.

Upon the next headland he found one of his men, for the smugglers kept a much sharper lookout than did the forces of his Majesty, because they were paid much better. Together with their hoist, which was hidden in the thicket of some bramble bushes, they managed to strap Lord Kepple and hoist him up like a bale of contraband goods.

Chapter Ten

LOVE'S UPS AND DOWNS

The news of Mary's narrow escape did not spread far; first because Uncle Popplewell did not want her parents to hear about it in case they might make her return home. Also because Mrs. Popplewell was not anxious to let the world know that the famous smuggler spent much time at Byrsa Cottage. In her role as friend to the free traders, Mrs. Popplewell valued what anonymity she had. As for the Anerley's, the Popplewells were successful at keeping the escapade quiet. But as for keeping quiet about Robin's frequent visits to the cottage afterward, Mrs. Popplewell had not counted on Robin the man, rather than Robin the free-trader. Mary was an obedient girl and she knew full well what her father would think of the many times Robin came to the cottage. "to see if Mary remained in good health."

Though the Anerley's did not hear about the rescue, there was one person who did. He also heard of Robin's visits to Byrsa Cottage. Lieutenant Carroway was not a man to be hindered from his duty. He subscribed to the epigram, 'all's fair in love and war.' Since Robin was the one in love, and the Captain made war with free traders, he could not sympathize deeply with the tender passions and certainly not with the wooing of a smuggler. Master Robin Lyth was in the contraband condition known to the authorities as love. Carroway knew this and reasoned that since a young man in love is seldom in his best wits, this was the best time to nab the smuggler.

"Tonight I shall have him," he said to his wife. "The weather is stormy, yet the fellow still comes between the showers to see his sweetheart. That old fool, the tanner, knows all about it but doesn't do his duty as he ought. Aha my Robin! As fine a robin as you are, I shall catch you wooing with your Jenny Wren tonight!"

"Charles, I beg you," replied his wife. "have pity on them. Do not catch him with his true love, but only when he is with his men and their goods."

"Matilda, exert your strength of mind. It would be nice to catch him then, for we would benefit from all his silks.   But everything cannot be as we desire. He carries large pistols when he is not courting, so when he is courting it will have to be."   He was quite convinced that his clever plan would work, because of his superior skill.   But he would never admit that the only time he could catch the young man, was when that man's mind was quite overtaken in the pitiful condition of love.

Because of the high seas that month, Captain Carroway reluctantly took to his horse to reach Filey.   He had sent several underlings on foot to spy out the land ahead of him, one of these being John Cadman.   Cadman still harbored a grudge against the Captain, and delighted in mocking the ungainly figure of the Captain seated insecurely on his horse, grasping at its main, so as not to fall off.   But if Cadman thought it was privilege that made Carroway ride and they walk, the Captain did not see it that way at all.   He had little experience with horses.   The jolting and bumping soon made him stiff and sore.   An old war wound on his heel was soon rubbed tender and painful by the stirrup.   Nevertheless, the little troop set out for Filey that day hoping to arrive before sunset.

Meanwhile, Robin's tender inquiries about Mary's health were altogether unnecessary.   That she was thriving wonderfully well, could be judged by the bright roses in her cheeks and quick smile when her rescuer visited. Yet inwardly, Mary was still struggling with what her father, as a king's man, would think of Robin's frequent visits. She could not help but feel happy and felt surely her father would too. Robin had saved her life—and Lord Kepple's too, so plainly she could not be blamed for thinking of the smuggler a little.

In fact, it is quite amazing how Mary's view of free-trading became increasingly different from her father's. Her uncle and aunt did nothing to sway her to her father's side. They spoke only of Robin with highest praise and insisted he stay for supper when ever he could. Often he had to leave before dusk, so that he might meet his men and tend to his calling.

The Popplewells, being in the rosy glow of their retirement and in their comfort with one another after so many years, could only wish the same wedded bliss for their niece. In fact, they left the two young people alone more than would be considered proper in some circles. Yet Robin was always the perfect gentleman and Mary devised many ways to keep her uncle or aunt by her side. Sometimes she was vexed when they left her in garden with Robin and so her face was cool and indifferent to Robin. Other times, she could not help but blush and smile at his most inconsequential comments. The poor girl felt she should not encourage his attentions, yet how could she not be charmed by his manners and the tales of his exploits? He always dressed in the most fashionable manner and complimented her in so many little ways, that even Robin dared to believe he might win her heart. In short, Mary was a long way towards falling in love with Robin, even as far as Robin was in love with her.

The days grew more windy and white caps dotted the grey sea. More than once Mary looking at them remembered her narrow escape and more than once her heart was renewed in its warmth towards her rescuer. Mrs. Popplewell seeing the long looks and sighs between the two young people knew just how to interpret them.

On the day Captain Carroway set off for Filey and Byrsa Cottage, Mrs. Popplewell communed with her husband. "Johnny, my dear," said Mistress Popplewell, "Things ought to be coming to the point soon, I think. We ought not to let them be going on in such a way forever. It is six months to spring and young people like to be married in the spring, when the price of coal goes down. We were married in the spring, my dear. It wasn't a sunny day but it should have been, for we have never repented tying the knot that day, you know."

"Never as long as I live shall I forget that day," said Popplewell. He stood up stiffly, and groaned. "Debby, I had good legs in those days. I could work longer hours than the best of them then."

"And so you could now, my dear, every bit as good if you had to. Lord, how everything seems to be different now!"

"Aye, five and forty years ago was ninety times better than these days, Debby. Except that you and I was steadfast, and mean to be so to the end, God willing. But look what the lasses are nowadays. Our Mary looks well enow, when she hath a color in her cheeks. Why Robin is taking so long in speaking to her, I can't think. When I was taken with your cheeks, Debby, and your bit of money, I was never that long in telling you."

"That's true enough, Johnny. But you was saucy. I'm wondering if we might get into a bit of trouble, over at Anerley Farm, if anything comes of this match."

"I'll look after that, lass. My back's as broad as Stephen's. What more can they want for her than a fine young fellow like Robin, a credit to his business and the country. Lord, I can't abide them coast riders. Rough men the lot of them. They'd better look out if they come around here! It spoils my pipe to think about them." He sat down heavily again, sucking hard on his pipe until his face was red. "Well you push her forward and I will stir him up. I will smuggle some schnapps into his tea tonight to make him bolder. He'll never know what I've done."

It was getting towards sundown that same day, when Robin Lyth appeared as expected. Always smart in his looks, he looked unusually sharp in snow-white sailor trousers, a velvet vest, lace at his throat and a smooth blue coat with gold buttons. His keen, dark eyes looked swiftly around for Mary. As soon as she came down the stairs, his eyes shone and he took her hand. Mary blushed and was half afraid to look at him. She felt in her heart that this night he was about to speak of his love for her, but her heart did not tell her what her answer should be. She was afraid of her father's grief and anger. So she tried to make sure he didn't have a chance to speak to her privately and kept close to her aunt's apron. But those tactics were doomed to defeat, for as soon as Robin remarked how good the tea was, Mr. Popplewell saw his chance.

"You shall come and have another one out of doors, my friend," he said graciously. "Mary, take the captain's cup to the bower at the end of the garden. It's a fine evening. I will smoke my pipe and we'll listen to some of your adventures."

Mr. Popplewell marched ahead of the young people, as fast as his stiff limbs would let him. He looked straight ahead so that they could share any flutters of loving kindness or whisper sweet things or just gaze at one another without wondering if he were watching them. But instead of any such thing, this self-conscious couple walked as far apart as the path would allow. They both felt the pressure of what the other might say and so they kept silent. The lad was afraid that she would say nay, and the lass was afraid she could not say it. So they kept silent.

The bower was set upon a grassy bank at the back of the garden, which overlooked a narrow lane. Here in this nook, Mrs. Popplewell grew all her many spices for the kitchen. In the damp evening air, the smell was more perfumed than if they'd been in a flower garden. Upon the grassy bank a few flowers grew and over it all draped a beautiful, tall, weeping ash tree.

"You young folk go sit under that tree," grumped Uncle Popplewell unexpectedly. "What I need is a little rum and water. Keep it in here I do." He turned off the path into a little wooden shack, leaving Mary and Robin to sit on the soft grass bank, watching the watery sun sink behind clouds. He stepped inside the little shack and after finding his store of rum, he fussed about with bits of potting moss and the like, giving the couple some time to themselves.

A few minutes later, his wife waddled a little as she made her way down the same path and into the shack. "Now you come in here out of the wind, Debby love," Mr. Popplewell spoke out loudly, making sure the two young people could hear him. You know how your back aches with the darning you did before the last wash." So Mrs. Popplewell did as he bid shuffling her feet noisily over the tiles on the floor to make sure Mary and Robin knew they were alone.

Mary was well aware of all this maneuvering and she cast her looks downward to avoid Robin's eyes. Robin led her to a little bench where there was scarce room for the both of them. Now Mary gazed off into the far distance as if studying the twilight clouds lit by the sinking sun. Robin, though a sailor, was not interested in the weather but only if he could detect the weather in Mary's eyes. She sat silently almost as if she'd forgotten his existence.

No fine smuggler such as he could put up with this stance for long. He made up his mind he would do as when on a smuggler's run. He'd run the cargo of his heart right through the breakers, risking all. With this thought, he took her hand.

"Mary, love, why are you so quiet tonight? Have I done something to offend you? That would be the last thing I would ever wish to do."

"Captain Lyth, you are always very good to me. I could never be offended by you." She looked quickly at him and saw such a loving gaze that she quickly looked up again and stared off at the clouds. "I…I'm just looking at that pretty cloud over there." Then taking herself in hand, she added, "And who ever said you may call me Mary," she rebuked gently, hoping to hold him off longer.

"It was you, yourself that told me so only yesterday."

"People shouldn't take advantage then," she replied just a touch haughtily.

"Mary, Mary," laughed Robin "Who are 'people'? Why are you treating me so coldly? You look so lovely tonight. As lovely as you always do." Mary made a small effort to draw her hand away, but he would not let it go. "You've known for a long while what I think of you, and now….now, I must be off tonight, as I told you yesterday. I have to carry out a big contract and I may not see you again for many months." At this Mary caught her breath in a sigh, which she could not hide. Pressing his advantage, Robin continued, "Won't you tell me you love me? Or have you maybe fallen in love with a coast rider. Is that it?" He knew that would move her.

"A coast rider! Captain Lyth, you are not thinking what you are saying," she couldn't help replying with a smile. "Those officers do not want me—they want you!"

"Then they shall get neither, you may trust me for that. But, Mary, do tell me love, how is your heart? You know you have had mine for such a long time now. Oh I've thought of girls before--"

"Oh really," Mary teased, "then surely you had better go on thinking of them."

"Never, Mary. Hear me out. I have only *thought* of them, nothing more than thinking, in a very foolish way. But you, Mary, I do not think of you. I seem to *feel* you all through me. I only know that I cannot live without you. I could only mope about ..."

"And not run any more smuggler's cargoes?" said Mary, softly but seriously.

"Not a single one. Not a keg of rum or bale of silk. I promise you Mary. This will be my last run, if you would only tell me that you care about me--"

"Hush!" said Mary suddenly looking about her. "I'm sure I hear footsteps. Listen a moment."

"No, said Robin warming to his task, "I will not listen to anyone in the whole world except you. I beg of you, do not try to put me off. Soon it will be winter. Oh say that you will think of me through the long winter. I know I am a poor sort of a man. I am not of a fine respectable family like you. Only the Lord knows where I came from. I know my business is not thought well of by some, but I am not a disreputable or dishonorable fellow. If you ask me to do it, I will give up smuggling. There are plenty of other trades that I could do. Only Mary, let me have your hand, not just for now but for always." He clasped her hand to his coat."

"Oh Robin," she whispered, a little frightened. "I have to consider my father. I cannot do just as I please and you know my father bears an ill-will towards free trade." Her eyes filled with tears at having to mention her obstacles.

"I know, I know. There are rogues enough about, but I am not one of them. Your father is a very particular man, Mary, I know, but I do not care about his objections if only you have none yourself. I know if any lucky fellow wins your heart, he will have it forever. I know, by your eyes and you pretty lips. If only I could be that lucky fellow—"

"You are very good and brave, my Robin," said Mary gently. "You are wonderful to me, but if you have this continual love of danger and adventure, what would your wife be doing all the while? She could only sigh, and lie awake at night."

"Not if you are my wife! I would come home regularly every night, before the kitchen clock struck eight. I would come home with an appetite for your cooking, I'd always wipe my feet on the scraper and...and...I'd come home and play with the baby while you set the table. I'd keep everything about the house in order and never meddle in the kitchen."

"Well!" exclaimed Mary, "you quite take my breath away. I'd no idea you could be so domesticated," she teased.

"I will do it all Mary, if only you would say, just once, 'Robin I will have you, and I will begin to try to love you.' "

"Ah, Robin," she gave him both her hands and spoke so tenderly, "Robin, it is too late to begin, for I fear I have already begun to love you, and now I don't know how to stop."

With all that stood between them now done away, all that was on their hearts was unleashed. They had so much to say and so many questions to ask. And all of it must be lovingly whispered in the other's ear. They entwined hands and laid heads together without a thought of anyone else in the world. Somewhere nearby a skylark rose to heaven, burbling its ceaseless song. It seemed there was only the two of them and their love surrounding everything, in the hush of the evening air.

But it was not so. All the while this had been taking place, Carroway's men were hiding under the hedge of the nearby lane. Nobler men would have sought another opportunity to capture their man, but they were not the noble sort. So they lay there and snickered to themselves at how easy it was to catch a man in love.

Mary and Robin had stood up, his arm around her waist, and were stepping softly across the grass, getting nearer and nearer to the treacherous hedge. "Mary, I vow to you as I stand here," said Robin for the fiftieth time as he pressed her trembling hand and gazed with deep ecstasy into her truthful eyes. "I will live only to please you, darling. I will give up everything and everybody in the world to start afresh. I will pay the king's duty upon every single keg. I will set myself up in an honest business, in tea and spirits, and the door lintel shall bear his Majesty's arms upon it. I will even take a large contract for the royal navy. I swear it. They never get anything genuine, -- not that any one of them ever knows the difference--"

With a roar, Captain Carroway leaped before them, flourishing a long sword and dancing with excitement at the success of his plan. "That's a dirty lie, sir! In the king's name I arrest you!" At the same instant, Cadman and his cohorts came bursting through the hedge, daggers drawn and then stood in a line awaiting orders. Robin Lyth, so taken by surprise, still in his passion of the moments before, stood like a little boy caught red-handed.

"Surrender sir! Down with your arms, you are my prisoner. Hands to your sides. Don't move or I'll run you through! Keep back, my men. He's mine. I've waited many a long day for this moment."

But Captain Carroway counted his chickens too soon. At any rate he overlooked one little chicken, for while he was making great flourishes with his sword, Mary flung herself upon his bony breast. She wrapped her arms around him, so that he could not move without harming her. "Oh please Captain Carroway, she begged as though terrified for her Robin, but she flung herself at him with such force that he fell backwards on his wounded heel. A flash of pain shot up to his very sword and down he went with Mary on top of him.

His three men, like true Britons stood still in position awaiting their captain's orders. Recovering his presence of mind, Robin ran at them and knocked them down like three skittles in a row. He looked back once to be sure Mary was unhurt. Now Uncle Popplewell came forth from the shack blustering loudly and Mrs. Popplewell added her shrieks and screams enough to frighten the whole coast guard service. Mary immediately signaled to Robin to take himself away. Seeing that his brave love was not harmed, the free-trader kissed his hand to her and disappeared into the bushes and darkness.

Chapter Eleven

"MARY, MARY, QUITE CONTRARY"

"I tell you, Captain Anerley, that she knocked me down. Your daughter there that looks as if butter would not melt in her mouth, knocked down Commander Carroway of his Majesty's coast guard. Like a Bengal tiger she was. I am not come to complain, you know. I admire her spirit, sir. My sword was drawn and no man could have come near me. But she did, and before I could think sir, I was lying on my back. Now what do you think of that!"

Stephen Anerley looked in shock at his daughter. "Mary, Mary, whatever were you thinking of, to knock down Captain Carroway?"

"Father, I didn't mean to knock him down. He was flourishing his sword about so and dancing around, that I thought someone would get hurt, so I wrapped my arms around him to calm him, and his leg gave way beneath him. With all my heart I beg his pardon -- but I must ask, what right had you, sir to come spying after me in my uncle's garden?"

It was now the next afternoon. Mary had insisted on going home at once from her uncle's hospitable house. Uncle Popplewell and his wife insisted on accompanying her to help the situation. All involved were still at council that afternoon about the whole matter when in marched the brave lieutenant.

Uncle Popplewell had already made his case clear. His premises had been intruded upon. His property which he had bought with his own money, saved by years of honest trade, his private garden, his ornamental bower had been invaded and trampled upon by this outrageous, scurvy coast-guarder and his low down crew of men. In the general commotion at the time, Mr. Popplewell had seized the lieutenant by the collar and demanded to see his search warrant. When the poor lieutenant could not produce one, Uncle Popplewell's fury was unbounded. "I'll have the law on you sir, he'd shouted. You see if I won't -- if it costs me two hundred and fifty pounds! I am known as a man who sticks by his word, so beware!"

This had frightened Carroway more than any sword fight. Fights he understood, but lawsuits, that was a different matter. Uncle Popplewell knew it and vowed long and loudly he would have satisfaction for this outrage. Poor Captain Carroway was well aware by now that his zeal had exceeded his duty.

Now at Anerley Farm, the tanner frowned fiercely at Captain Carroway. He squared his elbows and stuck his knuckles sharply out of both of his breeches' pockets. Mrs. Popplewell stood behind her husband and stared at the officer as if she longed to choke him.

"I tell you again Captain Anerley, cried the lieutenant, "I was only doing my duty. As for spying on young girls, well my wife who is right now having our eighth child will vouch for my character. If I intruded upon your daughter and it justified her knocking me down it was because… because …" he looked fiercely at Mary, "well Mary, I won't say it.... but you know the reason why."

"Did you say her eighth baby? Oh Commander Carroway," broke in Mrs. Popplewell, changing the subject. "What a most interesting situation! Oh I see why you have such high color, sir."

"Madam, eight is enough to make me pale. But I thank you for your sympathy."

"I want to know the truth!" shouted Stephen Anerley, fixing his eyes on his daughter. I don't care about eight children or Popplewell's rights invaded. Nobbut a farmer am I, but concerning my children I will have my say." He thumped his fist on the table. "All of you tell me what is this about my Mary!"

He looked at each one of them with a quick hard glance, and they all looked away from him. The Popplewell's wanted to tell him when he was in a better frame of mind. They looked at Mistress Anerley, but she knew better than to interfere with her Stephen when he looked like this.

"Come now Anerley," the bold lieutenant said. "It's nothing to get so upset about. I'd sooner have lost a hundred pounds than get Mary into such a trouble as this. Why bless my soul. It's not like she's broken the law in doing a little sweet-hearting. All the young girls do it."

"Not my Mary!" exclaimed her father. My daughter is not like the foolish girls. My daughter knows her own mind and what she does, she means to do. Mary, love, come to your father and tell him that they're all lying. I'd sooner trust a quiet word from you, than a whole crowd as big as Flamborough Head swearing against you, my little Mary."

Everyone held their peace as he walked towards Mary with open arms. He was sure she would tell him of some trifle and all would be solved. But instead, Mary Anerley arose from the corner where she had been quietly weeping. She looked at the people in the room and then met her Father's eyes. She did not flinch, though tears still wet her cheeks. Master Anerley looked at her face and knew that once and forever his little child Mary was gone from him.

She carried herself with dignity and the sad smile that passed over her eyes was that of a young lady.

"Every word of it is true," the girl said gently. "Father, I have done what they said. That is, all but deliberately knock down Captain Carroway. But I have promised to marry Robin Lyth –by and by—when you agree to it."

Stephen Anerley's ruddy cheeks grew pale and his blue eyes glittered with amazement. He stared at his daughter until she had to look away. Then he turned to his wife, who just said "I told you so." That was of little comfort to him. But he didn't break out into a fit of anger, he just turned back and looked at Mary, so coldly, that it seemed to her that he was saying goodbye to her forever.

"Oh don't Father, don't," the girl clung to him with a sob. "Beat me or do something, but don't turn your back on me. Not that!" she pleaded. "That is more than I can bear."

"Have I ever beaten you, Mary?"

"Never! Not once in all my life! But I beg of you, if I deserve it, do it now. Don't look at me so coldly."

"Only you know what you deserve," he said like an old man, his shoulders stooped. "Only from now on, do not call me Father." And he put her away from him and walked out of the room towards the porch.

When he got outside and he was alone with the earth and the sky, big tears arose in his brave blue eyes. He looked at his hay-ricks and his workmen in the distance. His favorite old horse whinnied and came up to have his nose rubbed, but he didn't see any of it. "Ah'd sooner heard the bank had gone broke. Fifty times sooner, if only my Mary was a little child again." he said to himself.

Mary ran upstairs to the landing window and watched her father grow dimmer and dimmer in the distance as he walked away from the house. And she shed a tender young tear for every sad old step that her father took.

For the next few days the master of the house was stern and silent, and heavy. He neglected his food and also his customary joking. Yet he settled in to strong, hard work with which to take his mind off his troubles. But it went very hard with him. Time and again he'd come up with a bright half crown and put the money in his pocket and think he'd a mind to give it to Mary. Then he remembered his state of mind towards her.

Things weren't any better with Mary. She, who used to be as happy as a bird where worms abound and cats are scarce, was now grieved, restless, lonely, and troubled in her heart and conscience. Surprisingly, her mother had shown some kind feelings towards her. For the more Mistress Anerley thought about it, there were good things to be said on both sides. She had never quite approved of her husband volunteering as a king's man. It took him away to drill at places where ladies came to watch for the men, and it kept him away from his own bed, and he ate things she'd never heard of and it wasn't as if he was any the better for all of it. If volunteering was the thing that turned him against free trade so bitterly, maybe free trading wasn't as bad a thing as being a king's man. Indeed, from the very first, she had always said that nobody knew what Robin Lyth might turn out to be in the end. Mary told her that Robin had spoken most highly of her and that proved he was a promising young man.

If Mary was comforted by her mother, the farmer was not. He felt badly used that his wife who used to be so hard upon Mary for next to nothing, should now turn against him for what he saw as downright womanish. Master Popplewell had continually told Captain Anerley what his opinion was about the matter. He said he'd never been far wrong in any of his opinions all his life – except maybe one time in a hundred. So he wasn't about to give an opinion now, except everybody would be sorry by and by, when things were too late for mending.

To this the farmer listened with an air of wisdom because he thought his brother had made a lot of money and so he should listen to him. He just let him talk and then contented himself with thinking what a fool he was, when he was out of hearing.

The third time John Popplewell came over, (the third time in a week that is,) he burst out in anger at his brother in law. "I'll tell you something," he said, "you are so thick-headed in your farmhouse ways, I'm worn out with you! Stephen you may rely on it, that you will be sorry afterwards. That poor girl, the prettiest girl in Yorkshire, the kindest and the best, is going off her food and wasting away, because you will not even look at her. If you don't want the child, let me have her. To us she is as welcome as the flowers in May."

"If Mary wishes it, she can go with you," the farmer answered sternly. Then hating his own words he went back to work.

But when he came home after dusk, his heart was pounding. Mary might just have taken him at his word and flown for refuge from his displeasure to the warmth and comfort of her uncle's home. Still, what did he care? he told himself. Nevertheless, instead of marching boldly in through his own front door as he usually did, he carefully and quietly went around the back of the house and began to peep in at his own windows as if he were planning to rob his own house. He sighed at the thought, for indeed his house might just have been robbed of that which he loved so fondly. There was no Mary in the kitchen, seeing to his supper. The fire was bright and the pot was there but only shadows around it. There was no Mary in the little parlor, only Willie half-asleep, with a stupid book upon his lap and the candle guttering. Then, as a last hope, he peered into the dairy where she often went at nightfall to see things safe. But no. The place was dark and cold. Tub and pan, and wooden skimmer and the pails hung up to drain were left to themselves. "She hasn't been there for an hour," thought he. "My little maid is gone. I must make up my mind I'll see her no more." He had always hoped to go through life in the happiest way, simply doing common work and heeding daily business. He was content to live the round of months and years, through the changes of earth and sky and most of all, to see his children dutiful, good and loving. When he should be carried from the farm to the church, he would have hoped to see his children ready and able to walk in his ways. But now he thought, like Job, "all these things are against me."

The air was laden with the scents of autumn, rich and ripe and soothing—the sweet fulfillment of the year. The mellow odor of the stacked wheat, the stronger perfume of the clover, the brisk smell of apples newly gathered, the distant hint of onions and the luscious waft of honey hung heavily upon the evening breeze. He shook his head sadly and said, "What is the good of all this, when my lassie is gone away, as if she had no father?"

"Father, I am not gone away! Oh Father, I never will go away, if you will love me as you did before!" She stood in the arch of the trimmed yew tree, almost within reach of his arms. And though it was dark, he knew her face as if the sun shone on it. Mary had to stop her voice, as a short little sob overtook her. She wouldn't let her father hear it. Her nature was too like her father's to let him triumph over her. She felt wronged in her heart as firm and as deep as he did. And her love of justice was quite as strong as his. They only differed as to what it was.

"Dearie, sit down here," he said. "There used to be room for you and me without two chairs, when you was my little child."

"I am still you child, Father dear. Were you looking for me just now? Say it was me you were looking for."

"Ah, well, there is always such a lot of rogues to look for at this time of night. You know...they come and set fire to the haystacks..."

"Now father you never could tell a fib," she chided, sidling up closer.

"He smiled a little, I said that I was looking for a rogue. If the cap fits..." and then quite without meaning to, he did a thing that signaled his utter surrender. He stroked his chin as he always used to do, when going to kiss Mary, so that the bristles might lie down soft for her.

"The cap doesn't fit! Nothing fits but you, my own dear father." She put her arms around him to protect him. "And nobody fits you but your own Mary. I knew you were sorry. You needn't say it. You are too stubborn, so I won't make you. Now don't say a word. I only want to make you good again. You are the very best of all people, when you please. You must never be cross with me again. Promise me immediately, or you shall have no supper."

"Well," said the farmer, "I used to think I was gifted with the gift of argument. Not like a woman, mind, but still pretty well for a man as can't spare time for speechifying when he has to earn bread for his self and young'uns."

"Father it is that arguing spirit that has done you so much harm. You must take things as though Heaven has sent them. Look now, Heaven has sent me to you, isn't that so?"

"So a' might think," Master Anerley replied, "but without a voice from the belly of the fish, I wunna' believe that He hath sent Bob Lyth."

Chapter Twelve

TACTICS OF DEFENSE AND ATTACK

While all this was going on at Anerley Farm, Robin set off with a light heart to put into effect his promise to Mary. He would carry out his contract and make this his last run --albeit a good one -- and then take up the life of a law abiding citizen. So much was his love for Mary, that it seemed but a small sacrifice to pay for the life of bliss that he envisioned for them. The fact that he was in love didn't make Robin any the less aware of his need for keeping a sharp lookout. He had for the first time in his career as a free-trader, allowed his guard to slip while at Byrsa Cottage. But it wouldn't happen again. Now, he was even more alert, for he felt that he had so much more to lose. If he could outwit Captain Carroway one last time, he vowed, he would keep his promise to Mary.

Thus, a few days after the incident at the cottage, he took off for Holland to set up the trade.

It was well known for several miles around the perimeters of Flamborough and Bridlington, that there was going to be one last run that late autumn, and a big one at that. Of course nobody could put his finger on exactly where, or when or whom. But the rumors wriggled through the hamlets and cottages, by the way of aunts, uncles and cousins who knew other aunts, uncles and cousins, who had it all on good authority.

Unhappily for Robin, the news of the coast guard's persistent failure to capture him, by being so often outwitted, had drifted back to the authorities. The coast guard authority didn't like it one bit that some upstart, young smuggler could run rings around their men. The smirks, jabs, sly smiles and knowing looks of the hardy villagers along the east coast of Yorkshire, served only to irritate the men of authority who were from further south of England than Yorkshire. They considered themselves to be not only their betters, but brighter than the men who were bred in the cold fogs, and northeast winds of the Yorkshire coast.

Because Captain Carroway hadn't shown that he was any better than the best of his enemies, three coastguard cutters were sent out under orders to station themselves off the coast of Yorkshire in readiness for the expected smuggling escapade. The head of this reinforcement was Commander Nettlebones. He was a Cornishman and predisposed to being a little bit superstitious. His sail north to Robin Hood's Bay, where the three ships planned to *rendezvous*, confirmed his suspicions that there was some witchcraft in the doings of Robin Lyth. His trim and usually lively ship was ploughing through the heavy seas like a cart horse plodding along a muddy cart track after six weeks of rain. It couldn't seem to make any headway. None of the crew could understand it. Some talked of currents and a mysterious 'undertow'.

The commander knew his little ship very well and knew something was wrong, but what he didn't know was that the mystery of the 'undertow' was in fact no mystery at all. It so happened that one of the very best hands on board the *Swordfish* was a hardy seaman from Flamborough—a man who was kin to Robin Cockscroft and no stranger to Robin Lyth. This gallant seaman had found a plug hole behind his berth. It was just above the waterline and out of sight from the deck. The sailor had passed a stout new rope through the hole. Then, while he was on watch on deck, he had fetched up the end of the rope, attached a long grappling iron to the end of it and lowered it down to the sea floor. The iron did not have large enough flukes to take hold a fast grip of the rocky sea bottom thereby bringing the ship to a halt, but it dragged along the bottom like a trawl. But because of its weight it would hitch up in some hole every now and then, thus hampering the voyage of Nettlebones' good ship *Swordfish*. The other two ships, the *Kestral* and *Albatross* meanwhile were already hove to, off Robin Hood's Bay, waiting and wondering what had happened to their commander.

Arriving late to meet with the two other ships' captains had set Commander Nettlebones on edge. They had lost precious time. Upon his arrival, the two captains were immediately sent for and soon presented themselves in their senior officer's cabin to report their latest information. But neither captain durst ask the reason for the commander's tardiness. It was obvious that he was in a short and sharp mood.

After the two made their report, each adding his own interpretation to the information they had gained, as well as their unasked for opinions, Nettlebones broke in, "I've heard your reports, but I believe none of them," he said curtly. "The reason old Carroway has made such a mess of it in the past is because he always listens to the country people's tales. They are all tarred with the same brush. They stuff us with a heap of lies to set us wrong. There isn't one out of ten of their fishing expeditions that isn't a sham. Their real business is to help those rogue smugglers."

"You have the right of it!" agreed the captain of the *Kestral*. "It's my opinion we need to pretend that we're listening to what they say and then pretend to be misled."

"And it's my own opinion says we'll never capture any of these fellows until we have a large sum of money placed at our disposal," said the captain of the *Albatross*.

"The villagers support them mostly because they are so generous. And so they can afford to be! They rob the king of his taxes and get paid well for doing it. The king pays little enough to defend himself against the robbers. If we had a thousand pound apiece, with no reckoning of it, we could soon stop the contraband in no time," he grumbled.

"We've no time for complaining," snapped Nettlebones. "We have to get the job done without a sixpence to spare for anybody. We know that all the fishermen and the people along the coast are in league against us. But we'd better make certain that this next landing of goods will not take place between the Tees and Spurn Point. If it does, we'll have to call ourselves a bunch of old women.

"Come, shake hands on it gentlemen. The sun will be down in half an hour and by that time we must be well under way. Here's what we'll do. You know how our every move is watched by land. I've let it be known that we plan to catch the smugglers in the open seas, not as they land the goods, as is usually done. So we need to be seen on the sail out to sea in very short time."

"Why, that'll never work," protested *Albatross.* "We can't catch them at sea, they're too nimble for us."

"You think I don't know that full well?" Nettlebones answered irritably. "My plan is to let them think we're out at sea, but every night we'll steal back close into land again. Then before morning breaks we'll move out again. We'll say nothing of our plans to the fishermen, for they're all spies. We'll make Robin Hood's Bay our center. *Albatross,* you take the stretch of coastline from Whitby to Teesmouth. I'll take from Whitby to Scarborough and the *Kestral* take Scarborough to Flamborough. As for Carroway, we can't rely upon him. From Flamborough to Hornsea is all that's left, and that's about as much as he can manage. I think you all quite understand our plans, so let's be off. We'll surely nab some of them this time. They're overstepping their marks, trying to do it on too large a scale and we'll get them this time, by King George we will!"

"If they runs any goods past me you can call me a donkey with four legs," stated *Albatross* stoutly.

"And if they slip in past me, I will believe more than all the wonders told of Robin Lyth," added *Kestral*.

"As for that fellow," said Commander Nettlebones, at the mention of that famous name, "we can only do one of two things— let Carroway catch him and get the money for him. Or, if we catch him ourselves, we must draft him off to the navy. That young fellow is a prime sailor and it's beneath us to get blood money from the capture of this man. We are gentlemen, not thief-catchers. Come, let's be off!"

So the three cutters set forth into the wind with shudders and creaks and cranks. With long shivers in the teeth of the wind, they turned around and flew, leaping and dipping towards the running hills of the sea. Away they went merrily, through the green hurry of surges, leaving broad tracks in the brine for all who cared to see, and hoping that they did.

Away, also, went three men who had been watching the rendezvous from the top of the cliffs. One went northward and one went south and the third rode a pony up an inland lane. As swiftly as the cutters flew over the sea, so the news of their flight path took wing across the shore. Before nightfall, everyone on land whom it concerned to know, knew as well as the ships' steersmen knew, what course they took.

Across the other side of the cold North Sea a wealthy merchant of the Zuyder Zee drew forth his ancient ink-horn, smeared with the dirt of countless contracts, and signed a deal in the captain's cabin, with a handsome young English smuggler. He signed the bill with a sigh as though signing his life away. But he was not sighing because of the money, but for the memories his transaction was ending. They were aboard on old bilander, off the Isle of Texel, off the coast of Holland. It was Sunday morning and Robin Lyth was putting together his greatest enterprise.

"I'm sorry to be troublesome, Mynheer Van Dunck. I cannot let you leave until you have given me your signed bill-of-trade showing our good faith transaction for this old ship."

"It is goot. You are very goot for the buziness, Mr. Lyth, but I waz married in dis ships. You poosh a hard bargain. Dis taime I tink you will have ze bad luck, sir." He wagged his finger at Robin as he was lowered carefully into his shore boat. The roll of the sea was getting heavier and Robin was anxious to get under way. He had gathered together his flotilla of free-traders and they were all straining to be free from their moorings. The Dutchman hated to part with his bilander, but the gold in his leather bag felt safe and full in his breeches' pocket and he secretly relished being a part of breaking English law. For the Dutch thought they were better sailors and ship builders than any Englishman and such argument had been advanced for centuries between the two nations. So he went his way over the windblown waves back to the land, grumbling still, but happy to count his golden guilders when he was dry and warm.

Robin's flotilla were three craft, all of a different rig --a schooner, a ketch and the bilander. All were heavily laden as far as speed and safety would allow, and all were thoroughly well manned. Robin was aboard his favorite vessel, the schooner *Glimpse*. The ketch was named *Good Hope*. The bilander appeared to be the most heavily laden, having a great capacity for carrying goods. It was an old Dutch coaster named the *Crown of Gold*.

This grand armada of invasion made its way leisurely towards Dogger Bank that shallow sand-bank in the North Sea, that was known full well to all who sailed in these parts. There they waited for the latest news brought to them from the Yorkshire fishermen. The news of the coast guard activity, did not deter Robin, though the fishermen urged him to return to Holland. To his mind the weather was ideal to carry out his last daring plan.

"This is my last run," he said, "and I mean to make it a good one." Then he dressed himself as smartly as if he were going to meet Mary Anerley herself and sent a boat to bring the skippers of the two other boats aboard. They held counsel in Robin's cabin where Robin soon made his cohorts aware of his scheme.

"I'm thinking that your notion is a very good one, Captain," said the master of the bilander. This skipper was a dry old hand from Grimsby.

"Capital! Capital! There never was a better plan," chimed in the skipper of the ketch. "Nettlebones and Carroway! What a lark! They will crack their heads together before they catch us!"

"The plan is clever enough ," replied Robin without a hint of false modesty. Then he looked thoughtfully through the port-hole. "But you heard what old Van Dunck said. I need good luck now as never before," said he, thinking of Mary. "I wish he had not said it."

"Aye and he's a stingy old thief at that. It doesn't bode good for us. 'Tis as bad luck to say it, as it is to see an old crow sitting on the fore-stay. I don't doubt but that's why he said it. Tha' knows there's no love lost betwixt us and them Dutchees," said the ketch master with some solemnity.

"It's all very well for you to talk," grumbled Brown of the bilander. "I'm the one that's saddled with the bad luck this voyage. You two get the best cargo and I get shot at!"

"None of that, Brown" said Captain Lyth quietly, but with a stern look that the other two well understood. "You're not such a fool as to believe that. You may get a shot or two fired at you, but what is that to a Grimsby man?"

Brown stretched his back and smirked. "Aye, you're right at that." He grinned a toothy grin. "And whose goin' to take a second look at me when they see what I'm carryin'," He gave a throaty laugh.

"Your game is the easiest that any man can play," spoke up the ketchman. "You share the profits, Brown, and what risk do you take for it? Even if they do catch you, which would be your own fault, but what can they charge you with? You Grimsby men are all the same, always grumblin'. I'll change places with you, if you want-- right this minute!"

"You could never do it half as well," retorted Brown coloring up. "A boy like you! I'd like to see you try!"

"Now, now," broke in Robin. "You're not here to do as you please, but to obey my orders, I remind you. If the coast-guard quarrel, we do not. Remember that. That's why we beat them every time. You will both do exactly as I have laid out. The risk of failure falls on me."

The two men relaxed, knowing the truth of Robin's words. "The plan is very simple and cannot fail," he continued, "The only thing you have to think about at all, is any sudden change of weather. If a gale from the east sets in, you both run north and I'll come after you. But 'tis my belief there'll be no easterly gale the rest of this week, although I'm not quite sure of it."

"Not a sign of it," said the ketch man. "Wind'll hold up with sunset 'til the next quarter moon."

"Listen to whose talking, responded Brown. "I've many a grey hair to show how long I've been on the coast and I'm telling you youngsters there'll be an easterly gale afore Friday, I'll lay a guinea on it with both on ye."

"Brown, you may be right," said Robin, "I know you have a weather eye and I respect you for it. But if the gale will hold off until Friday, we'll do well. And even if it does come on, Tom and I shall manage. But you will be badly off in that case, Brown. It could make it dangerous for you," added Robin, knowing full well how each man needed to feel his important part of the mission, and that neither was the man to shrink from peril.

"Aye, aye, Captain. You can rely on me. Every one pretty well knows what Bill Brown is. Just let them need someone with a bit o' pluck and they're sure to call on me. Now, no more about it. Orders is orders. Tip us your latest."

"Right then, these are your latest orders. Just before dusk, you, Bill, move about a league ahead of us toward the coast. Tom you go to the north of Bill, and I'll take the south. Everyone keep just within signaling distance. We know the coast guard cutters are to meet off Robin Hood's Bay at that very hour. Bill, you'll be sure to sight them before they sight us, because you'll be keeping a sharper look out than they ever do and you know where to look for them. As soon as you know, signal us immediately if there's one, two or all three. I heartily hope it will be all three. But not one of them will see Tom and me. Then you move on in as if you hadn't seen them. They'll laugh to themselves and draw inshore. They'll hug the cliffs so as not to be seen by you and then wait for you to run into their jaws. That's when Tom and I will bear off to the north and to the south with full sail and not a speck will they see of us. By that time it will be nearly dark, but you carry on in, Bill, until they know you must have seen them. Then 'bout ship and full sail ahead as if to escape them. They'll give chase and you lead them on a merry dance out to sea again. The longer you can get them to chase you the better for us. Just as they look as if they're going to close with you and grapple, you 'bout ship again as if in despair. Run back a'tween them and make for Robin Hood's Bay. They'll follow you and they may fire at you, though it's not very likely. They won't want to sink such a valuable prize as they think you are."

"Captain, I'll laugh at all their blazing brass kettlepots. They won't catch me," boasted Bill Brown.

"Very well then, you hang on, like a Norfolk man, through the thickest of the enemy. Admiral Nelson is a Norfolk man you know. You charge your way through, just like he does. All three cutters will race pell mell after you, if they don't run into each other first!

The other two skippers laughed heartily and rubbed their hands together in glee. "All right then," continued Robin, "I don't have to tell you what to do next. Turn into the beach, stern first. By that time it should be getting on for midnight, with the tide upon the ebb. Resist them as long as you can, for it'll be hard going with the tide against them. The longer you hold them off, the longer we have to do our part."

Clearly understanding Robin's plan, the two sailors quickly boarded the little boat to go back to their own vessels. Once there, they hoisted sail and set off to follow their orders.

All involved knew the moment for action had come. Both the coast -guarders and the free-traders were sure of their success, while the people on dry land shook their heads and were thankful to be out of it. Captain Carroway, meanwhile put everyone to shame with his unflagging zeal, riding, rowing, sailing up and down, and giving his men no peace, so certain was he on capturing Robin Lyth once and for all, and before anyone else did.

Chapter Thirteen

CORDIAL ENJOYMENT

The success of this great enterprise depended heavily upon the weather. It was now close to the end of November and few in this part of the world expected to see the sun again much before Candlemas. The color of the sky and sea together was as one. It was mostly foggy by day and a good mist at night. It was not such bad weather but Commander Nettlebones saw no benefit in it.

"What a damned fog!" he exclaimed in the morning -- and exclaimed the same again in the afternoon. He declared as much yet again through the megaphone as the two other cutters came up within hailing distance. They had approached their captain's ship carefully at the appointed rendezvous, hauling their wind under easy sail, shivering in the southwestern breeze.

"Not half so bad as it was," returned Bowler, in a cheerful frame of mind. "It's lifting all the time, sir. Have you seen anything yet?"

"Not a blessed thing except an old fishing boat. Why do you ask?"

"Why, sir, as we rounded up, the fog lifted for a moment, and I saw a craft standing about two leagues off coming straight towards us."

"The devil you did! What was she like and in what direction did she lie, lieutenant?"

"She was a heavy lugger under full sail, about E.N.E as near as I could say. Looks like she's coming in for Robin Hood's Bay, I'd say. If she stays on course, she'll be on us in an hour, if the weather keeps so thick."

"She may have seen you and sheered off. Stand straight for her and get as near as you can. The fog is lifting as you say. If you sight her, signal her instantly." He paused and swung the megaphone to his other ship. "Lieutenant Donovan! Have you heard Bowler's news?"

"Aye, every word of it. The fog carries it to me as clear as seeing."

"Very well. Go south a little but keep within hailing distance or sound of signal. The fog's clearing every minute, and we must nab them."

The fog began to lift in loops and alleys as the upward pressure of the evening breeze from the land began to freshen. Here the water darkened with the ruffle of wavelets; and there it lay smooth and quiet with a glassy shine as the line of the cliffs allowed the breeze to pass through ravines and dips. Soon the three ships saw one another clearly. They also sighted the approaching sail.

This was a full-bowed vessel of quaint rig, heavy and extraordinary build. Clearly, this was a foreigner. Her broad spread of canvas combined the features of square and fore-and-aft tackle. But heavily laden though she was, she was going through the water at a strapping pace-- her long yards creaking, her broad frame croaking and her deep bow driving up the fountains of the sea. Her enormous mainsail gave her the vast power.

"Lord, have mercy! She could run us all down if she tried!" exclaimed Commander Nettlebones. For a while it looked as though this was exactly what she would do, for she continued towards the central ship as if she had not seen any of them. Then, suddenly and beautifully handled, she brought about and was scudding before the wind, showing the coastguard her stern. The next moment, with all the coast guard ships chasing her, she led them in a brave chase out to sea.

"It must be that dare-devil Lyth himself," Nettlebones said as his ship strained all canvas after the foreigner, but gained very little on her. "No other fellow in all the world would dare to face us down in this style. I'd bet ten guineas Donovan's new gun won't go off if he tries it." A pop and waft of smoke came from the other coast- guard boat   as he watched. "Ah I thought so. Nothing but a fizz and a stink." growled Nettlebones testily. "But Bowler is further out. He'll cross her bows, if he's not a fool." He watched impatiently. "Don't be in such a hurry my fine Bob Lyth.   Well done, Bowler! You've headed him off!" he shouted as Bowler cut across the bow of the bilander. "What? By Jove! What's she doing now? I don't understand these tactics -- Stand by there! --She's coming back again!" Sure enough to the amazement of all the coastguard men, the bilander expertly swung around again like a top and bore down again upon her pursuers. It seemed she didn't realize that she could have outrun her pursuers or else she lost her nerve. Whatever the reason, Nettlebones thanked the Lord, for now he knew he had her. It was plain she must either surrender or run ashore.

"Such cursed impudence I never did see! Does the fool know what he's doing?

The fool, who was of course Master William Brown of Grimsby, did indeed know what he was doing. Every shoal, sounding and rocky gully was thoroughly familiar to him. The spread of faint light on the waves and along the shore, told him all his bearings. The loud cackle of laughter, for which Grimsby men are famous, wafted across the winds and water to the ears of old Nettlebones. He ground his teeth in frustration, for now he saw the plan. In the rising of the large full moon, he could now see the beach of the cove with black figures gathering rapidly. "He means to run in where we dare not follow. He'll smash the ship for the sake of the cargo. But we're not done yet! We'll land round the point and run back and nab him!" Nettlebones forwarded his orders to the other two coast-guarders.

By this time, the moon was beginning to open the clouds and spread her light on the waves as the sun never had done all day. Now there was a clear space between the vessels and the busy rolling of the distant waves as they crashed against the cliffs.

"There's little chance of hitting them in this light," growled Commander Nettlebones, "but let them have it men. There's a guinea in it for you, if you can only bring that big mainsail down!"

The gunner was yearning for this chance and he shot forth with enthusiasm, but only set up a long path of fountains as the bilander ploughed on as merrily as before. The gunner was noted as a successful shot, so these near misses fired him up to shoot again. He waited for the moment. The bilander was a sizable object. Not to hit her anywhere would be really too bad. He considered the sightings carefully. At just the right moment, he fired. The smoke curled over the sea, and so did the bilander's mainsail, for the mast beneath it was shot clean through.

Some of the men on board were a little scared, never having been shot at before. But the Grimsby man rubbed his horny hands. "Aye, and Robin Lyth says there'll be little danger in it for us. That might just as well been my head, if a wave hadn't lifted the muzzle when yon straight-eyed chap let fire." Then hailing the crew he bellowed, "Well come on lads! Cut away the wreckage he made. He's saved us the trouble of shortening that there canvas!" This was true enough and all the hands knew that the craft was bound to be beached as Robin Lyth had ordered.

It was William Brown himself who stood at the wheel and carried her into the beach, with consummate skill. "It cuts to my heart to do away with this good timber," he grumbled. "It's as steady as a lighthouse and as handy as a floor mop. Ah well, but it has to be. Hold on there now, my lads!" he shouted to his crew.

With a crash and a grating and a long, sad, grinding the bilander foundered on the beach.

"I done it right well," muttered the Grimsby man. The poor old bilander had made herself such a hole in the sand that she rolled no more, but only lifted at the stern and groaned as the quiet waves swept under her.

The beach was swarming with men who gave her a cheer and flung their hats in the air. Then in two or three minutes they were aboard her any way they could find. Immediately they began to roll and hoist out the bales and puncheons, with a thump and a creak, with laughter and swearing.

"Now you be partiklar, uncommon partiklar" fussed old Captain Brown. "Never start a tear, a scratch or a fray in any of the bales. This be powerful precious stuff. Gold, every bit of it, if it are a penny! They blessed coast riders will be on us around the point very soon. But it'd be better to let them have some of it than damage a thread of these goods."

"All right, Cappen Brown. Don't you be so wonnerful unaisy. It's not the first time we've handled such stuff."

"I don't know about that," replied Brown gruffly as he lit his short pipe and began to puff. I've run some afore, but never none so precious as this lot."

Both the men of the coast and the sailors worked with a will, by the broad light of the moon, showing their brawny arms and panting chests, hoisting and heaving and rolling the cargo. In less than an hour, three fourths of the cargo was landed and some of it even stowed inland, where no coast -guarders could penetrate.

Then Captain Brown put away his pipe and swaggered into a dark empty part of the hold, getting busy with some barrels of his own, which he had carefully covered with sail cloth.

Presently the tramp of marching men could be heard in the lane on the north side of the cove. "Now never you worry," said Captain Brown, calmly knowing what was to happen next. But the men under him could not maintain such calm. They fell into sudden confusion. There was a babble of tongues, everybody longing to be off, but nobody liking to run away without taking something good with him.

"Stand you still!" cried Captain Brown. "Never budge an inch, ne'er a one of you! I'll insist what we're doing is legitimate. I'll take full responsibility!" So the men huddled together on the beach, in the moonlight, scared of the soldiers and no one wanting to be on the outside of the group. As they were all striving to be in the middle, the coastguards marched upon them from either side, in their very best drill and with high discipline.

But the smugglers too showed high discipline, when they heard the next words of Captain Brown. "Every man ston' with his hands at his sides, and ask the soldiers for a pinch o'bacca" This made them laugh -- until Captain Nettlebones strode up.

"In the name of his majesty, surrender all you fellows. You are fairly caught in the very act of landing a large run of contraband goods. It's time we made an example of you!" he bellowed loudly. Now where is your skipper, lads? Robin Lyth come forth!"

"May it please your good honor and his Majesty's commission," said Brown in a full, round voice, as he walked leisurely down the widest available gangway, "my name is not Robin Llyth, but I am a family man of Grimsby. An honest trader on the high seas. My cargo is medical water and rags mainly for the use of revenue men, since they han't had a new uniform this twelve months." Several of the soldiers smothered a chuckle at this, for indeed their new supply of uniforms had failed to arrive, because of some government lapse. But Nettlebones marched up and collared Captain Brown. "You are my prisoner, sir. Surrender Robin Lyth this very minute!"

Captain Brown gave no resistance, but respectfully touched his hat and looked thoughtfully at Nettlebones. "Now I'm not going to deny that I've heard of Robin Lyth, but I can't think where? Weren't he a man in the contraband line?" he asked mildly, trying to look puzzled, but grinning inside at the success of Robin's plan.

"Brown, you're trying to provoke me! It will only make it ten times worse for you." Nettlebones sidled up closer to Brown. "If you surrender Robin Lyth, I'll do my best for you. I might even let a few of these tubs slip by," he muttered softly in Brown's ear.

"Tubs?" cried Brown loudly, "Tubs? Sir, I'm a stranger 'round here. What are tubs? Aren't they what women use for washing? Now Jack," he cried, "You know more of Yorkshire talk than I do. His honor here is speaking of tubs. You ever hear of tubs, Jack?"

Nettlebones was losing his temper. "Tie this villain fast to yonder mooring post and one of you stand by with a hanging noose! Now Master Brown we'll see what tubs are ... and what sort of rags you have to land on shore by night. I give you one more chance. Will you hand over Robin Lyth?"

"I'd be only too happy to give 'n up -- just as soon as ever I got 'un." replied Brown looking earnestly at the commander.

"You're a contumacious rogue if ever there was one!" cried Nettlebones. "Now then, one of you men, roll up a couple of those puncheons. We'll see what's in them. Bring over Mr. Donovan." he ordered. "Now sir, I've heard it said that you know fine spirits better than most people. Now come on over and taste this stuff."

Mr. Donovan trudged over to the commander, and a couple of men put a spigot into the barrel at his feet.

"Faith and I was weaned on it by my maither, Commander. Give me a taste and I'll tell you if it's the right stuff, sure'nough."

The Irishman took the mug offered to him. "Here's a health to his Majesty!" he said throwing back his head and taking a hefty swig from the mug…. "O Lord a'mighty!" he bellowed. "What ha' we got here? "Tis poisoned I am! O Lor', O Lord a' mercy!" He fell to the sand clutching his stomach. Bring me a dochtor, a dochter and a praiste an' all," he howled.

The commander jumped back, clutching Brown's arm. "What's going on here?" he cried in alarm. "Speak out now, Captain. Give me the truth!"

"Well now, Captain or commander or whatever you may be," Bill Brown of Grimsby said easily, with a glint in his eye. "Never you fear, sir. 'Tis medical water, is all it is. Such stuff as if you took it for a week your wife wouldn't know you. Your complexion will be like a h'angel's."

"You rogue!" shouted Nettlebones, drawing his sword in anger. "If ever I had a mind to cut a man down…why…"

"Why then, sir, you'd attack an unarmed man, and one as is tied up with thick rope too," cried Brown. "Well….if that's the way the honor of the British navy is, then do it. I've made my will and my wife is cared for. Go to it then! I'll die as a Grimsby man and be proud of it."

The commander knew he was beaten. He lowered his sword, though still panting with anger. "You're a brave man, Brown," he growled and I'd scorn to harm such as you.....but tell me now, on your honor and with not so much as a wink. Are all your puncheons filled with that stuff and nothing else? Tell me man!" He shook Brown by the shoulders in anger.

"Upon my word of honor they are, sir. Some a little weaker, and some a little more of the bilge water in them. But the main of them is filled with what comes out of what they call a spa. Right pop'lar it is among some folk on the Continent. Why captain, you must 'a lived long enough to know that no sort of spirits as were ever stilled, will fetch as much money as a gallon of a doctor's medical water."

"That's true enough, Brown," said Nettlebones, somewhat deflated, "but no lies now....on your honor you are. If all you were importing were doctor's stuff, why did you lead us such a dance?" The commander looked as suspicious as ever.

"Well, your Honor, you must promise not to be offended, if I tell you of the mistake we made. You see, we heard a sight 'o talk about some pirate craft as carried His Majesty's flag. So when you first come up in the dusk o' night, why we... we..."

"You are the most impudent rogue as ever I saw!" bellowed the commander. "You know well enough the difference between his Majesty's cruisers and a smuggling tub! Now show me your bill of lading and be quick about it."

"Ship's papers are aboard her, all correct, sir. Here, feel in my pocket for the keys, seein' as how my hands aren't loose to get 'em for ye."

"Very well, I can see I'll have to go aboard and see for myself. The locker's in the master's cabin, I suppose?"

"Yes sir, plain as can be on the starboard side. Only, yer Honor..." Brown hesitated with a malevolent grin on his face. Only I'd be smart about it if I were you. The time fuse an't got more 'n three inches left on it."

"Time fuse?" roared Nettlebones. "What do you mean time fuse, you old villain?"

"Nothin' but to keep you out of harm, your Honor, sir. When we decided we had to beach that old craft, it came into my head that it would be a shame to let her fall into the hands of pirates. So I just laid a half hour fuse to three big powder barrels as is down there in the hold. Aye, an' I expect to see her blow up almost any moment now. But you might be in time if you do it on the run and with a bit'o luck..."

With a great shout alarm to his men, Nettlebones cried "Back lads! Back every one of you! Get under the cliffs here! Push those smuggler fellows out to the front. They've laid a fuse to their powder barrels and the lugger will blow up at any moment!"

"Don't worry about me," said Captain Brown, "but shouldn't you be a doin' of your duty up on board and get those samples....?" stuttered Brown an insolent smirk on his face.

"Samples? I'll make a sample of you, soon enough, my friend!" cried the commander. The next moment, with a crash that shook the beach and rolled back and forth in an echo from cliff to cliff, the great bilander shattered into a great fountain of timbers, splinters, smoke and dust. The water was driven back in a white turmoil.

"Gentlemen, you may come out of your holes now," bellowed the Grimsby man as the roar echoed and re-echoed along the cliffs. "She blowed up handsome and no mistake! No more danger, and there's plenty of stuff to pick up afore next pay-day."

Nettlebones was now fairly dancing with rage. "What shall I do with this insolent hound!" he roared. "We haven't caught him in anything illegal......But...but... "a light glimmered across his features. "I have it! We'll make him drink to his health with his own health waters. That's what we'll do." He peered through the clearing smoke. "Donovan my man, leave off rubbing your stomach. You shall do the honors here. Let's give old Captain Brown a taste of his own medicine!" Donovan brightened up immediately, found a piece of rubble that could serve as a mug and for the next half hour they made Captain Brown of Grimsby drink a bucketful of his own medical waters. Then they left him tied to the mooring post to reflect on his mischief.

Chapter Fourteen

BEARDED IN HIS DEN

Robin Lyth's strategy fooled the whole coast guard. The contraband cargoes had been landed at each end of the coastline that was under coast guard watch, while Nettlebones and his other two cruisers were occupied with the bilander in the center area.

It might have been better for him, however, if Robin had been content to run his southerly cargo in at Hornsea or even Aldborough. But nothing would satisfy his sense of humor and justice until he had taught Captain Carroway a lesson. He still held a grudge against the lieutenant -- not for trying to catch him at smuggling, but for interrupting the very sweetest moment of his life at Byrsa Cottage. "You interrupted my privacy at the most sacred moment," he said to himself. "The least I can do is to pay my respects to Mrs. Carroway and your interesting family." Thus, in sheer bravado, he decided to land his cargo right beside the Captain's cottage door in Bridlington.

Meanwhile the vigilant Lieutenant Carroway was hurrying about here, there and almost everywhere. He carried his sword in one hand and his spy-glass in the other and at every thickening swirl of fog he swore until it seemed he turned yellow. He condemned smugglers, cutters, coast guard and even the coastline itself. Even more strongly he cursed the farmers, landladies and fisherman who all seemed to be working hand in glove to prevent him from capturing his prey.

At half past ten on the night that the poor bilander ended her long career, Captain Carroway arrived at the Ship Inn of Filey. John Gristhorpe, the innkeeper, and his wife were sitting by the fireside. John was counting the day's takings, when a thundering at the door made him upset a little pyramid of pennies.

"John, now don't be letting them in. Tha' knows it's past hours," his wife scolded.

"Copper cometh by day, goold cometh by t'night" the sturdy publican answered.

"In the name of the King, undo this door," bellowed a loud stern voice.

"It's that horrible Carroway again," whispered Mrs. Gristhorp. "Much gold comes from him, I doubt!"

"Open the door, or by royal command, we'll make splinters of it." The voice bellowed again, then the door flew open, and in marched Carroway and all his men. There were nine in all, and Carroway himself, the tenth. They were all sturdy fellows, and for the most part, tolerably honest: Cadman, Ellis, and Dick Hackerbody, one more man from Bridlington, and the rest were a reinforcement from Spurn Point, who were called up especially for the occasion.

"Landlord, produce your best and be quick about it," the Carroway said as he threw himself into an arm-chair. "We have to be gone again in an hour. So John, bring us something for our stomachs. A shilling per head is his Majesty's price and half a crown for officers. Now bring us a gallon of ale to begin with."

All, including Carroway, were in fact too hungry to criticize the fare Gristhorp and his wife brought forth. They set on the food, as hungry men do, by the light of three tallow candles. They were just getting into the heart of the meal when the rattle of horse-shoes on the pitch stones outside shook the wide, low window. The next minute a little boy came staggering in, dazzled by the light, his face all long and pale with hurrying.

"Why, Tom my boy!" exclaimed the lieutenant, recognizing his oldest son and jumping up so suddenly that he overturned the little table at which he had been sitting by himself. "Tom, my son, what has brought you here? Is there something wrong with your mother?"

"Naw," replied the boy gasping for breath and almost crying in relief at finding his father. "There weren't nobody would come, but me...an' I had to borrow Butcher Hewson's pony, and he's going to charge five shillings for it, an'... an'..." he wiped a grimy sleeve across his face.

"Never mind about that. What are you here for? Come on now lad, speak up."

"Ah've come about the men that are landing things, just across from our front door, Father. They've got seven carts and a wagon with three horses...and one of the horses is three colors...and ever so many ponies. More than you could count...."

"Well Ah'll be forever...." he glanced at his son, "Well I never!" he finished. "This is more than I can bear! To be running in a cargo right at my own front door!" He turned to his men, "You sons of --- have done guzzling and swizzling!" he snarled.

The new men jumped up, but the Bridlington squad, knowing Carroway's fits and starts, kept on munching. "Give us five minutes," said Cadman insolently.

"You're like an old pig at the trough, John Cadman," growled Carroway.

"That's one more mark against you," muttered Cadman under his breath. But one of the shrewd Spurn Point men heard him and noted Cadman's surliness.

While the men began to make their way down to the shore to pick up their little boat to transport them to Bridlington, Carroway paid the innkeeper and gave instructions to give his son some beer and some meat. "He's a fine boy," said Carroway looking proudly at his son who was struggling to tell the whole of his story while filling his mouth with food. "You're a chip off the old block. As good a rider as your father... as well as a good eater, like him. Mark my words, Mistress Gristhorp, he'll do well in the world and no mistake. To have stuck to his horse all that way in the dark! Wonderful! Quite wonderful! Now, Tom, ride on home carefully and slowly when you're done. You shall have a half-a-crown later. Now, come kiss me my son. I'm proud of you!"

Not many days later, little Tom had cause to remember these words and his mother cried over them hundreds of times.

Although it was getting on for midnight, Master Gristhorpe and his wife walked out into the road to see their guests off. All the fog had cleared now and there was a good full moon.

They watched the boy and his pony trot back towards Bridlington, growing smaller in the distance. Out to sea they could make out the white sails glistening and the splash of the oarsmen aboard Captain Carroway's boat.

"The world goeth up and the world goeth down" said the lady, her arms akimbo, "and the moon goeth over all of us, John. But I do pity the poor folk who don't have time for a sniff of their own blankets."

"Margery, I likes the moon as much as you do, but Ah'd sooner see the snuff of our own tallow candles a-going out, from the comfort of our own bed." Shaking their heads with wisdom, they managed to bar the door again and went peacefully to their own bed.

Later, when they heard of what happened that night, they could scarce believe it, because everything afterwards had seemed so peaceable from the warmth of their bed.

The stern commander bade his men set full sail and they pulled on all six oars, such was their haste to catch Robin Lyth. The wind and the sea ran after them, to help carry them on their way. After a league or more of berating his crew, Carroway cried, "Ha! I see something! Dick, bring me the night glass. What do you make her out to be?"

"Sir, she is the yawl that was sent to cover Spurn Point," answered Dick Hackerby. "I can see the patch on her sail."

"Aye and she'll be looking for us. Ship oars and bear up lads, so she can see us, for we're on the wrong side o' the moon."

In ten minutes' time the two boats came within hailing distance off Bempton cliffs. There were only two men in the Spurn Head boat. Not half enough to manage the craft properly, never mind stop a band of smugglers.

"Well! What is it?" shouted Carroway.

"Robin Lyth has made his landfall on Burlington sands -- opposite your Honor's door at that! There were only two of us to stop him."

"I know it!" said Caroway almost too angry to speak, "My eight year old boy Tom is worth the lot of you," he sputtered. "So you got yourself into a spot and ran back home to tell your mammy, did you?" he snapped sarcastically.

"Cap'n, I ain't got no mammy," the other man answered, with his feelings hurt. "I come to tell you something for your own ear and none other, if you want to hear it."

Somewhat mollified, Carroway answered "Hold on then, I'll come aboard and you can tell me."

The lieutenant stepped confidently into the Spurn Head boat and ordered his own to haul off a little. The stranger bent down to whisper in the Captain's ear.

"Are you quite certain of this?" Carroway asked, his grim face glowing in the moonlight. "I've had such a heap of cock and bull stories about those caves. Do you know it for a fact?"

"As certain as I stand here and you sit there, Commander. You can put me under guard, a pistol to my ear and shoot me, if it turns out to be a lie."

"The Dove-cot Cave you say, and not Kirk Cave or Lyth's Hole?"

"Sir, the Dove-cot and no other. I had it from my own young brother who got cheated out of his own share with the last run they made."

"Then by the Lord in heaven, I shall have my revenge at last -- and I won't stand upon the niceties of it!" said Carroway, his eyes gleaming, his bristly face gaunt in the moonlight. He went back to his own boat and turned her course inshore. Then he stood amidships and rubbed his hands with glee at the thought of the surprise he was about to deliver.

Soon he took the tiller and fetched a circuitous course towards the Dove-cot, sailing back and forth, choosing the dark waters and moon shadows of the cliffs, in case there was a lookout posted at the mouth of the cavern.

Hugging the cliffs as closely as danger would allow, Carroway ordered silence and with the sense of impending danger, he meditated seriously. "I shall probably kill this man," he thought. "He will not be taken alive, I fear. He is as brave as myself, or braver. If I were in his place I would never yield. I hate to kill a gallant Englishman…and such a pretty girl, and a good girl too -- loves him with all her heart, I don't doubt. Then there's that good old couple, the Cockscrofts, who depend upon him and who've had such shocking luck themselves. He has been nothing but a plague to me all these years and I've longed to strike him down. But tonight…I cannot tell why it is, I wish there were some way out of it. Like it or not, duty drives me, and do it I must. Life is such a fleeting vapor--" He stopped his thoughts abruptly, "I smell some man sucking peppermint!" he bellowed. "The smell of it goes a mile with the wind. Who is it? -- Oh, it's you again, as usual, Cadman." he snarled. "Get rid of it, old woman that you are!"

Muttering something under his breath, the man flung his lozenge away and his eyes flashed in the moonlight. But that same Spurn Point man who'd heard Cadman mutter under his breath at the Filey Inn, was sitting next to him now and saw him lay his hand on his musket. "Are your guns all primed and ready lads?" called Carroway in a hoarse whisper.

The first to answer was Cadman, with an angry answer full of meaning, "Ay, ay, sir."

"Then be sure that you fire only at my command. We'll try to get them without shedding any blood. But whatever happens we must catch Lyth!"

With these words, Carroway drew his sword and laid it on the bench beside him. The rest of the men were hoping they wouldn't have to strike out at anyone at all, for though they were irritated at the way the smugglers persistently outwitted them, yet the bad blood between them wasn't so bad as to warrant a killing. What's more, some of them had relatives and friends among the free-traders and wondered if they might not find them here along with Robin Lyth.

Meanwhile in the cave there was rare work going on, speedily and merrily. There was only one boat inside the cave, with six men and Robin Lyth himself. But the six men made enough noise for twelve, and the echoes made the noise as much as if it were twenty- four. The main part of their cargo had been landed and gone inland. The men who had worked heartily for many hours were now taking the well earned liberty of sipping their own booty.

Lights of bright resin were burning with a strong flare upon shelves of rock. Dark water was softly lapping around the sides of the cave and a quiet pulse of rise and fall spread across the kelp fronds with the smooth tide. The cavern, expanding from its long narrow entrance, was beautifully sculptured with snowy white chalk bulges and hollows here and there, peaked and fissured, all molded by the tide's coming and going. Above the tide line, darker hues prevailed. The jagged outlines were yellow, and spread with freckle patches of lichen. The whole vaulted ceiling was made up of ponderous grey slabs of mountain-like rock. The clear, smooth water flowed deeply into the cave. At the broadest end, the furthermost part of the cave ended with a narrow strip of shingle and pebbles. From its southern most corner went a deep, dry fissure, that ran back deep into the body of the cliff. Here the smugglers were merrily at work.

The nose of their boat was run high upon the shingle. Two men on board her were passing out the bales to four others who staggered up into the cranny to stow it away for the future. Here they hid the cream and jewel of their venture. Captain Lyth himself was sitting in the stern of the boat, keeping order of everything and jotting down numbers. Now and then the gentle wash lifted the old brown timbers and an occasional refrain of the sailors' song echoed around the vault.

There was only one more bale to land, and that the most precious of them all, being all pure lace, closely packed in waterproof coverings. Robin himself was by now ready to indulge in a careless song, for this, as he had promised Mary, was to be his last illegal act. He was thinking how pleasant, comfortable and secure it would be to be a grocer or shop-keeper.

Into the midst of his dream swarmed an unusually strong, surging wash of the tide that broke into his thoughts. In a moment all his wits, youthful vigor and coolness returned. With one hand he caught up a hand-spike and hurled it so truly straight along the line of burning torches, that only two were left blinking. With his other hand he flung the last bale out of the boat and leaped out after it quickly stowing it away in a nearby dark crevice. Then he sprang into the boat again and took an oar in each hand.

"In the name of the king, surrender!" shouted Carroway, standing tall and grim in the bow of his boat, which he had skillfully maneuvered through the entrance, leaving the other boats outside. "We are three to one," he boasted, "and we have muskets and a canon. In the name of the king surrender!"

"In the name of the devil, -- SPLASH!" shouted Robin to his men, who came running and leaping into the boat. Immediately with both broad blades of their oars, Robin and his men set up such a whirl of flashing white water in the cave, as though an enormous storm had suddenly overtaken them. Poor Carroway and his men were soaked, their guns and swords drenched in the deluge. All was uproar, turmoil and confusion as the boats reeled to and fro.

"Use your muskets as clubs!" roared the lieutenant, mad with rage. "Up and at 'em. Their blood be upon their own heads."

But as he furiously leaped at the smuggler chief, the roar of a gun and the smoke of powder mingled with the general uproar in the cave. Carroway fell backwards into his own boat, and died, without uttering another syllable or groan.

The terrible echo reverberated back and forth around the cave. Then as it faded a shocked silence was deafening. The revenue men drew back and sheathed their cutlasses and laid down their guns. Some looked in terror at one another and some looked at their dead commander, whose body lay across the heel of the mast and whose blood dripped into a pool onto the bottom of the ship's boards.

For several moments no one spoke or moved, until one of the older men who had seen a battle or two, propped up the limp head, lay his ear to Carroway's dead lips and put a hand on the too impetuous heart. "Dead as a door-nail he muttered." Then he looked up at the rest of the crew. "Who takes command now? This is a hanging offense, I'm thinking."

There was silence for a moment then two or three whispered, "Jem, you do it." "Aye" added others. "It be you as can do it, Jem."

"Awright," said Jem rising to his feet as one in a dream. Then he shook his head as if to clear it. "Lay her broadside on to the mouth of the cave," he ordered his men. Then looking towards the smugglers he shouted, "Let no-one move, without first killing me." He drew himself up to his full height and the men rowed the little boat across the entrance. Dazed, the smugglers all huddled together in their own boat.

"I'm not going to speechify to a bunch of murderers," cried the old sailor, "but listen to this: I'll blow you all to pieces with this 'ere four pounder, if you try anything." Then he cried to his men, "Burn two blue lights!" The brilliance of the blue lights filled the cavern revealing everybody's features-- especially those of the dead lieutenant. "A fine job you have made of it this time." said Jem scornfully.

The smugglers were beaten. They surrendered. They could scarcely speak to protest their innocence in this wicked deed. They allowed themselves to be bound and laid down in their own boat. "Put their captain on the top of these white-livered cowards," said the old sailor. "Now which is Robin Lyth?"

The lights had burned out and the cave was in darkness except for where a slant of moonlight came through the opening. There was some muttering among the smugglers. "Never mind," said Jem. "Tie up the boat along side us. We'll fetch her outside. We shall see him soon enough when we get outside."

But in spite of this confidence, when they got outside, they found they had only six prisoners and not one of them was Robin Lyth.

The Tale of Robin Lyth

Part Two

ROBIN, RENOUNCED AND REFORMED

CHAPTER 15

THREE MESSAGES DELIVERED

Mrs. Carroway was always glad to be up early in the morning, but this morning she was up later than usual, Tom having arrived from his trip to his father at Filey, sometime in the middle of the night. Suddenly there came a cry which woke her out of her late sleep.

"Oh, Mother, Mother, now what do you think has happened?" shouted little Tom as he rushed in from the beach in the early morning light, too excited to have slept late like his mother. "Father has caught all the smugglers, every one. His ship is coming home in a spanking breeze, with three boats behind her. They can't all be ours. One of them must belong to Robin Lyth himself. I would almost bet a penny they have been and shot him, though everyone said he never could be shot. He must be dead at last! Now instead of half a crown from father, I shall be sure to get a guinea."

"Tommy," said his mother, "you are always so impetuous. I can't believe in such good luck unless I see it with my own eyes; though you have been a wonderfully good and brave boy, going all that way to Filey. Your father will be proud of you."

Tommy ran off again to the beach and Mrs. Carroway became very busy, trying to make some good, fat gravy in the pan with whatever she could find among the left-overs, which was very little indeed. But she knew her husband would be hungry.

At this moment the door latch clicked. She turned around quickly, to see a young man standing there, looking at her with a sad, stern gaze and sorrowful eyes.

"Who are you and what do you want?" she asked, with the frying pan in her hand. Then she grasped her children to her, for the young man looked a little wild.

"Speak up," she said. "Are you mad? Are you hungry? What do you want? We are not very rich, but we can give you some bread, poor man. Captain Carroway will be home directly, and he will see what can be done for you." She looked past his shoulder to the door, hoping her husband would be coming sooner than later.

"Madam, have you not heard what has happened?" the young man asked her, speaking the words slowly and carefully, and steadying himself with one hand on the dresser, for he was trembling a great deal.

"Yes, I have heard it all. They have shot the smuggler, Robin Lyth at last. For which I am truly sorry, but it was needful. At least he did not have a family to feed like my husband has."

"Lady, ...I...I am Robin Lyth," he stammered. "I have not been shot. The man who has been shot instead of me was...was...somebody else." He could not bring himself to say the words. "With all my heart, I wish it had been me. He looked at the mother and her large family of children, then fell on to a stool and hung his head in his hands, his shoulders shaking.

Mrs. Carroway stood looking at him, bewildered, unable to comprehend his words. Her eldest daughter ran to him, and took his hand. "Don't cry," she said. "My papa says that men do not cry. I am so glad you were not shot."

Robin lifted his head and kissed the little girl on the forehead. "See how I kiss your daughter Ma'am? If I had done it, could I do that? Madam, I am hunted like a mad dog and shall be hanged on your flagstaff if I am caught. I am here to tell you just this: as God looks down from heaven upon you and me -- I did not do it."

The smuggler stood up, with his right hand on his heart and misery written all over his face, yet his eyes were crystal clear with truth. The woman barely understood that she was a widow yet, but she answered quietly, "You speak the truth, sir. I know it." Lyth tried to make a reply but his tongue could not do it. Having said all he could, with one backward pitying glance to the children, he rose wearily and slipped out of the cottage.

Mrs. Carroway wrapped her shawl around her. Gathering her children together, her face like a rock, she said, "I shall just go and judge for myself. Come, children. We are going to meet your father." Leaving the baby strapped in the cradle, she tidied each child, pulling each cap straight and smoothing their dresses as if they were marching off to church. Indeed that's where the younger children thought they were going, but the elder children knew from their mother's face that it was worse than that.

Then they set off in lopsided pairs, an older child holding the hand of a younger one. Their mother followed slowly and heavily behind them, holding the hand of the youngest of them all. Her heart was nearly choking but her eyes were wild as she watched the little boat come nearer and nearer.

At last they landed with their sad, cold freight. The men took off their hats and rubbed their eyes. Some of them wanted to put out to sea again immediately and land somewhere else. But Mrs. Carroway calmly said, "Please to let me have my husband."

When Mary Anerley heard that Robin Lyth had murdered Captain Carroway, she was at first angry. She had too much faith in his manly valor and tender heart to believe the tale. But persistent misery followed her anger. She had so hoped to rescue this man from his unlawful ways and make him a respectable character. He had such gallant gifts that endeared him to her. It was hard to think of him as a murderer. But now the wretched facts of the matter seemed that all hope was lost.

Her father and mother said not a word on the subject to her. "Let the lass alone," said Mr. Anerley to his wife. "A word against that lad now will do a sight of mischief. Mary is sorry for that rogue now. If you were to go speechifying to her now, you could never put up with her defense of him. As many times as you would run him down, so she would think the more highly of him -- and believe it too."

"Well, Stephen," his wife replied, "I will follow your advice this time, because it is my own opinion too." So the days at the Anerley Farm passed as though nothing had happened.

Mary was puzzled by her parents' behavior and she longed for some comfort. After a day or two, she asked if she might be allowed to go to Byrsa Cottage for a change. But her father refused her, even though his heart ached at having to do so. He believed that his brother-in-law would only encourage Mary further in her hopes for Robin Lyth. Though it hurt him to deny her, he knew it was for the best. Mary would come around eventually.

Soon after this denial, Mary crept up to her room and catching sight of herself in the little mirror Aunt Popplewell had given her, she was ashamed. Her spirit was aroused and her pride came to her rescue. "If nobody cares about what has happened," she thought, stubbornly, looking upon her pale face and tangled curls, "I won't let them see that I care! Not for another moment! I will cry no more." She looked at herself in the mirror again. "I declare, if ever he came back, he would think what a fright I had become. Besides, I will make myself look just as nice as ever, just to let them know their cruelty has not killed me."

So saying, she brushed the tangles out of her hair, dressed herself in her prettiest dress, donned a very graceful hat and trimmed it with a pretty blue ribbon she had been saving. Then she made up her mind to go out into the fresh air and see if she could put back some of the roses in her cheeks.

There was a favorite part of Anerley Farm that Mary often went to as a child, (for since meeting Robin, she no longer thought of herself as a child). In a gently sloping valley, a splashing brook passes into a small quiet lake. It was a friendly little place with cheerful sunshine on a sunny day that filtered through a few willow trees that lowered their slender branches over the pool. Under the largest of these willow trees, her runaway brother, Jack, had made a bench on which to sit, as he watched his toy boats cruising on the ripples. Mary often came to this place when she particularly missed her brother, or when she had something important to think about.

Though there was still a keen east wind, and the willow leaves were no longer shading the pool, this was still a sheltered place, where nothing could be heard but the murmuring of the distant sea and the silvery splash of a pair of coots at play.

Mary sat on the little bench, watching the pair of coots who were behaving as if spring was on its way and that winter had come and gone. Watching the playful pleasure of the pair, Mary began to forget about her woes.

Suddenly, the birds with one accord, dived with a little splash leaving only ripples behind. "Someone must be coming," thought Mary. "I'm sure I didn't frighten them." She drew in her skirt and shrank behind a tree. Perhaps it was a poacher. But the eyes that saw her first were keener than any poacher, and the light step was far from a poacher's tread.

"Oh Robin, have you come at last?" Mary said softly as a familiar figure came into view.

"Three days I have been lurking here in the hopes of seeing you. Heart of my heart, are you glad to see me?"

"I am certainly sure I am!" said Mary with a rush of joy. "It is worth a world of all the crying just to see you so again. Where have you been for such a long time? I have been so worried."

"Let me have you in my arms, if it is only but for a moment," said Robin hoarse with emotion. But then he stopped. "You are not afraid of me are you? Are you ashamed to love me?"

"I love you all the better for your many dreadful troubles. Not a word do I believe of all that the wicked people say. Don't you be afraid of me." She flew into his welcome arms. "You may kiss me, Robin," she said shyly. "You see, I trust you as much as ever."

"You look so beautiful, Mary and I am only fit to be thrown in the pond."

"You surely know I don't mind about such things. But when I look at you it makes me long to give you my best cloak. What has happened to all your fine clothes?

"Now don't be cheeky with me, because of your fine clothes, Mary my dear" Robin teased, holding her at arm's length to take in the pretty picture that she made. "Remember that I have abandoned free trade because of you --and the price of every article will rise because of that," he grinned, momentarily.

Mary not only smiled, but laughed with relief to see him still in fine spirits. She had never believed that her love had attempted to shoot Carroway, even though the lieutenant had often attempted to shoot Robin. Now, seeing him, she was sure he could clear himself, why else could he speak so lightheartedly?

"You see that I am scarcely fit to lead off a country dance with you, Mary," said Robin, still holding both her hands, watching the beauty of her clear bright eyes. "And it will be a long time before you see me in my fine, gay clothes again."

"I like you a great deal better this way, Master Robin," said Mary primly. "You always looked so brave, but now you look so honest too."

"Now that is a speech worthy of an Anerley," Robin laughed and then grew serious again. "How I wish your father liked me Mary! I suppose it is hopeless to wish for that."

"No, not at all Robin -- if you could keep on looking shabby. My dear father has a most generous mind. If only he could be convinced of how ill-treated you are...."

"Alas, I have no chance of that happening. Before tomorrow morning, I must say goodbye to England. This evening was my last chance of seeing you. I bless every star that is in the heaven that my wish has come true."

"Robin dear," said Mary still a little primly, "I think you should rather trust in the Lord than starlight."

"So I do, Mary. So I do. It has been the Lord that has kept me out of sight of my enemies until now, and brought you to me, my Mary. The Lord looks down on all His angels, Mary. You have made a man of me. But, my darling, I shall not see you again for years -- perhaps never again. But as long as I live, you will be here, in my heart." He laid his hand on his chest. "It is you, and no other. Oh, I will always be an honest man from now on. Perhaps I will serve in the navy. My captain shall be Lord Nelson."

"That is the very thing you were made for," interrupted Mary. "Oh, I wish Dr. Upandown had put you in the navy, then you would not have got into smuggling."

"I'm not so sure about that, Mary, my love," said Robin truthfully, for he never was of the nature to do peaceably what someone else wanted for him. "But you have not asked me about the killing of poor Carroway. I love you the more for not asking me. It shows what faith you have in me. But you have the right to know, so Mary, I will tell you all --if you are sure you can bear to hear it."

"Yes, oh yes, I must hear it all. Even if it is frightening I must hear it."

"But it is not frightening, what I have to tell you, because I did not even see what happened to Captain Carroway. We were almost through with the unloading, when he came upon us so suddenly in the cave. I saw immediately that we were caught, so I thought at least we should have a little fun for our pains. I knocked over the lights and began to splash with all my might and main and called to my men to do the same. I tell you Mary, we did it so well that the whole place was like a fountain or geyser. Then I sent a great dollop of water into the poor captain's face and that was the only assault I made on him. There was just enough light for me to recognize him, but I doubt he recognized me at all. He dashed the water from his eyes and became very excited, making wild thrashing in the air with his sword and lunged at me. That was the last I saw of him, for like a bird I dived overboard. Yet, just as I was in the very act of plunging in to the water, I saw a quick flash and heard a loud roar as I struck the waves. At the time I thought it was only the effect of striking the cold water so quickly, or at the worst, someone shooting at me. In a second I swam under the keel of the other boat and rose to the surface in the shadows at the far side of the cave. When I came up again the roar was still echoing around the cavern and I knew a shot had been fired, but at whom? That I did not find out until later. I expected to be followed, so I swam rapidly towards the entrance of the cave. I was amazed when I realized that no one was following me. But I didn't look back. I kept in close to the rocks and swam for my life like an otter with a whole pack of hounds after him. I had little time to think of anything else."

"Of course you didn't, swimming in the dark water like that, in the caverns and with guns going off. Oh, it scares me to even think about it."

"Mary, I thought my time was come," said Robin gazing earnestly at her. "The only thing that kept me going was your beautiful image in my mind! Though the water was very cold, it only seemed to freshen me. After a few minutes I found I could breathe very well in the gentle rise and fall of the waves. But I never expected to escape, because now I could see two more boats outside the entrance of the cave. At first I didn't know what to do. I could have stayed in the water in the cave and covered my face with kelp, but I knew eventually they would find me. So instead, I trusted in the Lord and with a long, slow stroke I swam against the tug of the tide out into the open. How they did not see me I do not know, for I dared not dive under again. I needed to see where I was going. Mary, my dear, if I had not been supported with continual thoughts of you, I'm sure I would have been dashed against the rocks or gone down to the bottom. You know I wouldn't have cared either, if I hadn't the hope of standing up one special day in front of the church altar, with a certain lovely Mary."

"Oh Robin, you make me laugh when I ought to be crying. If that ever happens, I shall expect to see you swimming up to the altar."

"It will happen Mary, my love. For what I set my heart on, I usually achieve. But let me finish my tale. I tell you I never enjoyed anything so much as the sense of danger I felt when I had to cross a strip of moonlight. I could see the very eyes and teeth of the men in the boats. Soon I rested in a smooth dark spot and watched them. They didn't know yet what had happened in the cave, so they sat there grumbling about what they ought to be doing. At first I thought the only way to escape was to round the little cape on the other side of the boats, but it was in full moonlight. Then I remembered there was another cave, before you get to the cape. It is called Church Cave, because some old legend says that there is a tunnel leading from it up to Flamborough Church. I have never found such a place. But I did know that there is a small fissure in that cave, just large enough to hide a man, though you have to be pretty nimble to climb up to it. Also, the cave has a very narrow entrance, so that no large boat could get into it, and even small ones would not risk it in the dark. But still I had to cross another patch of moonlight. I was just about to risk it, for I was growing very cold, when I heard a loud shout from the cave. The men in the two boats immediately turned their backs towards me and hissed through the water into the Dovecot. Nobody saw me and I laughed heartily to myself when I thought of Captain Carroway's rage at losing me -- little knowing that the fine old fellow was beyond all rage and pain. So I rested for a while on the little beach until the revenue boats passed by. That was when I heard them talk of what had happened to Captain Carroway. Such terror took a hold of me, for I could scarcely believe what had been done. I knew my men to be innocent, but I knew too that I would be blamed. The poor man deserved better, for all he thought of was doing his duty."

"How wonderful you are and what courage!" burst in Mary, with bright tears upon her cheeks. "What did you do next?"

"I must tell you the rest quickly, dear heart, because I want you to know that I am innocent, when people speak evil things of me. Have you heard that I went to see Widow Carroway? I knew I must do so, before the whole world believed I had killed her husband. So I went to see her right away. I don't think she understood what I was saying at the time. Did you hear, Mary, how in the midst of her desolation, as she stood beside her husband's grave in Bridlington Priory church-yard, she said in front of a hundred people, 'Here lies my husband, foully murdered. The coroner's jury has brought their verdict against Robin Lyth, the smuggler. But Robin Lyth is as innocent as I am. I know who did it, and time will show. I put my curse upon him who did it and my eyes are upon him right now.' Then she fell down in a faint. Did anybody tell you about that my Mary? Such a brave woman as she is. She knows I did not kill her husband."

"Robin, I had heard that she proclaimed you innocent and I blessed her in my heart for it."

"She did even more than that, dear Mary. Right after the funeral she sent a message to Robin Cockscroft, who has been as good to me as if he were truly my father. She told him in few but strong words, that I should have no justice here, if I were caught. She said that as sure as there was a God in heaven she would bring the man who did it to the gallows. Only she begged him to tell me to leave the country at once, for if I was caught and convicted, the one who is the real murderer would remain free. So you see Mary, my darling that is what I must do this very night. Above all that I have come to tell you, I now have to tell you.....goodbye." His voice broke a little and he clutched her hand to him.

"But surely I will hear from you sometimes," said Mary striving to keep her voice from trembling as she realized what the ending of all this must be. "Years and years without a word from you, Robin. Oh it will break my heart. And I will not even be able to talk of you. Oh Robin, it is too much."

He crushed her against him. "Think of me my darling. Never stop thinking about me even if you cannot talk of me. I shall never cease to think of you." He paused, and then took the earring from his ear. "Here take this, the token of the time we first met and you saved my life. You have been my life ever since and will always be, my beloved. Let me have this length of blue ribbon you have entwined so prettily in your hair. I shall think of your eyes every time I kiss it."

Mary untwined the ribbon and kissed, then gave it to him, and took the little gold trinket he offered in exchange. "But sometimes….sometimes, I shall hear of you shall I not Robin?" she whispered, lingering and trembling in their last embrace.

"You shall hear of me from time to time from Robin and Joan Cockscroft. But I will not ask you to be true to me, though I shall be true to you. For how or when we shall ever meet again my noble one, my everlasting love, I do not know. But now, I must go, before it is too late." With these words he wrenched himself from her with a sob and disappeared silently into the darkening glade.

Mary stood long afterwards gazing into the bushes where he had gone. Silent tears slid down her face as she prayed to God to bless him during this long sad time.

Robin had one more errand to do before leaving his homeland. He was to leave a letter for his good friend Dr. Upround. He slid it under the gate in the moonlight where he knew the rector would find it on his morning stroll around the grounds. And find it he did.

"Whatever is this?" the rector said to himself, turning it over and over. " 'Private and into his own hand: Dr Upround.' Well I certainly shan't know what is so private unless I open it." So he carefully slit open the edge with his thumb and began to read:

"Reverend and Worshipful Sir,

Your long and highly valued kindness requires at least a word from me, before I leave this country. I have not come to see you because it might place you in difficult circumstances. Your duty to King and State might compel you to arrest me. The evidence brought before you left no choice but to issue a warrant for my arrest. Though I am sure it grieved you to have to do so. Sir, I am purely innocent of the vile crime laid against me. I used no fire-arm that night, neither did any of my men. It is for their sake as well as my own that I take the liberty of writing this. Not finding me, the authorities might bring my comrades to trial and convict them. If this were to happen I would surrender myself and meet my death in the hope of saving them. But if the case is carefully researched, the authorities will find that there was no fire-arm of any kind in my boat, except for one pair of pistols in the aft locker, and they were unloaded. I beg of you to verify this, kind sir. It is my firm belief that the revenue officer was shot by one of his own men. His widow is of the same opinion. I hear that the wound was in the back of his head. If we had carried fire-arms not one of us could have shot him from that direction.

There is one more thing, though I fear to trespass so greatly upon your kindness. I have brought a young lady into sad trouble with her family -- a young lady worth more than all the goods I ever ran or ever could run, if I went on for fifty years. By name she is Mistress Mary Anerley, and by birth, the daughter of Captain Anerley of Anerley Farm. I know that this is outside of our parish yet if your reverence could only manage to ride that way once in a while, in fine weather, to say a kind word to my Mary, I would be so thankful. Perhaps you could say a good word too, about me, to her parents, if you can find in your heart anything good to be said of me. They are stiff but worthy people and I would not want to come between Mary and her parents. So it would truly be a Christian act for you to do this, such I know that you delight in.

"Reverend Sir, I must now say farewell. You always told me that my unlawful enterprise would one day end in sadness. Never did I expect anything like this.

In sorrow and lowness of fortune, I remain with humble respect and gratitude, your worship's poor pupil and banished parishoner,

Robin Lyth of Flamborough."

"Ah, Robin, Robin, you leave me with impossible tasks," said the Reverend Doctor Upround. "To put in a good word for you at Anerley Farm, where Mr. Anerley is so dead set against free-traders, and even more so, since this foul murder, and to turn the investigation away from your men towards his majesty's men! I fear I shall have little influence in either case." He put the letter in his pocket and with heavy tread he walked back to the house. Truly he felt no happy prospects in store for his pupil's future.

Unknown to all the unhappy people involved in Robin's present tragic circumstances, Fate was not yet through with this unfortunate young man. In fact, Fate had begun meddling in his life a generation of years before he was born and a hundred miles away.

Chapter Sixteen

THE WILL

Far from any house or shepherd's hut, in the depth of a dreary moorland, a rough unpaved road descends steeply to a rushing river and rises again at the other side for any traveler who dares to breach the ford. The North Yorkshire-men, a hardy breed, used to the edge of the North Country weather, call it "Seven Corpse Ford". Not that the name could be found on any map, but it was called thus by the locals in memory of a company of farmers who once wended their way home from Middleton Market, with their pockets full of cash from the sheep auction, and their bodies fortified with much brandy-wine. Their noisy bragging suppressed any thoughts of highwaymen who were known to infest these parts after market day. The best French brandy boosted their bravery and kept out the penetrating cold of the dank, foggy night.

The river, usually not much wider than the width of a barn, was in turbulent flood when the reveling farmers came upon it. With the foolhardiness of the braggarts that they were, the eight men, each challenging the bravery of the other, plunged into the torrent urging their horses to the other side. The frightful current swept them from their horses. In the turmoil each set upon the other with the clutch of a drowning man.

Eight men entered the water that night, only one reached the other side. He was Philip Yordas, the owner of that land. The bodies of the other men were found washed up on a ridge of rocks a hundred yards downstream. From that fateful day, the water ford took its fearful name.

Despite the name and reputation, and the fact that there was a good stone bridge some five miles upstream, the Seven Corpse Ford continued to be used by those in a hurry or unwilling to learn from the error of those gone before.

A generation or so later, one improvement was made to the ford by the son of the landowner. Aware of his father's narrow escape, Richard Yordas of Scargate Hall, stretched a long, heavy chain across the ford, and anchored it on either side in great, strong boulders of Yorkshire granite. This was done, not out of the kindness of his heart, but from stiff-necked pride. He reasoned that should anyone suffer a similar fate as those for whom the ford was now named, none could charge him with the fault of it. Any who might come by that way would at least have a marker of the shallows but also, should the waters attempt to wash him away, he could make a bold grab for the chain and thus save himself. Albeit, the wisest traveler avoided the crossing and made for the good stone bridge instead.

Forty years later, the original incident almost forgotten, although the chain hung as strong as ever, yet another event reiterated the ford's grizzly name.

It happened one gentle evening, a few days after Michaelmas of 1777. There was no flood upon the river that night, nor fog shrouding the black moorland. The night was light and the crossing could be made successfully by any man of reason, if his reason did not first persuade him to make for the stone bridge.

However, the man who rode down to the ford that night had little thought of reason. His temper was high as he crashed down the muddy trail. His thoughts were not on good stone bridges but full of headstrong anger. He was as stiffnecked and prideful as his predecessor, who had so begrudgingly set up the chain. He was Sir Richard Yordas' own son, now the father of a son himself; a son who gave him as much trouble as he had given to his own father. The deeply etched strain of arrogance, pride and willfulness had strengthened in the Yordas family with successive generations. Tonight it rankled Philip Yordas, like salt on an open sore, that his own son should display those very qualities that he clasped to himself as his own right. He would see his son cower and grovel for his living before there would ever be so much as a groat for him of the ill-gotten wealth his forbears had wrenched from the land and their tenants.

"It's done my boy!" he muttered to himself, while his eyes glittered with fire, like the flint sparks from the hoofs of the horse he had been hard riding since leaving his solicitor's office that afternoon. "Done my boy, once and forever! Never shall you step upon an acre of your own land, and the only timber you'll see will be that of the gallows." Philip, father of Duncan, struck his chest with a fierce satisfaction and heard the crackle of parchment of the new will which now nestled in his pocket under his heavy top-coat.

"Fool!" he continued with an oath. "To think that the blood of a Yordas could be mingled with a common farmer's wench and that I would stand meekly by." His horse was approaching the ford. Her speed was thrust on by his anger. But Philip had spied his father's chain. "Aye, Duncan," he cursed, "there hangs my father's chain. Ah, he was something like a man. Had I ever dared to defy him as you have done me, he would have hanged me with it."

The horse hesitated in her headlong gallop into the ford, but Philip struck her, spurring her on in his wild anger. The water was up to her flanks in a minute, and then she was swimming through the swirling waters, her eyes rolling in fear . If his fury hadn't driven him so, Philip Yordas could have turned back to safety. But the poor horse had thoroughly lost her nerve as Yordas urged her faster and forward.

"You think we'll drown, you wretched beast? Let the river do its worst. Ha! My own water drown me! That would be too much insolence!" He made a grab for the chain, but at that moment the horse balked. Yordas was shifted from the saddle like a heavy sack of beets grown on his own land. His great coat, weighted with the swift river, dragged him down. The horse gave a piteous gurgle of breath and sank with Yordas' leg trapped in the stirrups. He flung himself upwards for air, but as he surfaced, the river's surge dragged the horse downstream and Yordas was caught by the neck and held there on his father's chain. The weight of the swept-away horse, snapped the neck of the one who never knew what it was to bend to the will of another man in all his life.

He was found next morning, not drowned, but hung, with his eyes wide open while clutching his coat in a death grip, where sodden, but readable, nestled the new will of parchment, the cause of his jubilant death.

Chapter Seventeen

SCARGATE HALL

A score of years after the ugly event of her father's death, Phillipa Yordas, the eldest offspring of her stiff-necked father, continued to live with her sister at Scargate Hall, the family home. Duncan Yordas, the object of his father's deathly anger, and cut off from his inheritance, had not been heard of since his father's funeral. The parchment found on the body of Phillip Yordas that inadvertently led to his death, was never challenged by the family. All that was known was that Duncan had left the country with his new bride for lands afar, to make his fortune without benefit of family.

Life at Scargate Hall continued on without the benefit of a male heir. Indeed, it had been stipulated in that notorious document, that the Yordas lands were to be bequeathed to Philips's daughters, and not a coin was to be in any way put at Duncan's disposal. Any children of the sisters, should have the land divided between them. Philippa never married and her sister, Mrs. Carnaby was made a young widow, but not before she was made the mother of a healthy son. This young man, though he had half of the Yordas' blood in him, had been turned into a lazy, spoiled, and weak-willed brat, by his mother who devoted her life to encouraging the petulant nature of the youth.

It was a worry to Philippa at times as she watched her sister indulge the future heir of Scargate, but she, too was inclined to be as indulgent of her sister after the misfortune of losing her husband so early in the marriage. Consequently it was left to Philippa to look after the business affairs of the holdings and to be sure to extract the rent from the tenants of the land. Not having a man in the family, Philippa did the best she could to run the estate efficiently. But there was never enough income to cover the needs of the land, nor, in fact the needs of the tenants whose homes, bleak at the height of the wealth of Scargate Hall, were now more rundown than ever and badly in the need of repairs to withstand the harsh weather of a North Yorkshire winter.

About the time that Mary Anerley had her fateful encounter with Robin Lyth in Danes Dyke, here at Scargate Hall there was more than usual to worry the ladies of that mansion. Mrs. Carnaby had been fretting and fussing all morning. Philippa had been checking and rechecking the accounts daily since they had received notice in the mail of a certain Mr.Mordacks, solicitor of the City of York, who was to "wait upon their presence, Thursday next." Although he was their man of business, the sisters rarely had discourse with him. Philippa was afraid to show her abysmal knowledge of how to run the estate and Mrs. Carnaby too overcome with migraines and other ailments to warrant a long and uncomfortable trip into York.

Today was "Thursday next", and all the surmising between the two sisters could not bring to hand the reason for this visit. By turns they were sure it was to be dreadful news, or likely some long lost relative had left them a legacy.

"Oh, do sit down, Eliza do. There is nothing more to be done, and your constant fussing is making my head spin so that I will never be able to hold a sensible conversation with Mr. Mordacks when he does finally arrive." Philippa rarely spoke so sharply to her sister and Eliza recognized for the first time that this outburst was indicative of her dear sister's worried state. She meekly complied with her command and pulled up a chair to join her in the leaded glass bay window overlooking the long drive down to the once magnificent iron gates of the hall.

The late August afternoon sun shed its beams through the heavy leaded glass to light up the needle-work Mrs. Carnaby was forever working upon and with which she never seemed to be finished. She worked a few stitches and shifted her position while Philippa gazed from her chair unblinkingly down to the gates, where she had sat for quite two hours mentally going over the figures that caused her so much anxiety. Although it was August, there was a keenness in the air that already spoke of the harsh winter to come. The rains of late July had hampered the harvesting and yet again many acres of barley had turned black before the workers could cut and bale it. She heaved a great sigh.

Mrs. Carnaby lay down her work again, looking anxiously at her sister. "There Philippa," she said in soothing tones that trembled, betraying her own anxiety, "Like as not it will be some trifling legacy that will help us pay for coal or candles at least this winter."

Philippa flashed her a tired look and returned her gaze to the gates. Suddenly she leaned forward "I see some movement down there. He's here, Eliza," she announced standing up.

By the time the sisters had readied themselves, brushing back the stray hairs and shaking the folds out of their dresses, Mr. Mordacks was ushered in to the sitting room. The poor man's face was red and chapped by his long ride. He was more than thankful to be at the end of his journey, even though he dreaded the reason for it.

After being amply fortified by the good ladies' hot tea and some of Cook's gingerbread he gathered his wits and assumed the air that befitted a lawyer on business even if a little rumpled. It was an unpleasant business to be sure, he thought as he watched the two middle aged sisters make every attempt to display the niceties that befit ladies of their position. That was just the problem, he realized, concentrating his thoughts. Just what was the position of these two ladies he wasn't sure, but he was almost certain it wasn't as secure as they thought it was.

It was Philippa who began. She could wait no longer. Certainly the man needed refreshment but she needed ease of spirit. As soon as the plates were taken away and before Mr. Mordacks could help himself to a fourth piece of gingerbread, she plunged into the topic with as much delicacy as her impatience would allow.

"If I understood your letter clearly," she said, "you have something to tell us concerning our poor property here. A small property Mr. Mordacks when one compares it with that of the Duke of Lunesdale's, but perhaps a little longer in the family." She allowed herself a slight smirk of satisfaction.

"Ah yes," returned the upright, stiff and well-appointed Mr.Mordacks, settling into the inevitable. "Your estates have been longer in the possession of your family, than many another in the North Riding of Yorkshire." He groped in his mind for a way to convey his news as gently as possible.

Mrs. Carnaby, conscious that the future of the property was the future of her son, set about conveying to the lawyer how justly they were indeed the holders of the estate. "How often we have wished that our poor lost brother, Duncan, had not been deprived of the estate! But our Father's will was sacred you know. You yourself told us how fortunate we were to have rescued the will from his poor lifeless body, without damage to its contents. We had to abide by his wishes. We were helpless."

Mr. Mordacks, was so thankful that the opportunity opened up early in their conversation that he forgot his lawyer's verbosity and stated quietly, "That is exactly the question which has brought me here." The sisters caught their breath in unison, while Mr. Mordacks produced a small roll of parchment sealed in cartridge paper. "Last week I discovered a document which I am forced to submit to your judgment. Shall I read it to you?"

"What ever it may say, it will not for one moment alter our decision to abide by our father's will," observed Mrs. Carnaby obsequiously. "We were bound to do as he bid."

"Certainly, Madam. That is unquestionable. You are model daughters upholding your father's rights." He began to recover himself , "I had the honor of preparing your respected father's will and a finer document for clarity and turn of phrase there never was in all of Yorkshire. It was beautiful, beautiful…"

"Pardon me for interrupting you," said Philippa who had been holding her tongue with great difficulty. "Since I have always understood you to speak very highly of my father's will, what then can be the matter with it?"

"Miss Yordas, "began Mr.Mordacks, standing to his feet, unconsciously bracing himself for what he felt sure would be an unpleasant confrontation, "the matter is not with the will itself, but with the *will* of the testator, that is the one who made the will," he announced pompously. The sisters looked at one another and Philippa's face tightened. "Mr. Mordacks, will you be so kind as to use some of that clarity for which you are so renowned and tell us in plain words what is your meaning?"

"In plain words, Madam, I mean that your father could not decide to dispose of what was not rightfully his. In short, your property, the larger and better parts of the estates, including this house and grounds, were not his to give. They were his only for as long as he lived. At his death, the property, according to this title deed, must by law," he paused and tapped the parchment cartridge in his hand significantly, "it must revert only to the direct son and heir."

"But that would be Duncan and we do not know if he is alive or dead," squealed Eliza. "Indeed we have done all we can to ascertain that."

Philippa drew herself up to her full height and called upon all the pride of the Yordas family that she was heir to. "Are you denying the effectiveness of our father's will?" she asked in a steely voice. "Are you saying that we do not have the right to this property on which we have lived these many years?" Her voice strengthened with cold dignity.

"Exactly so, my dear Miss Yordas. Exactly so. Yet there is more, for we do know Mr. Duncan Yordas married, but we do not know if he had a son or even any children. Even if he did not, the rights of Mr. Yordas' widow must still take precedence over yours." Mordacks took a step backwards as he saw the black anger that clouded Phillipa's brow. But he continued valiantly with his task, knowing that worse might follow if he did not. "Thus you see that you cannot legally inherit this property until every effort has been made to locate any immediate family of Mr. Duncan Yordas, presuming he is dead."

Mr. Mordacks sat down again rather heavily, and took out a great white handkerchief to wipe his brow. The announcement had been made but he knew full well, by the battle light in Miss Yordas' eye, that he had better stay alert to her close questioning, or lose his reputation as a fine lawyer.

And a fine lawyer he was. Of that there was no doubt -- a fine lawyer, with a fine wife. It was as a direct result of his fine wife's conscientiousness that he had come into the possession of this old parchment he now held in his hand. It had lain in the bottom of an old box of papers for nearly two generations. The box had been turned over to Mr. Mordacks along with other items when he took over the business many years ago. A cursory look at that time had convinced Mr. Mordacks that the box contained little of value. All the important documents he had obtained were clearly designated and filed in his safe keeping. It was unthinkable that something had been overlooked. But it had. For this box had been stored in a dark cupboard, under the stairs in his home until earlier this spring, when his dear wife insisted on it being removed, to make more room for her sewing things. Accordingly, the lawyer removed it to his business office upstairs and on a day when business was slow, examined it more closely with a view to throwing away the contents. He dug through its contents of dust and grime, yellowed pieces of paper with faded ink, until almost at the bottom, filed along with the other names beginning with Y, he came across the name which stood out among all others: Yordas. Since Philip Yordas' will had been one of his first responsibilities, he had carefully removed the document and spread it out, noting that its signatures and seals were still intact. It was, as he explained to the listening ladies, only then that he realized, to his great concern, that this was the title deed to the Yordas property. How it had become hidden among these papers of much lesser importance he could not understand. It was of course well known that his predecessor had quarreled fiercely with Philip Yordas before retiring and dying soon afterwards.

Under closer scrutiny, the document Mr. Mordacks had discovered, clearly expressed, beyond all doubt, that the land and its settlements were given over in their entirety "to the rightful male heirs of Richard Yordas forever."

At this the ladies gasped their disbelief. It could not be so!

Yes, he assured the ladies, there was no doubt as to it being genuine and binding. As such it effectively nullified that other document for which Philip Yordas had given his life at Seven Corpse Ford. Philip could hold the land for only his lifetime. He could not do what he liked with it. After his death it must pass on to the next legitimate heir.

The ladies blamed Mordacks entirely, as he knew they must. Though he expected that it had been his predecessor's scheme to cause the Yordas family grief in later years, by hiding this title deed. But he himself had acted in good faith in drawing up Philip's will. He had, in fact, been intimidated by Philip Yordas' proud and haughty manner, and since he was newly come into the business, he did not question the right of Mr. Yordas to cut his son out of his will.

"I assure you madam, that I acted in all good conscience and have even now come in haste to apprise you of the situation."

"Whatever must be done?" moaned Mrs. Carnaby.

Philippa stiffened her shoulders and glared at Eliza, "Whatever is *right* must be done of course. We must act according to the rules of the family. Our first consideration must be thoroughly unselfish and pure justice."

Mr. Mordacks, nodded righteously, although he was uncertain as to her clear meaning. Mrs. Carnaby stood up to face her sister in a passion, her face flushed and not far from tears. "Philippa, I am amazed at you. Would you leave nothing for my son? Never was there anyone in this whole world so unfit for a beggarly life. How can you be so unfeeling?"

Being overcome with tears, Mrs. Carnaby sat down again. Mr.Mordacks, uncomfortable with any woman's tears, moved agitatedly away from the sisters.

"You mistake me, Eliza," Philipppa stated clearly and determinedly. "I said we must do what is right. We must maintain unselfish justice and a high sense of honor. Can there be any doubt what our actions must be? We must uphold what our good father intended and what his will dictates. As good daughters, can we do otherwise?"

Mr. Mordacks stopped his pacing in surprise and stepped back into the group. He thought rapidly. If the sisters decide to brazen the thing through, it might save him considerable loss of face for not having unearthed the title deed before ratifying their father's will.

"Excellent, madam," he said carefully. "I hadn't thought of the case in that way, but I believe you have the right of it." There would be fewer questions of his competence and he had not said one word to persuade the sisters in either direction.

"Oh Philippa, how noble you are!" Eliza cried and shed no more tears.

"Mr. Mordacks," said Phillippa stepping towards him and holding out her hand. "Please give me the title deed, and leave it here with me as I wish to peruse it more carefully."

Mr. Mordacks was shocked. Should he really do so, knowing the meaning of its contents? The look on Phillippa's face brooked no argument. Reluctantly he handed it over.

"You may trust me to do what is right and proper, Mr. Mordacks. Am I not a Yordas and has not this residence and all its lands belonged to the Yordas family for more than two hundred years?" She took the parchment and laid it carefully upon the table. Within a few moments Mr. Mordacks found himself ushered out of the door and onto his horse.

As he returned to York, Mr. Mordacks considered the fact that, had he cared to, he could perhaps have drawn up such a legal case over the parchment that would have taken many years to resolve, and upon which his grandchildren may have made a comfortable living. But all told, he felt it was better for his reputation to let matters lie as they were. The thing had been literally taken out of his hands. Nothing had been heard of young Duncan since he had left for India. In all likelihood he had died long ago or certainly he had made no plans to return to the country of his birth.

Nevertheless, as Mordacks approached Seven Corpse Ford, he felt the hairs on the back of his neck rise, as his horse splashed through the water. He almost thought he could hear Philip Yordas' curses in the noise of the water. Yes, it was better to let matters lie.

Chapter Eighteen

DOWN AMONG THE DEAD WEEDS

Unhappily for Mr. Mordacks, or perhaps happily, if he really wanted to be square with his conscience, several months later, a totally unlooked for event intervened in his life. As a result he found himself on horseback bound for Flamborough Village. This was a long journey, which was fortunate because Mr. Mordacks had something of great import to mull over as he rode.

The cause of his unease was an unexpected and unsettling letter he had received from India. The letter was from a Mr. Duncan Yordas. Now Yordas is a common enough name in Yorkshire, but the possibility of there being two Duncan Yordases was beyond belief. From the letter it was evident that Duncan was very much alive. Quite possibly he knew nothing of the of the original title deed of Scargate Hall or, and this thought was what caused Mr. Mordacks' unease, perhaps he chose to not to reveal his knowledge to Mr. Mordacks. At all events, from his letter, Duncan's concern seemed not to do with the Hall or his sisters, but with a ship which had carried his wife and son and which was supposed to have been lost off Flamborough Head about nineteen years ago. His request was simply to have Mr. Mordacks make discreet inquiries about the truth of the shipwreck in the village of Flamborough and report his findings to Sir Duncan.

Just to look at Mr. Mordacks, no-one would dare to think that money could be of any consequence to him. Stern honesty and strict propriety was so stamped upon him that any roguish fellow coming within hailing distance would turn and run and be thankful to have escaped. Yet now he was on the horns of a dilemma. To tell the Yordas sisters that their brother was alive, would embroil him in a family squabble. To reveal to Mr. Yordas that he might have been a party to the concealment of the original title deed to Scargate Hall would leave him open to severe criticism. Yet it seemed inevitable that the truth would come out eventually.

Thus after several days and sleepless nights, Mr. Mordacks decided that there could be no harm in undertaking inquiries for Sir Duncan. He decided he would wait out the question of the rightful heir to Scargate Hall until it arose in a more obvious mode.

In Flamborough, he made some casual inquiries about shipwrecks, of which there had been many because of the prevalent fogs and dangerous reefs. He dropped a little bait here and there, and knowing how close were the people with whom he was dealing, he made sure that he roused no undue curiosity. Flamborough was well known for its smuggling activities, but he could discover no breath of the village being involved in the art of 'wrecking', as was the case in the southwest of England.

After two days he returned to the City of York, but not before hiring an old Flamborian known as Veteran Joseph, a retired sailor with but one leg. He lived in a shack by the old tower which served as a beacon for lost vessels and was so anxious to earn a golden guinea that he agreed to hold his tongue but leave his ears wide open. As soon as he learned something of a wreck in the specific time frame Mr. Mordacks gave him, he agreed to report to the factor's business residence at York. Mr. Mordacks then returned to York to allow time for his Flamborough inquiries to bear fruit.

Mr. Mordacks, however was far from content during these waiting weeks. With regard to the title deed, events were moving too fast for his peace of mind. He'd done what he thought was best, but evidently that may not have been enough. Yet as far as his inquiries on behalf of Sir Duncan those events were taking far too long. It was now a month or more since his contact with Veteran Joseph. He could only presume now, that the ship which Duncan was inquiring after was the one that bore his wife and child. Since the area was so rife with smugglers and perhaps wreckers, Sir Duncan was right to be suspicious. But why now, nineteen years after the event?

The more he rambled everything over in his mind, the more he had the strong conviction that there must be something there -- and he was doubly sure because there was no sign of it. But something in Mordacks restrained him from committing to action in the one matter before he had resolved the other.

At last, one day, while he was rubbing his wiry head with irritation over these matters, a great knock on the door sounded through the house – like a thumping of a mallet on a cask of beer.

"One of my Flamborough men I'm sure," said he, jumping to his feet with anticipation. "They don't knock at a door, but thump at it.".

"Ah mine ancient man of the tower!" Mordacks exclaimed with satisfaction holding open the door. "Veteran Joseph, if my memory is right. You make your place of settlement by the old tower in Flamborough, isn't that right? That's where I met you. Come in, come in. Now let me get you a glass of grog."

The old man pulled off his cap, revealing the white band where it had resided above the red and weather-beaten, leathery face and wiped his head with a shred of cloth. Then he began hunting for his pipe.

"First time I ever was in York City; and don't think much of it either," Joseph grumbled.

"Joseph, you will see things better through a glass of grog. You have had a long journey. Rum shall it be, my friend? Rum like a ruby of the finest water I have. Aye, and no water shall you have with it. Am I not right?"

"First time I was ever in the city," repeated the ancient watchman, "and so grog must be done as they does it here. It's a good thing as I don't reg'larly have to travel such a distance as this for my beer."

"Aye and for all you're a man of the world, home brew's best," said Mr. Mordacks pouring the sparkling liquor into a glass and putting it into the old man's hand.

"Sir, I'm obliged to you," said the Watchman of the Tower, taking a deep draft from the tumbler. "I could never live a month without my beer. Same as it is with all my sea stuff around me in me home at the Tower. I miss the dipping of the land and the noise of the water all around, let alone the changing colors of the sea and sky. Ah, those I miss and I'd miss even more if I didn't have all my bits and pieces of sail nets and ropes around me as I do at 'ome."

"Well I can understand a thing like that," said Mr. Mordacks with a kindly nod. "My water butt leaked for three weeks. Pat... pat...all night long it went, upon a piece of slate, and when I had a man come and caulk it up good, why I could not sleep a wink any more there in the quiet. But you may trust a Yorkshire workman that it wasn't very long before it began to leak again and I got my sleep. So now tell me what you came so far to tell me."

"Well now, your Honor, I had rare luck. A son of mine comes home, as I'd thought as was lost at sea. And he came back with a handful of guineas and the memory of his father. Lord, I could 'ave cried. He had done his work well against the Frenchies and earned a good conduct with fourpence-halfpenny a day so long as ever he shall live."

"Good Lord! Whatever did you do with all that money, Joseph?"

"We never wasted none of it, not half a groat, sir. We finished out the grog cellar at the Hooked Cod first, and gave Mother Precious money enough to fill it up again upon the understanding that we'd come back when it was ready. Then we went into Bridlington and spent the rest of it like two posh gentlemen until there was nothing left a'tween us. It was then my boy, though he was a few sheets in the wind, goes a-rummaging in his packs, and sure enough he finds five good guineas tied in the tail of an old handkercher he had clean forgotten. So he says, 'Now, father, you take care of them and we'll go up to York to see that gentleman as you have picked up some news for.' That was you he was meaning of course, sir. So we set a course for York on an old schooner as far as Goole and then in a barge as far as here. So here we are, high and dry your Honor and my boy's down the street whetting his whistle."

"Wonderful, quite wonderful!" cried Mr. Mordacks. Then prodding the old man forward he added, "So go on man, tell me all of it."

"Aye, Ah'll be doin' that. But first you have to hear how it came about or you'll not be taking our word for it. 'Twas while we was at the Hook and Cod. We was there many long nights – and mornings too. And we stood drinks for every man that came in. They came from miles around to enjoy our company and Widow Tapsy's grog. And we sent 'em home through the lanes as merry as could be many a night. And some there be who wouldn't come in at first, but eventually, if you keep the beer taps goin' long enough, they all come in, saints and sinners alike.

"Well, your Honor at the last, the tardiest came along in and he were as big a sinner as ever you clap your eyes on. My son and me was sitting on the floor among the sawdust, for it'd been a long night and he looked at us down his long thin nose, as sober as a judge, shook his head and spread his hands out over us like we was the sinfullest of men. And then we heard the other men laughing at us and he snickering the loudest. But we took the care of him all right. Come the next day, we found out from Widow Tapsy that he was one of those long shore beggars that turn up every now and then, who makes their way galley wrecking, raking through the wrecks when the tide goes out, like a stinking ray fish. Not having the courage for a bit o' honest smuggling, they make their way on other's misfortune.

Mr. Mordacks nodded enthusiastically, to encourage him along.

"So," Joseph continued, "my son Bob and me remembered what you told us about a ship as went down off the 'eadland and we took thought as 'ow this man might be knowin' some'at about your missing ship. A man like 'im uh'd know, I'll be bound. So Bob and me, we came up with a plan. We made up a brew as would have had the cockles turn up their toes. We boiled it down to a nice tidy soup, and got a bottle with 'Navy Supply' written on it. Then we filled the bottle with the soup, French white brandy and a noggin of molasses and shook it all up well together. And a better rum never came into the admiral's stores," stated Joseph with a mighty wink wrinkling his leathery face.

"Joseph, Joseph, please to get to the end of your story," broke in Mordacks.

"Your Honor is like a child hearing of a story," complained Joseph. "You wants the end first and the middle last. But you shall have it all and judge for yourself.

"Mother Tapsy was ready for us. The man's name was Rickon Goold who lives down upon the rabbit warren the other side of Bempton. She never did like him because he scarcely ever came to the Hook and Cod and when he did he'd eat and drink all she put before him and leave a tab as long as your arm and never pay it. And being a lone woman, she doth feel it.

"Well, your Honor, we goes on that night with great restraint. We gave him at first the usual grog, and as others joined us, we all tippled like usual. 'Cept Bob and me, we never touched a drop, except from a gin bottle full of cold water. When we see the others with their scuppers well awash, our Bob began grumbling about the brew – Lord how beautiful he done it – 'Mother Tapsy,' he called, 'I'm blessed if I won't stand to buy that old guinea bottle of best Jamaica. The one as you put by for the Lord Admiral whenever he comes. The one with the cobwebs on it down in the cellar. Hoist it up here now.'

Ricken Goold pricked up his ugly ears at this. And Mother Tapsy played her part bootiful, she did. She brought out our special bottle of Navy Supply and sure enough, he downed the lot. To cut a long story short we spliced him, good and proper we did, Captain, with never a thought of what would come out of it. All we wanted was our revenge."

"Yes, yes, Joseph. Get on with the rest of it, do," cried Mordacks nearly beside himself with impatience.

"With all this Bob and me was as sober as two judges, but we had to take old Ricken Goold to the weed room, as it is called, and left him there. They call it the weed room for Mother Tapsy does have all kinds of sea weeds and shells all over it, like it was the very bottom of the sea.

"So now we went down again to have a little drop for ourselves this time, leaving him upstairs in the dark. We'd been there only a little while when suddenly there came a great groan, like from the depths of a heathen's heart. Bob and me scampered up to the weed room and there the thundering rascal lay in the middle of that there menagerie of sea-stuff. Blest if he didn't think he was at the bottom of the sea among the starfish and cuttles, waiting for the Day of Judgment. 'Oh, Captain McNabbins,' he cries, 'the hand of the Lord has sent me down to keep you company here. I never would a' done it, Cap,n, hard as you was on me. If only I know'd how dark and cold and shivery it would be down here. I cut the big bung hole out, I'll not lie. No lies is any good down here with the devil's wings coming over me. But it were a score of years agone, it were. And no-one ever even spoke of it.' Then he let out another blood curdling scream. 'Oh pull away on those oars, pull, for God's sake pull – the wet woman and the innocent babe they're crawling all over me like conger eels!' and old Ricken Goold lay writhing on the floor like the conger eels theirselves. With that my Bob gets down on the floor and wriggles up to Rickon through the sea weeds with a hiss like a great sea-snake. Then he gripped him and in a big deep voice, like old Nick himself coming from a sepulchre, 'Name of the ship you sinner,' he boomed. 'Give the name of the ship.' Goold gave a groan as seemed to come out the whites of his eyes, '*Golconda* of Calcutta,' says the fellow, and down went his head with a thud on the floor and we heard no more from him that night.

"Well now Captain, you scarcely would believe but Bob and I never gave another thought to it, having had our revenge, until the day our money ran out and Bob came up with them five guineas. That was when we remembered how you'd commissioned us all those weeks ago. So we decided it was best to come and let you know what we'd heard. So here we are spinning this yarn to your Honor's honor. And we hope as how you have a liberal twist to it, so's we can take our orders and draw rations. After all, it was all our dibs that's gone in doing you the service."

Mordacks was satisfied. He nodded. "You have done wisely and well in coming here, but we need further particulars, my friend. You seem to have hit upon the clue I wanted but we must look for more." He tapped the side of his nose thoughtfully. Do you know where to lay your hand upon this villain?"

"Certain sure your Honor. I could clap the irons on him any hour you gives that signal."

"Capital!" said Mr. Mordacks gleefully. "Here, take these two guineas and take your son to see the sights of our great city. I'll call upon you again when I have need to see the matter through."

With that the old sailor had to be satisfied, because Mr. Mordacks trundled him out of the door without a half-penny more.

Chapter Nineteen

THE CLUE OF THE BUTTONS

For all that Mordacks now had some good information, he still wondered what had aroused Sir Duncan's suspicions of foul play, all those thousands of miles away in India and so many years after his son's death.

It was a fact that Sir Duncan Yordas was a man of great self-reliance, quick conclusion and strong resolve. These had served him well in India and insured his fortune. Even so, unpleasant events and the bitter losses of his wife and son softened that stiff-necked nature that ran so strong in the Yordas family. The illness and death of his wife, to whom he was so deeply attached, overwhelmed him. For years he was satisfied to believe both losses were a matter of fate and that he could do nothing to bring them back. And so he might have still gone on believing, except for a strange little accident.

About the time Mordacks called upon the Yordas sisters to inform them of the discovery of the original title deed, Sir Duncan was called to Calcutta upon government business. Strolling down the street on his first evening there, he happened to see a pair of English sailors, lazily playing in a shady place by the side of the road. One of them seemed to have lost his last penny to the other and was trying to convince his mate to take a couple of trinkets in exchange for money. "'Ere Jack," said the one, "you give the change for one of these and I'll give you another game. That I will."

The other swore that they were "naught but brass and not worth a copper farthing."

"They's real gold, Ah'm tellin' you. 'Ere ask this gen'leman. What say you, sir? A man of the world such as you look, you'd know real gold. 'Ere, look at them and give us your judgment." The sailor in his excitement pushed three yellow-gold hollow buttons into Sir Duncan's hand.

A weaker man might have shown his excitement, but other than losing a shade or two of his sun-browned face, Sir Duncan held himself steady. He recognized the buttons immediately as the ones on his little boy's dress when last he saw him in his mother's arms. There was no mistaking them, for they had the peculiar design and workmanship of a man in the village of his district who made them.

"Well now," said Sir Duncan, in a gruff voice to hide the emotion he felt. How'd you like for me to give you thirty rupees for each of them...?"

"Done" cried the sailor and made to grab at the buttons again.

But Sir Duncan was too quick for him, as well as being much taller. Swiftly he closed his fist around the buttons and held it up high. "Not so fast, my jolly seaman," roared Sir Duncan, and the sailor jumped back again. "You must tell me every detail of where you got these buttons and be prepared to swear and make an affidavit if required. Whereupon, the sailor eagerly agreed, for he had been carrying them around long enough now, that if he were to make a profit on them it would be a whole lot better than having them sit in his pocket along with his penknife, bits of string and some grubby looking mints.

The sailor told a tale that had the marks of truth as far as Sir Duncan could tell.   It seems the sailor had been keeping company with a nice young woman of Scarborough, about a twelve month back. She was a servant girl whose name was Sarah Watkins. He kept company with her for some time, meaning to get spliced to her one day. Then the day was set, and the night before as many a young lad does, he took off with his friends for a night of tippling. When he came to the next morning, he was twenty leagues from Scarborough, press-ganged on board His Majesty's recruiting brig, *The Harpy*. When he'd felt in his pockets, he found naught but these three beads which Sally had given him as a keepsake. Sir Duncan expressed his sorrow for the poor man's misfortune and gave him an additional ten rupees to help him get over it. That persuaded the sailor to remember that Sarah was the daughter of a rich pawnbroker in Scarborough, whose surly attitude and avarice had led him to kick his children out of their home as soon as they were old enough. Apparently Sarah was pushed out before her turn and she took on the job of a serving girl, but not before she took the gold buttons from her father and a warm jacket too, to disgrace his memory.

Having the three buttons now safely in his possession, Sir Duncan resolved upon making some inquiries through Mr. Mordacks of the City of York who had, so he heard, great wisdom, tenacity and strict integrity. This Duncan had heard from his father's rantings, the day he departed from his family vowing to get on in the world without the help of any other Yordas. So he had contacted Mordacks.

The months had dragged by with no word from Mordacks. Sir Duncan was an impatient man as his father had been. Nothing could normally have driven him from his post in India when times were troubled, but now, events in his district having quietened down for some time, the buttons burned like a fever in his mind. Having heard nothing from Mr. Mordacks for more than two months, he resolved to go to England himself.

Sir Duncan was not a man to wait for action, so as soon as he could, he arrived on the doorstep of Mr. Mordacks.

It happened to be only days after the visit from Old Joseph. Mordacks knew the time had come to move events forward. Sir Duncan was not a man to be trifled with and what is more he was here in the flesh.

Yet, to Mordack's amazement not a word did Duncan say about the will and title deed to Scargate Hall but only the investigation of the *Golconda* and the fate of his wife and child. To aid in this investigation, Sir Duncan had brought with him the three buttons. Mr. Mordacks looked them over, but could make little of them. It was a thin thread to link three small buttons to the loss of a wife and son some twenty years before.

"I'll tell you what I'll do, Sir Duncan. If you would be so kind as to let me have one of those buttons, I think I have made enough friends in Flamborough from my past visits, that I might be able to find the missing links. I don't make any promises, and it wouldn't do for you to go, for the people of that village are over suspicious of outsiders. They might think you were a revenue man and then you'd get nowhere. Me, -- some of them already know for what I am and it's to them I'll go."

At this, Duncan drew himself up and fixed Mr. Mordacks with a steely eye. If it's my son we're going to find then it's me that will go with you. I've waited too many years to sit here and do nothing when I might be finding out if my son's dead or alive."

It was then that Mr. Mordacks thought of the issue of the title deed. Thinking that it might be something with which to please the man if nothing came out of their visit to Flamborough, he agreed to Sir Duncan's presence on the journey. "Well if you insist. But there is another matter of business that I'd like to take up with you that we can discuss along the way. It might also be to your advantage."

"Mr. Mordacks, sir," roared Sir Duncan, for that was the way he was used to conducting his business abroad, "I'll have you know that nothing is as important to me nor that could be of any like advantage as knowing what has become of my son."Through   the gruffness of the man, Mr. Mordacks perceived a glitter in his eye, which betrayed the emotion of the moment. Yes, he decided, this man should have his money's worth. He deserved it. Those old ladies are reveling in the land from which they have ousted their brother and maybe granting leases not worth a straw, now that Sir Duncan is known to be alive. Duncan's yearning to see his son had quite touched the heart of the upright Mr. Mordacks.

Taking the buttons with them, the two men left for Flamborough the next day. As they journeyed, Mordacks recited all the information he knew about Scargate Hall, the title deed and the uselessness of the spiteful will made by Duncan's father. Sir Duncan was unimpressed. The land mattered little to him if he had no son. His interests were all abroad. But if his son were found to be still alive then Duncan would claim the land as his right and for his son and heir. Thus he informed Mr. Mordacks. "In the mean time I have only one object here and that is to find my son, as I conveyed to you from the beginning, Mr. Mordacks," stated Sir Duncan with rigid finality.

Mordacks accepted this without comment and set his thoughts on discovering the son. This time he resolved to take the direct route for his information. So after a strenuous journey, they put up at the Hooked Cod. Mistress Precious took one look at the important button and did exactly what Mordacks expected. Her face closed up, her eyes hardened and with a firm smack of her lips declared she knew nothing of the offending button. Mordacks knew that had she really not recognized the button she would not have been able to contain her curiosity and would have made it a topic of conversation and speculation for more than an hour. Mordacks was sure she was familiar with the buttons. This he had to convey vigorously to Sir Duncan, who did not know the ways of the close-mouthed Flamborians.

Being even more strongly convinced that there was a clue here, the next morning Mordacks dressed carefully and with Sir Duncan and the buttons, he set out for the home of Dr. Upround. There, they were shown into the best parlor where they sat only briefly before the good Doctor entered.

"Ah, Dr. Upround!" Mordacks exclaimed leaping from his seat and stretching forth his hand, "How good it is to meet you, for I do believe that Flamborough, as small a village as it is, and you being a man of the cloth as well as a man of the law, must already be acquainted with me, though perhaps not with my friend Sir Duncan Yordas here. That I have visited the village before I'm quite sure you know for I'm also quite sure nothing takes place in this village without your esteemed approval -- that is nothing lawful."

The good Doctor straightened his glasses on his nose, since they had slipped a bit at Mr. Mordack's enthusiastic greeting. "I would certainly hope that I know my business as well as that of the Lord's," he said mildly. "but as to who you are, and I have known of your presence in the village -- and your questions, I…ah…I have no knowledge of your vocation, unless it has something to do with the Revenue service. In which case I tell you, you have come upon a fruitless mission if you come to me for information. The sorry business in the Dovecot a few weeks back, has put an end to the foolishness of free-trading in these parts for a while." It was true that nothing had grieved Doctor Upround so deeply in his years of ministry as the death of Captain Carroway and Robin's ultimate flight.

A small frown creased Mordack's brow for he was not, as yet, aware of the death of the coast guarder and the implication of Robin Lyth. Nevertheless he ploughed on. "No my good man, I am not here about any events of a few weeks back but of nigh on twenty years ago. You have been in this parish I hear for at least that number of years and much good does it speak of you to persevere in this harsh country. I am here investigating on behalf of Sir Duncan, who is a man such as you; a leading man of society; a man of large intellect and commanding character and, though he does not boast of it, an extremely wealthy man."

Dr. Upround cast a subdued look at Sir Duncan who was remarkably calm and let Mr. Mordacks do the talking -- at which the solicitor was well skilled.

"Reverend Sir, prepare your mind for a highly astounding disclosure," began Mordacks dramatically. "I have been here in Flamborough on several occasions as an agent for Sir Duncan Yordas, to follow up the long lost clue to the whereabouts of his son and only child, who was for many years believed to be dead. It is my penetrating mind that has brought me thus far and now I believe I will soon identify him with certainty. But only with your help."

Poor Doctor Upround was now more than ever confused. He was used to the slow, plain talk of the fishermen and their wives, not the fancy word playing of this citified gentleman. "I will do what ever I can," he grumbled. "But what can I do when I do not know what you are talking about?"

Mr. Mordacks put his hand deep within his pocket and pulled out the button with a flourish. "Do you know what this is, dear Doctor Upround. Hold it, feel it, examine it closely and tell me if you do not know whether you have seen others to match this and in whose possession."

Dr. Upround took the button, straightened his glasses on his nose again and then under the pretense of seeing it in a better light, he took it to the window. There he tried to marshal his thoughts. At last he turned around and gazed steadily into the agent's face.

He drew a deep breath. "A babe was brought to me some twenty years ago. On his dress were such buttons. Perhaps I should not have remembered so clearly except that as the babe grew to be young man, he had two of them made into earrings as many a sailor does."

Mr. Mordacks' ears were ringing as he heard these words. Not only had he struck upon the truth of what happened to the ship, but perhaps he could unite father and son! He looked at Duncan who was dumbstruck and holding his hand to his chest. What a satisfying and profitable turn of events he thought. "And the young man's name is....." he prompted.

"Robin Lyth, beloved by the family that raised him and by me who schooled him," Dr. Upround stated simply.

"Aaahh!" exclaimed Mr. Mordacks expelling his breath in a deep, satisfying sigh. "Just as I believed," he said. "I have every reason to believe that this young man is the long-lost son of Sir Duncan. What skill I have! Wonderful! Wonderful!

"I congratulate you upon your wonderful success," added the Doctor, but I wish you had enlightened me about the reason for your research when you first came to Flamborough. I understand the need for such secrecy since Sir Duncan is such a wealthy man, but if I had only had your confidence sooner, I could have saved you a vast amount of time and indeed seen you through to the end of your mission. But now.....I fear Robin is well beyond your reach."

"Beyond my reach! Is he indeed? How can that be?" Mr. Mordacks was not a man to give in to adverse circumstances when success was so close.

"He sailed for the Continent last night, which I know is in itself a vague description of a destination, but necessary in times like these. My position forbids me to express my opinion, but the evidence compelled me to issue a warrant for his arrest. I received this from him this morning." With these words Dr. Upround produced the letter Robin had left for him only hours before.

Mordacks took it and read it carefully and then passed it to Sir Duncan to read. His sharp mind quickly grasped the predicament. Mordacks looked away from Sir Duncan, whose emotions were now carefully in check. He asked briefly, "You believe all this?"

"Indeed, I most certainly do sir. Robin is a free-trader. He is not a murderer. Poor Carroway was shot from behind and the smugglers had no firearms except the two unloaded pistols and Mistress Carroway is not a person to deceive herself. If she believes Robin is innocent then she must have reason. However, John Cadman, the most intelligent of Carroway's crew, insists the Captain turned around for one moment to give an order and at that moment received the shot in the back of the head."

"Hmm, his evidence may well hang those six poor fellows, but... but...I trust our man will be far away. Am I right?"

"I believe not, Mr. Mordacks. If even one of them is condemned, or even transported abroad for his crime, the Robin Lyth I know will surrender immediately. You smile. Do you doubt me? Do not. I am a man who has known Robin's true nature nearly all his life."

"Well, let us not go too deeply into that just now," replied the Doctor's visitor. "Yet there is one point in Robin's letter that really does demand immediate inquiry: the guns of the preventive men. They should be examined. This John Cadman, do you know anything about him?"

"Only of his villainy in another way. He led away a nice girl of this parish, an industrious mussel-gatherer. The rogue already had a wife and large family of his own. Her father thought to kill him, which I readily restrained. So John Cadman rarely comes near Flamborough now."

"I must pay a visit to Mistress Carroway," muttered Mr. Mordacks. She is the very person. After what Robin says here, Mistress Carroway may have some enlightening information. It must not be overlooked. Matters are crowding upon me fast, Dr. Upround. I must see Mrs. Carroway as soon as possible. Good morning and my best thanks to your Worship." With that, Mordacks ushered Sir Duncan before him and they both bade the good Doctor goodbye leaving him shaking his head at the abrupt ways of city men.

Once mounted upon their horses again, Mordacks realized that Sir Duncan had not said a word during the entire conversation with Dr. Upround. As he looked closely at the man, Mordacks could see that he was thoroughly distressed. "Do not be discouraged," he cried. There appears to be more to this terrible crime than would implicate your son."

But Sir Duncan was so overcome, first at the joy of finding his son and in the next moment losing him again so fast, that the memories of the unpleasant leave-taking he had had with his own father many years before, arose before him and quite overwhelmed him. He could hear the strident voice of his father "…cut you off without a penny…" He could see the stiff-necked anger in his father's red face, the veins standing out on his neck. No, no, it was too much. His son was of Yordas blood. He was a murderer and a free-trader. How could he be otherwise? Duncan's own father, hot-blooded, unreasonable; his own sisters scheming to cheat him of his birthright. The truth had to be faced. His new-found son was a wastrel of true Yordas blood and on the wrong side of the law.

He pulled up the reins of his horse and called upon Mordacks to stop. "No more, no more, Mr. Mordacks," he called above the blustery wind. "I've heard all I need to hear. My son, if not a murderer, has spent his youth as a free-trader, scoffing at the law. I'll have no more of it. You go on to Mrs. Carroway if you wish, but I'll have no more to do with it. And I want no more to do with my son." His face was red and twisted with disappointment and anger. "I'll away to York to make the old deed a present to my sisters, if they haven't already destroyed it."

Mordacks sat amazed trying to bridle his horse, which was overset by such a sudden stop. "It's been a fool's errand from the start," continued Duncan bitterly. "When I've settled with my sisters, I'm going back to India. My life's there. I was a fool to think otherwise. If you ever find my son, you may tell him he's a Yordas and much good might it do him!"

All Mordacks' efforts to persuade Sir Duncan otherwise were useless. The man was as stubborn as his predecessors. The more he tried to convince Sir Duncan, the more Sir Duncan sat on his horse in surly silence. The more Mordacks was unable to convince the man, the more Mordacks convinced himself of the innocence of the youthful offender, Robin Lyth. Being a man of law, he could not like leaving Robin Lyth to his consequences if there might be further evidence to prove his innocence.

Since there was no reasoning with the father and the matter of the land was about to be resolved by Duncan refusing it, Mordacks felt his way clear to do someone some good from this business. He disliked unraveled ends, and injustice. He therefore concluded that it was incumbent upon him to discover if Robin Lyth was in truth the murderer of Captain Carroway.

Thus, the two men set off in different directions -- Mordacks to the home of Mistress Carroway, and Sir Duncan to Scargate Hall to settle the ownership of the land once and for all.

Chapter Twenty

THE SCARFE

Duncan set off at a good pace to reach Scargate Hall before dark. His thoughts were full of as much darkness as that which he hoped to forestall. His heart was scarred deeply by the now clearly evident death of his most beloved wife. His son, whom he had hoped to clasp to his breast as the last link with his wife had turned out to be a wastrel and his elder sister, Philippa, schemed to deprive him of his rightful inheritance. That Eliza, the one of the two sisters for whom he held in greater affection, could aid and abet in this scheme to defraud Duncan, rankled like salt on the wound which was already an open sore. Her treachery, turned her past seeming affection for Duncan to hypocrisy in his eyes. He was through with the Yordas name, the Yordas land and any thing else which might be tainted by the Yordas blood -- and that included his son, Robin. As soon as he had dealt with the matter of the deed he would return to India and be done with the lot of them.

Meanwhile, the news of Sir Duncan's return to his homeland had filtered through the villages and hamlets of Yorkshire until it reached Philippa herself. Until now, the fateful deed lay hidden in a secret drawer of her accounting desk, which only she knew how to open by means of releasing a small spring on the underside of the desk. It had lain there safely since the day she had gained it from Mordacks. Even Eliza did not know of the drawer, since she had never had a head for figures and left the task of running the Hall to Philippa. But if Duncan were to return to the Hall, Philippa reasoned, it was entirely possible that he would know of the drawer. Before his father had so forcibly denied him his inheritance, Duncan had from his early years been trained in the running of the estate. He was bound to know of its existence. In addition, since Mordacks knew he had left the deed with her, albeit temporarily, she would have to remove it. Until now, Philippa had just enough respect for the law not to destroy the offending piece of parchment. If it was out of sight, it was out of mind, she'd told herself. She could always protest that she had had every intention of returning it to her lawyer.

But now, the danger of its contents being brought to light could destroy the living she and her sister so carefully and frugally maintained. No, it was clear the deed must be destroyed, she thought, and it was entirely possible that Duncan did not know of its existence. What she did not know, and in fact had not even considered, was that it was entirely possible that Duncan would have met up with Mordacks, nor that even now Duncan was on his way to the Hall.

There was no immediate emergency right now as far as she knew, but the manner of her ways was such that once she had made up her mind on something she would not delay in doing it. With Philippa there was no room for delay between resolution and execution. She was never one to halt between two opinions. She had set up her plan last night.

Thus at about four-thirty of the next day, she called her butler to her and bade him prepare some tasty turbot to be taken up to her sister, whose appetite demanded some gentle persuasion because of her delicate nature. The butler had his own opinion on the subject of Miss Carnaby's appetite but knew it could not be expressed. Therefore, he bowed in silence and retreated to the kitchen to carry out his instructions.

Philippa had her beaver hat and mantle by the shrubbery door and sent for her little pony and went quietly to her room where she had stored a flat basket with a heavy clock lead weight in it.

"Much better to drown the wretched thing than burn it," she had been saying to herself, "especially at this time of the year when the fires are weak because of dampness and our own necessary frugality. And burning parchment makes such a nasty smell. Eliza might come in and suspect something. No, she thought, the Scarfe was a much more trusty confidante than the fire.

The Scarfe is a deep pool, supposed to have no bottom, (except perhaps in the very bowels of the earth). It was set upon one of the very wildest headwaters of the Tees River. A strong mountain torrent from a desolate ravine springs forth with great ferocity casting itself upon the air from where it falls, for one hundred and twenty feet. It falls with a tremendous roar and gives off bright streaks of white foam and even little sun-bows in fine weather. But once it reaches the foot of the crag in great violence, two white volumes of water roll away with a clash of waves between them. They sweep round the craggy basin, meet again and swirl back in coiling eddies and rushing foam. And there in the middle is the pool, deep and dark, waiting for something to suck down into its depths. Many a sheep had been engulfed there, never to see her lambs again.

"If it could swallow up a sheep," thought Mistress Yordas, "how much better to engulf this tiresome work of a lawyer." Indeed, in her frame of mind, she thought it would be an even more pious action of the pool to swallow up the meddlesome lawyer himself. Although a lawyer was not a sheep (except in his clothing, and his eyes perhaps), yet there were many no doubt, who would not feel horror at the thought of such an end for busybody lawyers.

She came resolutely down the dell to the ravine, with a strong determination. The clock-weight and the deed-poll itself, were stitched firmly into the small two handled basket. She had chosen the basket with its two handles so as to give her a firmer grip when she cast the bundle deep into the pool below. The deeper she went into the ravine, the more the towering crags shut out the late afternoon sun. There were great boulders and sharp-edged walls of rock along her way and everywhere they could find root, thick brambles covered the ground. There, in the middle of this jungle was the caldron of the torrent, called the Scarfe. Though the rocks surrounding it were green in the daylight, now they were black and the spray and mist spewed upwards in a smoky wreath and hovered over the chasm.

Miss Yordas was a strong lady with staunch nerves, yet she disliked this place and never came near it, even in the summer when the fury of the scene changed into grandeur and even beauty. Her reasons stemmed from a story she heard as a child when a long ago Yordas had, in a fit of cruel anger, flung a man into its midst because he had been threatening him with a lawsuit. Even more unnerving was the story, though never proved, that a favorite maid of hers, when hearing that her sweetheart had been exiled for some misdeed, had in her loneliness, jumped into the swirling basin.

Now Philippa was out of sight and sound of anything but the roaring gorge. "I must be getting old," she thought, "or this path is much rougher than it used to be. Why it seems to be getting quite dangerous! My father used to ride this way sometimes, but how can a horse get along here now?" So she abandoned her pony and scrambled over rocks and tree trunks, down the track. She had no choice. For a moment, she was sorry that she had not chosen some other method to dispose of the deed and risk the chance of arousing suspicions. But having thus begun, she would not consider turning back. She was angry at her idle fears.

With her hereditary stubbornness she thrust aside doubts and continued down the steep, perilous path, until she stood on the brow of a sheer rock, directly overlooking the torrent. She stood to recover her breath and regain her strength in readiness for the great casting throw that would be needed to rid her of the parchment forever. The crag on which she stood was trembling with the power of the water's thundering crash below. The white mist from the deep moved slowly like a shroud, here and there revealing the slippery walls of the gulf. With the basket in her right hand, she planted her left foot on the edge and swung herself backwards for the hefty throw it would need. But just as the throw should have been completed, the heavy weight in the basket slipped and instead of the basket being flung into the deep abyss, it fell back and hit her in the chest. She lost her balance and fell backwards. Her feet flew up and she fell on her back. Her smooth beaver cloak began sliding upon the slippery rock. Horrible death was pulling at her. Not a stick or stone or branch was in reach of her hands. She gave one long shriek which echoed pitilessly around the crags, and above the roar of the waterfall. She tried to turn over to grab the tufts of grass but only felt herself going faster. Her descent increased and the sky itself was falling.

Just when she was about to plunge into the abyss below, powerful hands fell upon her shoulders. A grating drag against her swift slide was the last thing she remembered. Sir Duncan Yordas grasped her shoulder and threw himself back on his heels. The long Indian spurs on his boots dug into the rock and held like the talon of a falcon. Without knowing who she was, Sir Duncan had leapt from his horse at hearing her despairing scream. Without another thought, he had risked his life to save hers.

Breathless, he dragged the lady to a place of safety. There she lay still in a stupor. Clenched in her hand was the basket. Sir Duncan tried to remove the basket from her tight fist. "Allow me, madam, I will not steal it, I just thought to use it to place under your head." He could not move it until suddenly the stitching gave way and Sir Duncan spied the roll of parchment. The lady opened large, dark eyes, and met his startled gaze.

"Philippa!" he gasped.

"Yes," she answered faintly, still so shaken by her experience and now overcome by the sight of her brother.

"Are you all right?" he cried. "What were you thinking of doing?" For his sharp mind immediately grasped the implications of the scene he had interrupted. "What is this that you risked your life for?" He picked up the parchment. Philippa tried vainly to take it from him. He looked at her and then again at the parchment. Gently he unrolled it and read the title. A shadow crossed his features. There was a silence between them for a moment. All that could be heard was the thundering roar of the water. Then Duncan released his breath in a heavy sigh.

"Look up at me," he said firmly. "Don't be afraid to look. Surely you know your only brother! I have lived for years in India and now am returned, but only for a little while." He paused, still kneeling beside her. "I used to be very kind to you when we were children. Don't you remember when you tumbled in the path down there? Your knee was bleeding and I tied it up with a dock-leaf and my handkerchief. Don't you remember? It was primrose time and we searching for them down there."

"To be sure I do," replied Philippa gathering strength from her brother's gentle words. "And you carried me all the way home. Eliza was dreadfully jealous." She gave a small smile.

"That she was," replied Duncan, "And you were not much better than she. We had our squabbles then, but now we are older, and getting on in life." He looked at the parchment in his hand. "We don't need to have too much to do with one another if we can't get along. Still, we surely ought not to try to kill one another out of petty jealousy for land and property. What is land in comparison with life?"

Sir Duncan stood up, placed the parchment in the basket, pulling the stitches tight again. Holding up the basket he cried, "See now, sister. Stay where you are for a moment and see what I care about this." Grasping the basket with the deed in it, he took three steps to the edge of the chasm and hurled it with one strong arm, out into the midst of the white mist. It dropped straight down into the murky waves of the whirlpool.

"No-one can prosecute me for that," he said returning to his sister's side with a smile. "Though Mordacks may be somewhat upset by it." He dusted his hands together dismissively, as though with a job well done. "Now Philippa, although I cannot carry you back home as I did all those years ago, for, my dear, time has added to us both, but I can help you home, my dear, and then get on with my business. He grasped her hands and pulled her to her feet.

The pride and esteem of Miss Yordas had never been so crushed, as she now stood before her brother's kind words, knowing the ill will she had felt for him only moments before. It was too much for her. She put both her hands upon her brother's shoulders and burst into a flood of tears.

Chapter Twenty-One

MRS. CARROWAY

Unfortunately for Mr. Mordacks, winter came early to the little headland. While Duncan out-rode the storm that descended upon the north moors, Mr. Mordacks had to hole up at the Hook and Cod for several days until the snow-storm blew itself out. When he finally set out on the road to Bridlington to see Mistress Carroway, the cliffs were snow-mantled and the cold North Sea storm-ploughed the sands. Dark grey billows frilled with white, rolling and roaring to the shrill east wind, made Bridlington Bay a very different sight from the warm and happy scene of August last, when chance brought Mary and Robin together for the first time.

But if everything looked cold and dreary in the harsh winter wind, the solitary cottage of the late Lieutenant Carroway, standing on the shallow bluff and beaten dreadfully by the bitter blasts of wind, looked more desolate than anything within view. On the windward side, the snow was piled up in a deep drift. There was no footpath to the front door or any footsteps in the snow. There was no smoke from the chimney and all the windows had the blinds pulled in honor of the dead one.

"I am pretty nearly frozen," said Mordacks to himself, "but this place sends shivers down my back." After peeping through a window with a torn blind, Mordacks first turned pale and then red with anger at the thought that no neighbors had evidently seen fit to stop in at the cottage. A pathetic sight met his eyes. Several of the youngest children were huddled together by a cold fire place. A dirty blanket half covered them and judging by their dirty clothes their mother had not seen to them in several days—probably not since the death of her husband.

Mordacks turned his horse swiftly and headed to the public house that abutted the quay. He marched into the parlor and stamped about until the landlord came to him.

"Will you have a glass of hot toddy sir?" asked the landlord.

"Never from such as you!' was Mordacks' fierce reply.

The landlord sniffed haughtily, "Well if that's all you've got to say…"

"It is not all I have to say. Bring me a bottle of your best Cognac and all the victuals you can lay your hands on. You're a fine scoundrel when you laze back here with food and warmth. Your next door neighbor is a woman with many children, whose father and husband has just been murdered and you've done nothing about it."

"Well…" stuttered the landlord, "well, these be hard times tha knows…"

"You'll know this!" roared Mordacks . As his host turned away with a careless shrug, Mordacks planted a highly energetic kick, in a well padded place. "Take that as my neighborly contribution for the poor family," he cried. "Now be prompt about it. Don't give me any airs or there'll be more where that came from!" He stepped towards the landlord who immediately became very active.

"I've done you a world of good today, sir." Mordacks continued, "You've learned to be benevolent ... to look to your neighbors' welfare. Remember the lesson well!"

In five minutes all the resources of the inn were at the disposal of Mordacks. "Now take a leg of mutton," he commanded, "and begin to roast it. Then warm up your biggest bed for a lot of frozen children." With that he clapped down a bag of cash on the counter and bade the owner look to his horse. At that moment, the landlord's wife came shambling in. Holding all he could carry in his arms, Mordacks beckoned to her to carry the rest of the food and follow him. They set out in the snow and the freezing wind and made tracks for the lonely shack.

"You can't come in," said a weak little voice after Mr. Mordacks had knocked at the door in vain. He turned the handle and began to push against the poor little body that was trying to hold it shut. "Oh you musn't come in. Oh please, whatever shall I do? Mother is so poorly and she said no one was to come in."

"Where are your brothers and sisters?" asked Mr. Mordacks in as kindly a voice as he could muster after the blustery walk over to the cottage. "In the kitchen are they? Oh you poor little mite, how many of you are dead?"

"None of us are dead, sir, unless it is the baby," wailed the little girl bursting into a storm of tears. "I gave them every bit of food I could find, even the rush-lights, but they wouldn't eat them, sir, so I tried to eat some of them. Mother is gone off her head and the baby... the baby..."

Mordacks set down the supplies, "Here's hot bread and milk. Come now, pour it out and feed every one. Where is the baby?" In the kitchen there was no spark of a fire, just barely warm ashes. Tommy, the brave lad who had ridden to Filey to deliver the fateful message to his father, was nowhere to be seen. Mordacks looked at the little crowd of children. If once they had been scrubbed clean by a bit of soap and flannel, it couldn't be told now.

"Please sir, I couldn't keep them clean," said the oldest watching his eyes and choking through her tears. "I had to feed Tommy down in the coal cellar and then I had to hunt through all the places in the house for a bit of bread or whatever I could find."

Three little children at the grate, sat among the ashes, peeping over their shoulders at the tall strange man, half-afraid and half-ready to toddle to him for comfort.

"Here woman," said Mordacks to the landlord's wife. "Take two of them in your apron to the inn and put them in the warm bed. They need warmth before they can eat properly. I'll bring along the other three."

"But please, sir, won't you let our Tommy out of the coal cellar first?" cried the oldest girl, as the woman ran off with the other two. "He has been so good and he was too proud to cry. It was as black as ink going down there into that cellar. But Tommy never minded."

"Show me where little Tommy is my dear. Whatever made your mother lock you all in like this and Tommy in the cellar of all places?"

"I don't know, sir," she replied but her eyes fell and the blue lids trembled.

"Now, now, you know right well," he said gently. "Don't be afraid I shan't let any one hurt you. Tell me all about it. You must tell me quickly, else how can I put matters right? Tell me what happened and we'll let Tommy out and try to help your mother."

"All I know is this," began the child, beginning to shake again with large tears welling up in her eyes. "It was the very night after....after.... my poor dead father was put in that deep hole. Mother was sitting in the window, sir," said the girl bravely trying to keep herself together. "I was at one side of her and Tommy was at the other. None of us was saying anything when there came a bad, wicked face at the window. The man shouted to m' mother through the window, 'What was it you said today at the grave, today ma'am?' he said. Mother stood up and opened the window and she looked right in his face and said, 'I spoke the truth John Cadman. It's between you and God now.' And the man said in an awful voice, 'You shut your bad mouth up, or you and your brats shall all go the same way. I'm giving you this one warning.' Then Mother fell down in a dead faint and she lay upon the floor and kept on moaning until the morning. After that she had no more milk for the baby and she rushed our Tommy in the cellar and locked him in, for fear the bad man would come and get him."

For once in his life Mr. Mordacks held his tongue. He'd been almost too late and still there was more to do. The little girl looked up at him, "Oh please come, sir." She ran to the cellar. Swiftly she unlocked it and called to her brother, but no Tommy appeared. Then she climbed down inside and took his hand and pulled him out. The poor little fellow was quite dazzled with the light. Then tears mixed with the grime on his cheeks followed by loud howls at the injustice of it all.

Suddenly a voice sounded from behind them. "Who is come into my house like this, talking to my children. My house and my baby belong to me she moaned, rocking back and forth on her feet. Go away all of you. How can I bear this noise?"

As soon as he observed her, Mr. Mordacks didn't know what to do or say. She stood there in bare feet with her husband's heavy night coat draped over her almost to the floor and the long white clothes of her dead baby which she still held in her arms, draped over its poor dead father's coat.

"I have come to help you ma'am," said Mordacks. "My dear madam, please to consider your children. See how cold you are. Allow me to conduct you to a warmer place. You don't seem to understand the situation," Mordacks added gently.

"Oh yes I do sir, thoroughly….thoroughly. My husband is in his grave; my children are following after him. But they shall never be murdered. I will lock them up first, so that they shall never be murdered."

"My dear lady, I agree with you completely. You did the wisest thing under the circumstances. See I will never harm them." He sat down on a box. "Come my child," he said to Geraldine, the eldest. "Come sit on my knee and you too Tommy on the other side." They did as he said, with Geraldine leading the way, since she had had the food. Tommy did as she beckoned to him.

Mrs. Carroway seemed to be emerging from her dream, as she saw her two children being safely held by a man with a kindly face. She looked around her, towards the kitchen, where she could smell the fresh bread and the milk. "I scarcely know what is happening," she said faintly. "My husband is not here to help me."

"Exactly so, Madam. So now you must take it on yourself to decide for the best of your children. Of course, you are waiting for the government supplies that you are entitled to at the death of your husband. But they have not come and your children are starving within and freezing without. Now I will see that you get what you deserve, only come with me now, and let me take the children. You are a noble wife of a very admirable officer. You are safe under my protection and so are your children. Soon you will understand what has happened and when you are warm and fed and you see your children happy you will come around, yes, you will come around."

Mrs. Carroway scarcely understood what he was saying, but looking at him miserably, she murmured, "I will do whatever I am told." And she followed him slowly through the snow to the inn at the quay side.

There they gently took the dead baby from her and laid it out in some snow white clothes. The landlady, whose conscience was now smiting her, had unearthed them in an old chest of clothes from her laying-in time.

Chapter Twenty-Two

A TANGLE OF SKEINS

It was evident to Mordacks, who liked things to be nicely tied up with no loose ends, that there was still a tangle of skeins left at Flamborough. It was true that the main object of his task had succeeded. He had at least discovered the fate of the *Golconda,* -- and Robin Lyth, but it rankled with Mordacks that he'd been unable to accomplish the reconciliation of Duncan and his son. What's more, Robin Lyth, who may just be innocent, and was now known to be born of a respectable family, would have to stay abroad and deny himself the love of his adopted family. Yet another thread was the truth that Mrs. Carroway and her children could not sleep peaceably at night while John Cadman was free.

Yet unhappily for Mr. Mordacks, who was nothing if not a man of purpose and some impatience, winter had now so thoroughly set in and there was little more that he could do until the winter gave way to spring and traveling became more comfortable.

Although it was a trouble to him, Mordacks knew he needed to return to York. Before they had parted, he had promised Duncan that he would meet him there after Duncan had settled matters with his sisters. This part of the tangle could only be unraveled in York. So after ensuring that Mrs. Carroway's future was well cared for by her neighbors, Mordacks left for York.

He did not have to wait long before Sir Duncan Yordas came to visit him once more.

"Well, roared Duncan in his usual manner, "I've come to settle with you and then I'll be off. My sisters are well cared for. We'll see no more of that wretched title deed. I've bought a place in the army for that miserable son of Eliza's. Perhaps it will make a man of him. Perhaps not. At all events, Scargate Hall will eventually be his. I've no interest in the place. I've grown too used to the climate in India to struggle the rest of my days against the bitter winters of Yorkshire -- nor enjoy what passes for summer in this place."

"But what about your son?" blustered Mordacks. "I'm gathering evidence right now. You can't abandon him surely."

"Aye and a right good son he's turned out to be," exclaimed Duncan bitterly. "No, he's a Yordas through and through. The smuggling is a trifle. Our family never was law-abiding. They used to be cattle-stealers and even the slaying of a man in hot combat is no more than I myself have done, and never felt the worse for it. But to run away and leave six good men to be hanged after he brought them into the trouble himself... then hide, quivering like a bat in a cave like the coward he is, far away enough to escape justice. That is not the right sort of dishonor for a Yordas." He paused. "No, I've been a fool....though I did love his mother so...but blood will tell." He thrust out his hand with a leather packet in it. "Here's what I owe you, and more, for wasting your valuable time."

Mordacks protested and argued, though his hand clasped the packet Sir Duncan had given him. With many explanations and remonstrations he followed Duncan to the door. But Sir Duncan turned and clasped his hand once more. "If you ever find my son, tell him he's a Yordas, and much good may it do him." With that Duncan stomped out of the door to his horse and his words echoed down the narrow street, mingled with the clatter of his horse's hooves.

The snow swirled after him as Mordacks shut the door and leaned heavily against it. Ah, but it was a sad business, Mordacks knew.

What Mordacks knew, but was unable to convince Duncan of, was that money was lodged and paid as punctual as the bank, for all the needs of the six free-trading sailors in jail. They may have grumbled a little because they had no ropes to climb, but they were too wise to have any fear of an unfriendly rope awaiting them. They knew they had not done the deed and they felt assured that twelve good jury men would believe them.

Robin knew it too. He had little doubt of their acquittal. 'The Chancellor of the Exchequer of Free-Trade', Master Rideout of Malton himself, had told him he would take care of it all.

The long winter days and dark nights passed slowly in York as they did in Flamborough. The north-east wind cut its teeth on the headland, terrorizing the gnarled, sloping hawthorn trees into bending yet further before its might. Widow Precious had laid in her stock of beer that was to comfort the stout-hearted Flamborians who leaned into the wind to reach her door. Mistress Carroway, in Bridlington was settled again in her cottage by the bay, stronger now that she knew her safety was in the good hands of Mordacks. Yet she still jumped at the loud cracks her cottage made on a frosty night or when the wind howled like a voice down her chimney. But she took comfort in the regular dole her family received from the government, thanks to Mr. Mordacks. Now she and her family ate as well as they ever did when Lieutenant Carroway was alive, having one less mouth to feed. Even kindly Dr. Upround presented his weekly dissertation without obstacle, having only to cross the street, hugging his robes close to him before they blew away down to the lighthouse – or over his head to obscure his view on the slippery church path. His parishioners, being hardy fisher-folk, came as they always did, summer being so often like winter, to hear the good Doctor proclaim his thrashing message, tempered with a powerful dose of mercy in his 'upandown' way. Though good old Monument Joe and his son Bob might have benefited from such a sermon, they were happily engaged most days in Widow Precious' rooms, enjoying the spending of Mr. Mordacks' liberal funds.

As soon as the winter days gave way to the warmer days of spring, Mordacks set off for Flamborough again. There were still too many tangles and he could not leave matters as they were. He had heard rumors about that wicked ship-wrecker, Ricken Goold, and nothing would satisfy him until he knew how Mrs. Carroway and her family went on.

Before he called on Mrs. Carroway, Mordacks stopped in at the Tower to see Joe of the Monument and his son Bob. He soon discovered that Ricken Goold had been nicely disposed of by these two worthies. According to their story, they engaged the ship-wrecker in several nights of drinking, being careful to restrain themselves, until he eventually died of an apoplexy in front of Joe and his son. "Neither of us," explained Joe, "could find it in ourselves to shed a remorseful tear for such a wicked villain." Mordacks understood their reasoning. There is indeed honor among thieves he thought to himself on hearing of Goold's fate. A little free-trading hurt no-one, but shipwrecking was a murderous occupation.

With that thread of the skein nicely tidied up, Mordacks set off with a greater degree of equanimity to visit Mistress Carroway.

By now, the weather had turned mild and all the snow had gone. The wind was blowing from the land instead of the cold grey North Sea. The cottage which had looked so bleak before was now warm and smelled of good wholesome food. The children were a delight to behold. Geraldine, recognizing him flew through the door and jumped upon his shoulder. He immediately found that Mistress Carroway had greatly benefited from the kindnesses, although belated, and care of her neighbors. Mordacks was delighted to find her in her right mind though still a little weak from her ordeal.

Although pleased to see him, she was a little restrained, for she guessed why he came. She couldn't help trembling a little with the memory of it all. Yet she would never be at peace until that evil Cadman was caught.

"It is all very horrible, very horrible," she murmured as Mordacks settled down with his pipe and the children were all in bed. "Yet for my husband's sake I shall endure it," she resolved with a small sob. She wiped the dust from the low table with her apron and from the arms of the chair she was about to sit in. Then she looked around the room at other dust covered objects and sighed.

"Dirt, sir, dirt was his only weakness. Oh my blessed, blessed Charley. I used to drive him wild with all my cleaning and scrubbing; but now...I leave everything as he would have liked it to be. Every table and chair has dust that you could write your name in. But I leave it so, for my beloved Charley's sake. Yet I cannot leave it o'er long, because it would be such a bad example for the children to be brought up among the dirt. But I haven't touched his pipe. There it lies upon the shelf with the old tobacco still in it. And I never shall clean that out." She clamped her lips shut and straightened her back. "No never."

"Mrs. Carroway," began Mordacks afraid that she might develop another fit of crying. "Mrs. Carroway, we must get down to the root here. You shall never live in this place in peace until we have Cadman. Your husband was a wonderful man and a wonder indeed. He did his duty with zeal and ardor. He set a shining example for very little pay. Yet I fear it may have been this very truly British character of devotion to duty and a stern sense of discipline which may have led to his downfall. What do you think of that thought Mrs. Carroway?"

"Yes Mr. Mordacks, it was all of that. He could never put up with a lazy man. All his men were kept in line at his word and no arguing upon it. Honest men can take that kind of discipline but wicked men fight against it. And all along we have a very wicked man here."

"True, Mrs. Carroway. Very true. Yet the question is, -- innocent or guilty? There you have it. If he is guilty shall he get off and innocent men be hanged instead of him. Six men are in jail for what we believe to be his crime and one, Robin Lyth himself, is to be hunted down if he should return to this land. While John Cadman is at large, your life is in peril, ma'am. I am sorry to have to use such harsh words, but I need to know what provocation had this man? What cause for spite against your husband?"

"Oh, none whatsoever, Mr. Mordacks. My husband rebuked him for being worthless and a liar and a traitor. He did threaten to remove him from the force; and he once pushed him down a small ledge of cliff on to the sand below. But whatever Charles did, he did it for Cadman's own good and so he should have known."

"I see," murmured Mordacks making notes as she spoke. "Was Cadman ever heard to threaten him?"

"Many times and in a most malicious way, -- when he thought no-one was listening. The other men may be afraid to say so, but my Geraldine, she has heard him."

"Capital!" exclaimed Mr. Mordacks. "What better is there on the witness stand than a child! A wonderfully, pretty child as shall tell the jury what she has heard." Then he added thoughtfully, "But I need more than that….aah, here is an important point. What happened to all the coast-guard muskets? They were all returned to the station I presume. I wonder did they all still have their charges in them?"

"I'm sure I cannot say about that, replied Mrs. Carroway. But I do know that one of them is lost and was never returned to the station."

"One of the guns never came back at all!" Mordacks almost shouted. "Whose gun was it that did not come back?"

"I can't say. There was such confusion. Every man is responsible for his own gun, I believe. Cadman declares that he brought his back and nobody contradicted him." Then she caught her breath, startled by an idea. "But Mr. Mordacks, if I saw the guns I should know whether Cadman's is among them."

"How can you possibly know that ma'am. Surely you never gave out the guns to the men."

"No, Mr. Mordacks. But I have cleaned them. Not the insides of course. Nobody sees that. But many times I have observed a disgraceful quantity of dust in the station. Dust upon the guns, dust and rust. I would make Charley take them down and be sure they were empty. Then I would clean them till they were a credit to my Charley's coast guard station. I found it quite pleasant to polish them, knowing that there was nothing in them to make them go off, and for me to have such wicked things at my mercy, so to speak. I noticed the wooden handles most, on account of being familiar with the polishing of tables and chairs. One of them had a curious pattern of grain, on the left side behind the trigger. It was just like when a child trickles treacle upon bread. It was Tommy as noticed it first. 'Look mother,' he says, 'look at this wood. It's all crinkly crankly,' that's what he called it sir. And at that very moment Cadman came up to us in his surly way and said, 'I want my gun missus. I never shoot with no other gun than that.' And so I always called it Cadman's gun. I hadn't thought of that till now. If that gun is the missing one I shall know who it was who lost it that dreadful night."

"All this may prove to be most important, but I will have to proceed most warily," pronounced Mordacks. "Cadman is a villain. I must not let him slip through our grip. We will start by taking a look at those guns. In the meantime, you look after yourself and your children. I will make sure your supplies from the government continue to come through. I thank you Mrs. Carroway. You have been most helpful."

Chapter Twenty-Three

THE PATH OF TRUE LOVE...

Meanwhile, those at Anerley Farm were content to hear the creak of their wagons and to live off the carefully stored produce their hard work of the past summer had earned them. Though Mary was sometimes too quiet, yet Mistress Anerley knew how to deal with that.

She reminded her good husband that her predictions were always found to be true. Hadn't she begged the lamented Captain Carroway not to shoot at Robin Lyth, because he would come in for a thousand pounds of trouble instead of the hundred pounds reward? And didn't it come true, she asked her husband? So now she made it clear to him that every word she said to him must turn out to be Bible true. From this time out, there was no excuse for Stephen if he ever laughed at anything his wife said. Now she had something else to tell her husband, only on no account was Mary ever to hear of it.

"Now look here, Stephen," she said, "You and I well know that a bird in the hand is worth two in the bush, and this bird in the hand is worth fifty of the other, who has gone abroad and is under serious accusation. Now Harry Tanner, he comes from a good family."

"Aye, that he does Sophy, but his father's an old skin flint. Why, how many times have I seen ol' George go to his pocket to for a sixpence for a poor old beggar chap, and then he'd think the better of it and back his hand would go with the sixpence, into his breeches. While out comes I with my shillin' to give to the starving chap, and I do it on the sly so as it was never mentioned. Ah well, for all that, ah think like enough, ol' George maught a' managed to get up to heaven."

"Stephen I wish to hear none of that. The question concerns our family, not his. Now what is your desire to have done with our Mary. When our Willie makes his great discovery on perpetual motion, nobody need look down on us."

I should like to see anyone look down on me," Master Anerley said straightening up his back and looking fierce. "He mought do so once, but a' would be sorry afterwards. Not that I'd be hindering 'im of his way, only he'd better keep out·of mine. Now my dear, how is it that when you go thinking of your own ideas, you never bear in mind, what my considerations might be? So why now?"

"It's because of the quickness of the way I think and you cannot follow my thoughts. You know you always say that, my dear."

"Well, well, quick churn spoileth butter," grumbled the old farmer. It's like Willie and his perpetual motion. What good to come of it, if he hath found it out? A nice thing 'twould be for fools to say that perpetual motion come from Anerley Farm!"

"You never will think any good of him Stephen because his mind comes from my side of the family. But wait till you see the money he'll get."

"That I will and thank the Lord to live so long! But enough of this talk. Let's get back to common sense. How was Mary and Harry a'carrying on this afternoon?"

"Not so very bad Stephen, and yet nothing so good to speak of," replied Mrs. Anerley. "He kept on looking at her from the corners of his eyes, but she never responded, so to speak, like as how… well you know….."

"..as how you used to do when we was young. Ah well, like as not she'll come around. Did he ask her about going to the hay-rick?"

"That he did. Three or four times over, exactly as you told how. He knew that was how you won me over and he tried to do it the very same way. But the Lord makes a lot of things change in thirty years of time. Mary quite turned her nose up at him and he had to pull his spotted handkerchief out of that new hat of his and it fair matched his poor red cheeks. Now, you know Stephen, if I had behaved like that to you, you would have marched off and stayed away for a week."

"And that's the right way to do it too. I'll tell him so. Long sighs only leads to turned up noses. He doesn't know how to go about it. You have to go on very mild at first with your sweetheart, just feelin' for her finger tips, so that she believes that you are frightened. Then you brings her round to peep out at you under her bonnet as if you was a blackbird ready to pop out of sight. That makes 'em wonderful curious and eager. But you mustn't wait too long like that. Next you has to come on like a large bull – but with a goodness in your heart that keeps you out of mischief, and you makes like you could smash a gate for her. Then she comes up all sweet as honey and thinks 'poor fellow!'"

"Stephen! I do not approve of such goings on! It may have worked for you once, but not for our Mary. Although she may not have my sense, she always must have her own opinions. But the more you talk of what we used to do when we was young, the less I feel inclined to force her. And who is Harry Tanfield after all?"

"I'll tell you who he is, Sophy. First, we know all about him, not like t'other chap, Robin Lyth," the farmer answered. "And that's something to begin with. Then we know his land is worth fifteen shillings an acre more'an ours, though it's full o' kid-bine. For all that, he can keep a family and is a good home dweller. T'other lad's naught but a slippery young free-trader, playing games with his majesty's men. Even so, like the rest of us, when it comes to women, young Tanfield must make his own way to win her."

"Father," the mistress of the house replied, "our Mary deserves better than that. What would it hurt us to encourage the lad? He's a good man and we know all about him, as you said. Harry Tanfield should have his chance, I say."

"Aye, so a' may for me, mother, so a' may for me. If he was to have our Mary, she'd know where he'd be at night, and there'd be no coast-guarders knocking at her door."

At that moment, Mary came into the garden from behind the hedge where she'd been feeding the chickens.

"Why poppet, we were just talking of you, exclaimed the farmer. "Fie, fie – you weren't listening were you?"

"Now, father," Mary replied calmly with a smile, though she couldn't help hearing part of the conversation as she'd approached the garden, feed bag in her hand. "You ever love to find fault with me, I think," and she kissed her father to soften the words. "But if you are plotting against me – for my own good – as mother loves to say, you best shut me in the barn or somewhere, before you begin to do it, so I can't hear." Truth to tell, Mary's heart was hurt, though she loved her father. It was Harry Tanfield again who they wanted for her and her heart was given so completely to Robin. But she said nothing of it, for she knew her father would never allow it.

"Why, bless my heart and soul. The lass has got her own mother's sharp wit and now she's telling me what to do in my own house. What a time is this, when the childer tell us what to do, and their mothers tell us what not to do." He laughed heartily at his own joke. "Soon you women'll be taking my farm off my hands, and be selling them turnips as is rotting. Ah knows you. You'd be putting the best ones on the top of the barrow with the rotten ones underneath and telling the buyers they all be sound and good. Well you'd better mind one thing – if I retires from business like brother Popplewell, I shall expect to be supported. Cheap but very substantial," and he chuckled again at the very thought of his womenfolk supporting him

But underneath it all, his heart was sore, for he knew Mary had heard them talking and he knew he'd never be able to give her where her heart was settled.

Winter reluctantly gave up its hold and spring coaxed the broom in the dyke and the gorse on the headland to break into their bright yellow, sunshine blooms. The primroses were plentiful on the cliffs once again and bluebells carpeted dells in Dane's Dyke.

One rare, late spring morning, a little boy ran through a field of green wheat and hid himself in a hawthorn hedge to see what was happening at Anerley Farm. His eyes were sharp, being of true Danish descent and nothing escaped him. He saw Farmer Anerley trudging up the hill, with a pipe in his mouth, to the bean field where three or four young men were enjoying the air without too much exertion. He saw the mistress of the house throw wide a lattice and shake out a cloth of crumbs for the birds, who instantly skipped down from the thatched roof, by the dozen.

Then he saw Mary going round the corner of the house carrying a basket of feed, and clucking for the hens to come running from their scratching-places. They came running from the straw-rick, the threshing floor and hedge rows with skinny legs and scrawny wings. Swiftly the boy slipped from the hedge, following the tails of the chickens across the rick yard. With that, he tossed a note wrapped around a stone, to Mary, with true Flamborian style and scampered off like a rabbit, as quickly as he'd come, not waiting for the twopence Mary had taken from the pocket of her apron.

Now the fowls came and helped themselves to the wheat in her basket, on the ground where she had set it while she collected the note. Her cheeks were redder than the master-cock's comb in all the yard, for she made no doubt about where the note had come from. It was short, being of only a few words, but it was sweet in its promise: *"Darling, the Dyke where first we met, an hour after sunset."*

Mary never doubted that she would go. She was firmly convinced in her own mind that she was now no longer a child but a loving and reasonable woman and that Harry Tanfield would never be her choice. So at the appointed time she went. It was almost a year since she had saved Robin's life. Patience and loneliness – as well as the opposition, which she had felt but not heard, from her own father- - had ennobled and enlarged her heart. Indeed no purer or sweeter example of maidenhood could have been found in all the land than this daughter of a Yorkshire farmer, as she went to the dyke in her simple dress, carrying all the dignity of true love in her heart.

The sunset deepened into dusk. The glen was shadowy and the bushes dark. But Mary continued, her delicate cheeks flushed pink with a little anxiety. Would he come? But she was not left to doubt long, for soon he emerged from the shadows.

They clasped hands. "Oh, where have you been? How long it has been! How much longer will you have to be away?" Mary's questions tumbled over themselves and Robin was hard put to answer them all so quickly. But soon the first excitement of their meeting settled into an orderly, though heartfelt pace.

"I am a true blue navy man as you now may see," said Robin delightedly showing off his uniform in the dim evening twilight. I am a warrant-officer already and when the war begins again, as they say it must, I shall very soon get my commission. I am already fit to command a frigate," said he with a hint of pride. You see my Mary, I am become respectable as I promised you...," he paused, " except that I have a price upon my head, not only as an outlaw, but because I am a suspected criminal. Of course, I am innocent as everyone knows, at least I hope that everyone does, especially the one who should know it the best." He held her gaze for an instant, with just a little uncertainty in his eyes.

But Mary didn't hesitate. "And am I not the very one who should know you the best?" she declared earnestly. "Ah Robin...."

"No more 'Robin', if you please," Robin interrupted. "I am Mr. James Blyth, captain of the fore-top, once the coxswain of a barge and now master's mate of H.M. ship of the line, '*Belleisle.*'" He grinned at her surprise and then sobered instantly and continued, "But the one who should have trusted me, next to you my own precious love, is my father, Sir Duncan Yordas."

"Whatever are you saying?" said Mary quite bewildered by this talk. "A warrant officer – an arrant criminal – your father Sir Duncan Yordas! Stop! Stop! You make me dizzy with all this joking."

"But it is no joking, Mary, my love. Every word of it is true," said Robin, his arm instantly encircling her waist, because of the dizziness she was feeling. "It has been clearly proved, long before I ever knew it, that I am the only son of Sir Duncan Yordas. He is a very rich gentleman from India, who is the heir to a large, though not very profitable estate, only a day's ride from here. But I am only his son for the moment, for he is ashamed of my present circumstances and has taken steps to be rid of me as his heir."

Mary didn't know what to think. All of this coming at her like a gust in a sail. "But Robin, if you are this man's son, how can we ever marry? You must know we cannot. If you belong to great people and I am just a farmer's daughter, you know we cannot. She clasped her hands, keeping down all sign of tears.

"Do I? Why?" asked Robin Lyth calmly, knowing well what she meant, but willing to prolong her doubts, so that he would reap the reward so much more soon after. "A little while ago, you were the one who was above me," he teased. "I was nobody's son, and only a castaway with a nickname."

"But that has nothing to do with it," cried Mary, tears glittering in her eyes.

"Mary, Mary, I am not worthy of you. What has birth to do with it? In every way you are above me. You are good and I am wicked. You are pure and I am careless. You are sweet and I am violent. I can only rival you in truth, for I know what I am and what is my duty. I would be a pitiful scoundrel if I did not do that. "

"But", said Mary, her lovely eyes gleaming with unshed tears, "I like you very much – but it is not exactly a duty, Robin."

"You look at me like that," said Robin softly, gently brushing her cheek with his hand, "and you talk of duty. Duty – this is my duty!" He touched her cheek with his lips. "This is the duty I should like to be discharging, for ever and a day."

Mary was silent for a moment, her eyes telling him all he wished to know. Then she said a little shyly, "I did not come here for this," but she smiled sweetly belying her words. "Ah Robin, free-trade made you bad enough but it seems the Royal Navy is worse." He touched her cheek again with his lips.

"Now, Robin, dear," she protested weakly, "be sensible. Tell me what I am to do."

"You are to listen to me, for I have such a tale to tell you. When my father, who has a great quantity of money, came back from India, he had no other purpose than to find me, his only child of the only wife he ever had. For twenty years he believed me to be drowned, because the ship I was sent home on to be educated, was wrecked and all hands were lost. But something caught his fancy that made him believe that somehow I had escaped the wreck. So he employed a gentleman of York, named Mordacks, to find out all he could about the ship that was lost, and if somehow I might be alive. Mordacks, who seems to be a wonderful man from what everybody says. He is most kindhearted to everyone, including poor Widow Carroway. Well, he set to work and found out in no time, everything about me, my earrings and how I crawled from the cave, and so much else that I do not have time to tell you."

Mary settled comfortably in his arms as he continued. "Mordacks even arranged a meeting in Flamborough with Sir Duncan, who had by now arrived in England to find out for himself, being an impatient man. So Mordacks intended to bring me to meet him and everything might have turned out well. But in the meanwhile that horrible murder of Captain Carroway took place and I was obliged to go in to hiding as you know only too well my dear. My father, as I suppose I must call him, took a hasty dislike of me before I could even speak for myself or be proved innocent. Mordacks whom I saw last week tells me that worse than the free trading, Sir Duncan supposed I had taken off and left my partner free-traders to bear the full brunt of the law and be hanged. For that he will never forgive me. He says that I am a coward and a skulk and unworthy to bear the name of Yordas."

"Oh what a wicked man he must be," burst in Mary, "to take you in such dislike, without having even met you."

"No, responded Robin thoughtfully. I am told he is a very good man. He regards me with scorn because he knows no better.

He may know the laws of our land, but he knows nothing of the ways of the free-traders. If he did, he would have known that my men were not in any danger. If I had been caught that night in the cave, I would have ended up on a gibbet on the cliff top before any trial was held. As it was, I am convinced no good Yorkshire jury would have found those poor fellows guilty."

"Oh I am so glad those poor men were acquitted," sighed Mary.

"Aye, and I was there to see justice done," replied Robin with a glint in his eye.

"You were there then to see it?" asked Mary, her blue eyes opening wide at the thought of the risk her Robin had taken.

"To be sure I was. Though few men knew it was me. I came dressed as the father of one of my men. It was Mr. Mordack's idea. The story I told the jury about my son's innocence was so convincing, even the Judge wiped his eyes. Why, my poor eyes have scarce returned to normal after all the sobbing I had to do in front of the court. I even had a crutch that I stumped with, so that all the court could hear me. Well, even the hardest hearts were moved."

"Oh Robin, I hardly know whether to laugh at your antics or to scold you for taking such risks. But what if the verdict had not been in your men's favor, what then?"

"Well then, Mr. Mordacks had a paper in his hand, signed by me, which he was to read to the court saying that Robin Lyth himself would surrender to the Court, upon condition that the men on trial should be declared innocent."

"And you would have given yourself up?" said Mary incredulously.

"No doubt of it!" stated Robin decisively, "though giving you up would have been much harder." His voice softened and he took Mary's hand in his, "Now Mary, my dearest, you must be brave. Though my men are freed by the court, I must still keep out of sight until more evidence of the real murderer is found."

"But how can that ever be," said Mary a tear trembling upon her eye lids. "When will I ever see you again if you are to stay in hiding?"

"Now don't worry, Mary my dear. Mr. Mordacks has taken to me like a father to his son. He has such a love of justice that he will not rest until the real guilty one is found. After the trial, he, Widow Carroway and I had a long talk. He is convinced that the murder was committed by a villain called John Cadman, -- a sneak and a skulk, whom I know well. He's one of Carroway's own men. They told me that Cadman's gun was missing and that Mistress Carroway can swear to that fact. If only I was free to show myself, I'd lay my life on finding it thrown away in that unlucky cave. Mordacks has taken down all I know about the cave, for no-one knows the cave like I do. Why I'd run all the risks, just to do it myself."

"Oh Robin! That would be too much risk!"

"Yes, but I'd do it all gladly if it meant that I could be free to return from my exile and marry you, my sweet Mary."

There followed a sweet silence, while Robin sought to show his Sweet Mary, his love, rather than talk of it.

At last he drew away with such sadness in his eyes that Mary's heart sank.

"What must be done, Robin?" she asked softly, yet fearing to hear his answer.

"Ah, sadly my love, only certain times of weather, tides and clear water, will allow us to find that gun we are looking for. So I must go back to my ship and leave all in the hands of Mr. Mordacks.

He has talked of a diving-bell and some great American inventions. But that will be of no use here. There must not be a word breathed of what we are doing. Whatever is done, must be done by a man who can swim and dive as well as I can, -- and one who knows the cave almost as well as I do. I know such a man and have told Mordacks where to find him. I have also shown my own dear, good and better father, Robin Cockscroft, the likely spot the gun will be found. So now I can do no more. All has to wait until that moment when everything comes together. Meanwhile I must return to my life as a sailor. I must remain Captain James Blyth and trust my friends to find the guilty one."

"But how long will that take?" asked Mary with despair in her voice.

"That I do not know," replied Robin, "But will you wait for me my Mary?" He paused and looked earnestly into her eyes. "Here, I have brought this for you." He pulled a small packet out of his pocket. "Here is a ring, not worthy of you my love, yet it is to go on your precious hand. Let me put it on for you. There! What do you think of that lovely Mary?"

She blushed with pleasure and admiration, "But it is too good...too beautiful...too costly."

"Not half good enough for you," answered Robin, "though I must admit that it cannot be easily matched by any other, any more than you can be matched by any other sweet Yorkshire lass. Now promise me to wear it, Mary, and when you look at it, think of me, my dear. I know your father still hates my name, but be sure to tell him every word I have told you, who my real father is and what I have been doing all these months. Perhaps it will help to bring him round to favor me a little. I'm sure he will come round eventually, but it will take time, I do believe. When he sees how much I have been wronged, perhaps he will change his mind."

"Oh Robin, Robin, perhaps he will, but he is a stubborn man, though he says I am the one who is stubborn, though he loves me still." Then because the subject was painful to her, she said hastily, "But now Robin, what am I to call you? Though you may be Captain James Blyth to the Navy and your father's name is Yordas, you can never be anything else but Robin to me. No, I must ask you to make me a promise. I shall never call you anything else, for it suits you. So promise me please."

Now no promise is complete without a seal. So in the old but expected way, Mary and Robin pledged their love and many more promises too, as they slowly headed back to the farm. The air was sweet with summer fragrance and the breath of night and the two in the Dyke were ripe with sweet dreams of hope and happiness, until, after long lingerings, they were forced to part at the very lips of the house itself.

But at the farm's edge, the perfumed air beheld another noble and strong presence each unknown to the other. Farmer Anerley stood in the darkness, in his shirt sleeves, puffing on a long clay pipe, and grumbled, "Wherever is our Mary, all this time."

Chapter Twenty-Four

NICHOLAS THE FISH

With Captain Carroway gone and things needing to be investigated, Mordacks contacted the diver Robin had described to him. Nicholas the fish, as his neighbors contemptuously called him, lived not far from Teesmouth and would be the ideal man to explore the waters of the cave where Carroway was murdered. The temperament of the man was to be slow and lumbering as often deep-chested men are. His thickened skin and extreme hairiness, such as would be admired by those with very little on the head, seemed to give him excessive ability of flotation and insulation from the cold temperatures of the often unfriendly North Sea. In addition, his deep chest gave him a rare capacity to take great lungs full of air that enabled him to remain under water for extraordinary lengths of time. His size rendered him clumsy and awkward on land, so Nicholas spent many days down at the shore often half immersed in the brine.

Mordacks was sure the gun he was looking for would be found in the cave and Robin would be exonerated, Unhappily for Robin and Mr. Mordacks, the precise combination of tides, the calmness and clarity of water were not expected to occur for several months.

Finally, it was about an hour before noon of a beautifully soft September day, when little Sam Precious, the same boy that carried Robin's note to Mary that spring, brought to Mr. Mordacks a bit of plaited rushes. This was the sign agreed upon by he and

Nicholas, (who did not know his alphabet), that the long awaited moment had arrived. Immediately, Mordacks, who had been staying at the Cod and Hook in Flamborough whenever his business allowed, put on his hat and girded himself with his riding-sword and pistol belt. Then he hastened to Robin Cockcroft's house; but not before sending young Sam with a letter to the Bridlington coast-guard station, just as he had previously arranged with poor Carroway's successor.

The Flamborough fishermen were out at sea. So without attracting undue attention, Robin Cockcroft's boat was quietly launched at North Landing, manned by the veteran fisherman himself, together with Old Joe from the Tower and his son Bob. Their orders were to slip quietly round the point of the bay and wait in the ill-fated Dovecot cave until the diver arrived. Mordacks watched them launch from the top of the cliffs and then strode up the deserted path that struck away toward a northern cove, where the diver's little boat was temporarily anchored to a clump of tough, brown seaweed. There he found Nicholas the Fish spread out on the golden ruff of sand, like a basking turtle. The wavelets broke gently over him, leaving a beaded silver fringe upon his hairy body. He was perfectly relaxed. His huge chest, inflated with the soft fresh air, kept him afloat as the waves encroached upon the sand.

As Mordacks approached, he awoke with a grunt of reluctance, realizing business was at hand and swam lazily to his boat. Embarking Mr. Mordacks, he pulled the boat and its passenger across the placid bay to the cave where the fishermen were assembled.

"Let there be no mistake about it," Mordacks shouted after they'd arrived in the cave, "Our friend Nicholas here, the great diver, will first determine whether the thing we seek is actually here." His voice echoed with a hollow sound as the voices of the free-traders had done so many months ago. "If he finds it, he will leave it exactly where it is until we have summoned the coastguard. You understand of course that we must keep the matter so secure that no lawyer can pick any hole in the evidence we hope to find here. Now, Nicholas, let us be about it. Go down at once."

Without a word, the diver plunged under the water, leaving scarcely a ripple. The watery floor of the cavern was as smooth as a mill-pond in July. There was not a sound for several minutes except for the lapping murmur around the walls of the cave. Everyone seemed to be holding their breath, with every ear intent for the first sound of the surface water breaking.

Finally, with a gusty breath old Robin, peering down into the dark depths, muttered, "Ta goop has got 'im. God niver mahd man to pree into his own warks". Old Joe and Bob grunted their agreement. Mordacks himself was beginning to believe that some dark whirlpool had drowned the poor diver, when there was a gentle noise, like a dabchick playing beneath a bridge. Over in the darkest corner of the cave, Nicholas had quietly surfaced and was inhaling air, not in greedy gulps, but leisurely encouraging his lungs with small mouthfuls, as a doctor gives soup to a starved boat-crew. The men hailed him loudly in their relief, but he didn't answer, for he was not talkative by nature. Instead he turned his great body to the side and with scarcely a ripple swam to the side of the boat.

"Have you found the gun?" cried Mordacks. Nicholas made no reply for a full minute, while he stood upright in the water supporting himself by nothing more than a gentle movement of his feet. "O' coorse I has," he said at last, "Over in yon little corner."

"And you can put your hand on it in a moment?" cried Mordacks excitedly. The diver nodded. "Admirable!" burst out Mordacks. "Now then Joe, and Bob, the son of Joe, do what I told you. Fetch the coast guard, while master Cockscroft and I get the lights ready."

The torches were fixed on the rocky ledge, as they had been that fateful night, but they were not yet lit. Joe and his son who had been sent in the smaller boat, soon came back with the news that the Preventive men were rounding the point and approaching swiftly, with a lady in the stern whose dress was black.

"Right!" cried Mr. Mordacks, his brisk voice ringing around the echoing cave. "Now Nicholas, when I lift my hand, dive down and do as I have ordered you."

The cavern was soon lit with resinous fire, and the dark, still water heaved in the eerie light. The coastguard boat came gliding in. The crew in white jerseys looked like ghosts slipping into some fantastical scene. Only the officer , darkly clad, standing up with the tiller lines in hand, and the figure of a woman sitting in the stern, disturbed their spectral whiteness.

"Commander Hardlock, and men of the coastguard," shouted Mr. Mordacks, when the wash of the boat, the drips from the oars and the creak of wood gave way to silence. "The black crime committed upon this spot shall no longer go unpunished. The ocean itself has yielded its dark secret. A good man was slain here, -- in cold blood. He was a man of remarkable zeal and gallantry, discipline and the noble father of a very large family. Worse yet, the villain who slew him, would have slain six other men by perjury, except he was foiled by an enlightened jury of Yorkshiremen." Warming to the drama of the moment, Mordacks drew himself up to his full height. His face glowed in the flickering light. "Now I will show you the truth. When I lift my hand, you will have to wait less than a minute before you will see rising from the watery depths of this abyss, the gun that was used in the murder."

The coastguard men, though honest, scarcely understood his meaning --except for one of them, who knew only too well that his treacherous sin had been found out. He tried to look as the others did, but knew if there were more light he'd have given himself away. Then the widow who had been watching him through her black veil, lifted it and fixed her eyes on him. Deadly terror seized him and he wished he had been shot himself.

"Stand up, men," shouted the commander. "We'll see this through to the end. This crime has been laid at our door. We scorn the charge of such treachery. Stand up men and face the charge like the innocent men we are.

The men stood up and the boat rocked dangerously. The light of the torches fell upon their faces. All were pale with fear and wonder. But one of them was as white as death itself. Yet calling up all that evil anger that had made him do the murder in the first place and never repent of it, he stood up as firmly as the rest. He forced a smile to his face, but his eyes were riveted to the spot on the water where he knew his fate was sealed.

Then, without a sound or even the sight of the hand that lifted it, a long gun rose from the water before John Cadman and the butt was offered towards his hand. He stood transfixed, unable to move nor speak.

"Hand me that gun!" cried the officer sharply. But instead of obeying, Cadman plunged over the gun into the depths of the water.

But Nicholas was there, as swift and deadly in the water as he was awkward on land. He caught Cadman like a dog catches a worn-out glove, and brought him to the surface. "Strap him up tight," cried the captain. The rest of the men were glad -- and relieved to do it.

Months later he was tried and the jury did their duty. His execution restored goodwill among the people and revived that faith in justice, which subsists upon so little food.

Chapter Twenty-Five

ALL'S WELL THAT ENDS WELL

It was more than a year before the news of his proved innocence reached Robin Lyth, now Lieutenant James Blyth. His time at sea had been extended several times now as the pressure of the French forces came to bear upon England and Robin had been forced to serve at His majesty's command wherever His majesty saw fit. His latest orders found him upon the HMS Victory, serving under one of England's greatest men. But the joy the news should have brought him, along with honor of doing his duty under Admiral Nelson was tempered by additional news that reached him by the same messenger.

The ship was making all preparations for a great battle looming in but a few hours. The men of the *Victory* were wound up tight ready to let fly at their admiral's command. But for now, the wind was dropping. A sullen swell was rolling and canvas flapped giving all aboard some respite to consider what the morrow would bring.

"For this moment of battle I have lived, and it would be worth my while to die, having no one left now, in all the world to care for me." So spake a disheartened Lieutenant Blyth, whose true name was Robin Lythe, who had once been the captain of all smugglers. Now he had fought his way up the ranks in the navy, by skill, spirit, patience, good temper and most important of all, self-reliance. But without good fortune all these talents would not have been enough. And one of Robin's truest gifts was that he usually earned a great amount of good luck.

But this night, he was not in his usual high spirits and his anticipation of tomorrow's battle meant unusually little to him. For Robin Lyth had heard last night, when a schooner joined the fleet with letters, that Mary Anerley was going to marry Harry Tanfield. Mordack's news of Cadman's justice arrived with the same batch of letters. But the bad news far outweighed the good. He told himself many times, that it was his own fault, for he had not been careful about the safe dispatch of his letters. Changing from ship to ship and from sea to sea, he had found but few opportunities to write. To Mary herself, Robin had never written, knowing well that her father forbade it. So his letters to Flamborough had been few.

The people of Flamborough itself, being sure that Robin could never exist without free trade -- and missing the many generous gifts he had brought to them while at it -- were certain he was dead and lamented it mightily.

But Robin knew none of this until now, when the dispatches finally found him. He did not blame Mary, for how was she to know whether he was alive or dead.. Indeed, Robin knew her mother was always promoting Harry Tanfield, and since the villagers considered Robin dead, what else could an obedient daughter do?

It was providential then, that the mighty battle, which history would record as the greatest victory, the battle of Trafalgar, was to be fought the very next day, giving Robin little time to brood on the news he had received.

And a great battle it was. Many a British sailor, who mercifully survived that day had much to tell about the furious uproar, the choking smoke, the din of roaring metal, and the clash of cannon-balls as the French and Spanish ships fell upon his majesty's navy. It was said that no less than seven ships set about destroying Lord Nelson's ship, itself.

In the storm and whirl and flame of battle, when shot flew as thick and close as the teeth of a hay-rake and fire blazed into the furious eyes of blazing men, many men fell, never to rise again. Nelson knew that it would be so, and when he himself had to be carried down to die, it was Robin Lyth who was close by him. It was Nelson himself who told that officer not to tell the men of the admiral's fate, but to get back into the thick of it and fight.

At that moment, the French attempted to board the *Victory*. The heavy British guns had momentarily ceased to throb and to the French captain it seemed that there were more dead bodies than living on the quarter-deck. So he seized his moment, with a cry of "Forward, my brave sons! We will take this vessel of war, and Nelson too!"

But it was not to be. Though few of the British sailors aboard the *Victory* could understand French, there was one, whose roots in free trade gave him that skill. Hearing the French captain's words, Robin leaped up and with a holler called up the Britons from below. By this time a swarm of brave Frenchmen were gathered in the gang-way, waiting for the swell of the sea to lift them onto the British ship. Scarcely a dozen British sailors were left there alive to confront them and no officer to take command until Robin Lyth appeared with his band of men from below. In the midst of the drifting smoke, the flare of fire, the pelting of bullets and the screams of the Frenchmen exalting in what they thought was their success, their came a mighty sound. Above the explosion of powder and metal and crash of timber, came the roar of a British cheer. Onward came the vigorous and powerful charge of Robin Lyth and his men. The sudden and unexpected onslaught and the fury of the cheer caught the French unawares. Robin and his fifty men behind him came up and carried all before him. Although Nelson was gone, the ship was not lost.

The war over, the English hardly knew whether to rejoice or mourn, since with the winning they also lost their greatest hero, Lord Nelson. And though Robin was the hero of that day, few knew of his exploits. The news did spread as far as Flamborough, who was justly proud of him and quick to claim him as one of their own. In fact, to have fought under Nelson in his last fight was in itself a passport to the strong, right hands of men and into the hearts of women.

One staunch Yorkshire man, who had never been known to change his mind before, was even seen to raise an eyebrow in approval when he heard of Robin's bravery, though he said not a word, in case his wife and daughter think he was growing soft. But to prove his broadmindedness, the next Sunday, Mr. Anerley put on his best uniform of the Yorkshire Invincibles, draped a heavy sash of black crepe over it, in memory of Lord Nelson, harnessed the white-nosed horse and drove his family to the neighboring parish of St. Oswald's church at Flamborough. It had been announced that Dr. Upround was to preach on the Death of Nelson.

The sermon was of the noblest order, eloquent, spirited, theological and so thoroughly practical that seven Flamborough boys set off on Monday morning, to destroy French ships of war. Mary did her very best not to cry, for she wanted to watch her father's reaction. But when the good Doctor began to speak of the distinguished and brave part played by a gallant son of Flamborough who had previously endured unwarranted scandal, she could not but prevent a quiet sob escaping. When the Doctor went on to claim that, but for the bravery of this young man, England would be mourning her greatest hero without the privilege of burying him, for he would have been in the hands of the French. And when he proceeded to ask who it was that foiled the enemy's attempt, up stood Robin Cockscroft and other equally ancient captains, and respectfully touching their forelocks, they answered, "Robin Lyth, sir!"

Mary allowed another quiet sob to slip forth from her tight control. Her mother pulled out the stopper from her smelling-bottle and looked at her husband as if he were Bonaparte himself. So uncomfortable did that man feel that he looked for his hat and fumbled about for the button of the pew door to get out of it. Fortunately, the church clerk awoke to see the men standing, and hearing the noise from Mr. Anerley, thought that the sermon was over and pronounced "Amen," decisively.

During the whole drive homeward, Farmer Anerley's face was clouded with thought. He knew that his wife and his daughter watched him, but he did not choose to let them know his thoughts, before he had decided them for himself. So he let them look at him to their heart's content, while he looked at the hedges, and the mud, and the ears of his horse and the weather. And he spoke only two words during the whole of the journey, one of which was "giddyup," and the other was "whoa!"

The two women looked at one another, and said not a word. Knowing what kind of a man he really was, they knew too, that he would be better by-and-by, and perhaps try to make amends handsomely. And this he did, without any doubt --just as soon as he had dined and smoked his pipe -- while he sat on the butt of the old tree by the rick-yard.

When he returned to the house with his mind made up and the details settled in his head, he found that there were visitors at Anerley Farm. Mr. Simon Popplewell and his wife, Deborah were visiting. "Aye and they are probably here to witness my humbling," thought Farmer Anerley. But humbling or no, a man had to admit when he was wrong, especially when that wrong involved his beautiful daughter who had so filled his heart that there was no longer room for any false pride.

As he entered the room, a lively talk was stirring and at first he stood unnoticed. He stomped his feet in the doorway to shake off any excess mud that the door-scrapers might have missed and the talk died down to a mumble. "Ah! You was talking about me," the farmer said.

"We mought be, and yet again we mought not," Mr. Popplewell returned, a smile on his jovial face. "Brother Stephen, a good man seeks to be spoken of, and a bad one objects to it, in vain."

"'Tis true, brother Popplewell. You have the right of it, and to show I bear no ill will, come, our Mary, you know where I keep that old Mydeary wine that we kept since your baptism. Bring you up a bottle, for we have a toast to drink."

"Well said, Brother Stephen!" cried Popplewell, for he had a weakness for Madeira, while the others all kept silent, wondering what was to happen next. Mrs. Anerley took out her best glasses and Popplewell poured the fine wine into her fine crystal decanter. It shone in liquid beauty, not too gaudy, not too sparkling with a shallow light, not too ruddy with a sullen glow, but vivid -- like a noble gem, with a mellow depth of luster. "Wonderful Madeira," stated Mr. Popplewell, with a sly grin. "No wonder you have discouraged free trade all these years, with your cellars full of this." He gently swirled his glass and gave a quiet wink to his wife, who quickly looked away, as if she had no idea what he was talking about.

"Such things is beyond my knowledge," growled Farmer Anerley. "But nothing is too good with which to drink to a man's health. Brother Simon, fill you up a small glass for our Mary and listen to what I have to say.

"Now here I stand, and I drink good health to a man as I never clapped eyes on yet, and would have preferred to keep the door closed between us. But the Lord has ordered otherwise. This man has wiped out all his faults against the law and he has fought for the honor of old England as well. In spite of all that, I could have refused to unspeak my words against him, if it had not been that I have wronged the man." Here Mary let out a little sob, not knowing where her father was going with this speech.

"Hush, Mary," Mrs. Anerley murmured, drawing the young lady close to her, "You know your father is a fair man and a kind one." Mary said nothing, her eyes fastened on her father's face, grasping every word he spoke.

"I have wronged the young fellow, and I am man enough to say so," continued the farmer. I called him a murderer and a sneak, and time hath proved me to have been a liar. Therefore, I ask his pardon humbly, and what will be more to his liking perhaps, I say that he shall have my daughter Mary, if she abides agreeable. And I put down these 'ere twenty guineas for Mary to look as she ought to look on the day of her wedding. She hath been a good lass, and hath borne with me better than one in a thousand would have done."

At this Mary left her Mother's side and ran, arms outstretched, to be encircled by her father. "Now, now, Mary luv," said the old farmer, his wind-worn face crinkling with emotion. "Watch out for my glass, lass. I'm not done speaking yet."

Mary, moved just enough so he could raise his glass for all to see. "Mary, my love to you, and if you're all in agreement, here's to the very good health of Robin Lyth!"

"Here's the health of Robin Lyth!" shouted Mr. Popplewell, his fat cheeks shining merrily. "Hurrah for the lad who saved Nelson's death from a Frenchman's grins. Stephen Anerley I forgive you. Ye've done the right thing --though we hardly expected it of you, by rights of your confounded stubbornness. But now I'll be behind no man in doing what's right. I may be a poor man, a very poor man, but the day our Mary goes to church with Robin Lyth, she shall have 500 pounds to tek wi' her, or my name's not Popplewell."

At this, Mary was so overcome that she had to leave the room, after first giving her father and uncle a gentle kiss each, with trembling lips. She could not express her gratitude to them. Now she knew she might start thinking about furnishing a cottage. Though still, she couldn't help feeling some small anxiety. It had been so long since she'd last met with Robin in the lane. Perhaps he might have seen some-one he liked better. Perhaps he might have heard that stupid story about her having taken up with Harry Tanfield and therefore have married a foreign lady. But none of these perhapses cut very deeply into her heart, for she was both equally trusting and trustworthy.

It was not long before her confidence in the future was justified, for but a few days later, word came that Robin Lyth was about to arrive at North Landing. A large group of Flamborians was on hand to greet him. His 'best and dearest' father Robin Cockscroft was there, along with Dr. Upround. Even Mr. Mordacks enjoyed the pleasure of greeting his protégé. Farmer Anerley was the first to shake his hand, and brother Simon Popplewell looked on, smiling with satisfaction. Mary hardly dare look at her faithful hero's face, but he had eyes for no-one else.

It was Mr. Mordacks who put the question that was lurking in the minds of many who were there to greet him. "Now, my lad, what of your relatives and Sir Duncan Yordas?" he asked, knowing the answer before he asked the question, but knowing too that there were those present who needed to hear the answer from Robin's own lips.

"What care I for the name and riches of Yordas, when I have all that is best in all the world, here at Flamborough," exclaimed the one time free- trader, turned honest gentleman.

And Mary's heart was near to bursting with pride as she saw the satisfaction that reflected upon the faces of the little gathering on the shingly shore of North Landing.

So it was, when the spring was fair with promise of green for the earth and of blue for heaven, and of silver grey upon the sea, the little church close to Anerley Farm was filled with color too. There was the scarlet of Dr. Upround's hood, the rich plum color of the coat of Mordacks, the delicate rose and virgin blush on the brow of Mary, every tint of the rainbow on her mother's gown, and gold, rich gold, in the tanned leather bag belonging to Squire Popplewell, his gift to his favorite niece.

In the years that followed, Mary had no cause to repent of her long wait for the truth to emerge and the steadfast power of her quiet love. Yet Robin was still often at a distance as he finished his term of duty. But Mary prayed for his safe return, and safe he was. And when Captain Lyth came home to stay, he trained his children in the ways he should have walked, and the duties they should do -- and pay!

Christine Jones is available for speaking engagements and personal appearances. For more information contact the publisher at:

Christine Jones
ADVANTAGE BOOKS™
PO Box 160847
Altamonte Springs, FL 32716

e-mail: chris@flamboroughhead.com

To order additional copies of this book or to see a complete list of all **ADVANTAGE BOOKS™** visit our online bookstore at:

www.advantagebookstore.com

or call our toll free order number at: 1-888-383-3110

Longwood, Florida, USA

"we bring dreams to life"™
www.advbooks.com

Printed in the United States
32612LVS00005B/160-204